JOSEPHINE LIGHT

EVERNIGHT PUBLISHING ®

www.evernightpublishing.com

Copyright© 2025

Josephine Light

ISBN: 978-0-3695-1191-1

Cover Artist: Jay Aheer

Editor: Melissa Hosack

JOSEPHINE LIGHT

DEDICATION

To my husband, thank you.

JOSEPHINE LIGHT

Josephine Light

Copyright © 2022

Chapter One

I'd always believed an omission of details didn't constitute as a lie.

Or was that a lie?

Either way, it was too late to change my mind. Today was moving day: the busiest day at Braker Academy as all the students moved into their dorms and said goodbye to parents, roaming around campus looking for the best places to eat, study, and hang out. I was technically a junior, although this was my first year at the Academy after spending the last two years at the state's community college. Luckily for me, I didn't have anything to unpack. The school provides us with the rooms, beds, and nightstands. All I had was underwear, socks, and all the pillows I'd managed to acquire and stuff into suitcases that were probably supposed to hold cherished belongings.

Since I didn't belong to a pack, or even a prospective pack, I had the room to myself. The space barely fit all the stuff the academy put in here, but there were worse things than having to turn in a small circle in the shower so my whole body got wet. The benefit to a room to myself? I didn't have to worry about being surrounded by alpha pheromones.

That led me to my lie: I wasn't *technically* a beta.

In all fairness, no one asked whether I was or not. To attend the formerly named Alpha Academy (now the Braker Academy finally allowing Betas to attend) every student had to get their pheromones tested so they couldn't lie on the application about their designation. New dorm buildings were built so the two designations wouldn't have to mix. I just so happened to be a rare omega that didn't send out the proper pheromones signaling my difference from a beta. Was it my fault the test didn't plainly demand an alpha, beta, omega answer? No.

I was an omega at a school where I didn't really belong, but there was no way I was going to go to the Omega Compound. Despite the claims, it wasn't a school in the same way as Braker Academy. Omegas learned how to take care of the house and children and how to please their bondmates. And I respected them for it. Even wanted that one day. But I wasn't ready to stay in the house all day. With the chance to go to Braker Academy, I took it.

After graduating high school—which, to my knowledge, no omega had ever done—I spent two years attending a local community college on the state's dime because of my superior grades. It may have also helped that a new legislation passed a few years ago to help betas attend higher levels of education.

Braker Academy opening their doors to betas was the most recent result of this. Social pressure to include betas even at fancy-ass academies forced their hand, not that I was complaining. There were still protests and plenty of disgruntled alphas, but I grabbed this opportunity with both hands and refused to let go.

A knock on my door pulled my attention away from stuffing all the pillows that didn't fit on the bed into the closet. While I may not smell like an omega, I definitely had all the omega quirks, like hoarding pillows so I could make a nest with the scents and fabrics I liked. I just needed to make sure everyone thought I had a weird pillow fetish, or something, if they ever came into my dorm.

I opened the door just wide enough for my body to squeeze through, closing it behind me and forcing the female that knocked on my door back a few feet. Much taller than me, she wore an athletic outfit, showing off her toned muscles. Her skin was even lighter than mine, more white than tan, with dark red hair I wasn't sure was natural considering how perfect it looked.

"Oh," she said, looking at my door with a frown like she had expected me to invite her in. When I didn't offer her an explanation to my antics she seemed to jump into motion, forcing a smile. "Well, hello. I'm Knox, an alpha. Now, I know what you're thinking, and yes, I am in my fourth year and also the person in charge of the dorms in this building, but that's no reason we can't be friends, right?"

On instinct, I sniffed the air to confirm she really was an alpha. Omegas had the strongest noses, able to scent designations more easily than the others which was probably why she felt she had to tell me her designation. I was sure if I went to the Omega Compound, I would've learned why that was, but I would rather discuss Lagrangian mechanics.

"So, even though I know who you are," Knox said, tapping the clipboard like it held all answers, "it really is more polite if you introduce yourself. That way I don't seem as creepy when I know all the information about you like your name and age and designation."

I waited for a moment before actually introducing myself because I wasn't sure if Knox was going to continue speaking. But she paused and then raised her eyebrows as if queuing me to speak. Instead of offering any sort of introduction, I gave her the information she already had, as if I was verifying what she knew.

"Koda. Nineteen years old. Beta."

Technically, the designation tests all stated Beta, so it wasn't a lie when I filled it out on the form requesting a dorm. Technically.

Knox's nostrils flared as she scented me. I got over my nerves a long time ago when it came to alpha's scenting me. Some professors scented new students, landlords did the same with new occupants, and then there were just the social norms of alphas tending to randomly scent the air as if they were waiting for an omega to suddenly appear. Of course, it helped in these instances that my inner omega didn't care to try and entice her by flaring my scent. Knox's alpha scent of pepper—the spice not the vegetable—didn't call to me. Not gross, but nothing to get my inner omega purring.

"Great." Knox clapped her hands together. "Now I have your scent. I'm going to go and make the rounds, but I want you to know if you need anything, I am on the first floor, room one-oh-one. And I also have a note you're a scholarship student, is that correct?"

Pure luck had me graduating from high school at the same time as politicians pushed to help betas attend higher levels of education. Good grades, a path in astrophysics, and maybe some luck got me a partial ride to Braker. Considering I had two years—three if you included the summer classes—worth of classes done, a partial ride was all I needed.

The money left over from my initial grant to attend the state college was how I paid for food, my phone, pillows, and even kept a savings for once I graduated and the academy kicked me out of the dorm.

My eyebrows rose, as if tempting the Alpha to criticize how I got my place in her posh school. "Yes, I am."

"Okay, well if you have any issues with the deposit or questions about the requirements to keep your scholarship, the counselor for you is in the main office across campus. Elder Building."

"Got it." I moved to head back into my room, but Knox stopped me with a hand on my shoulder causing all my muscles to tighten on instinct. Scenting, I was familiar with. Touching? Not so much.

"Wait. Aren't you going to the orientation? It's across the campus, so you need to leave now to make it on time."

I was about to tell her I had no intention of going to an orientation, especially this one with both alphas and betas but decided against it. Better to just make myself scarce and ignore any lecture or disapproving stare Knox might have had in store for me. She seemed the rule-following-to-the-letter type.

"Yes, I was just heading out before you knocked." I grabbed the key on my makeshift necklace, forcing my body to fold in half in order to lock my door. It wasn't just the fact I was hiding an unusual amount of pillows in my room—but another omega quirk—demanding that without a proper secondary room for a nest, the whole room became one. Which meant any alpha trying to enter without my permission would enrage my inner omega. And if the stories—and my instincts—were true, an omega rage usually ended in the omega and all nearby alphas dead.

"Good. I would walk with you, but I want to make sure everyone else in the hallway is on their way. Why don't you head that way and I'll look for you when I arrive?"

I had no intention of actually going to the orientation, but I gave Knox my brightest smile and headed off. There was a coffee shop not too far from this building that sold some nice pillows I didn't own yet. Might as well get them now because I wouldn't be able to stop thinking about them. Plus, I hadn't had any coffee since I bought the espresso when I arrived on campus this morning and that was like, four hours ago. I needed a constant line of caffeine in my system to maintain control over both my omega and beta instincts. Really, I just needed it to stay alive, so the coffee shop it was.

Chapter Two

I was too early to my first class. I needed coffee to ensure I could sit still for two hours so I had put in extra time in the morning ensuring I could wait in any potential long lines and make it to class on time. As it turned out, the baristas were prepared for the long line, and I waited maybe ten minutes to order and then got my drink. Now, I was slowly sipping my Flat White so I had some for the class because if history was any indication, I would fall asleep without something to drink.

It wasn't a lack of sleep or even an innate desire to be somewhere else—I wanted to be at college. I wanted to learn. My body wanted me to sleep whenever a professor droned on. At first, I had assumed it was an omega-thing, but if movies were any indication, omegas felt supercharged and excited around alphas, so it was really just a Koda-thing.

Adding to my present humiliation, not even the professor had arrived yet, so I was suck sitting outside. This building, an add-on to the older part of the academy, had 'hallways' outside which meant I wasn't even sitting on a nice plush carpet, but red dirt staining my jeans and ruining the cute little flowers along the bottoms. There were a few other doors, none of them open, and the whole quad was vacant except for me. My only saving grace was the sun already out and, despite the small chill from the wind, warming me up. The weather would only get colder, though, so timing my coffee runs would be imperative to keeping all my fingers.

I smelled the company before I heard them. Six people. Three intoxicating male scents and three flowery female ones. The perfect numbers obviously indicated a pack which did nothing to make me feel better about sitting on the ground with zero friends and too much time before the door to the class would even open. I wasn't sure how classes worked for pack members—if there even were any—that was probably something covered at the orientation.

Deciding not to look too much like a loner, I stood up and moved a little farther away from the door, taking a bunch of little sips of my drink as if actively drinking made me look more natural.

The closer the pack got, the stronger their scents became, giving me details to the newcomers. My first sniff told me the males were alphas and the females betas. The next sniff blocked out any other distinction since the couples were covered in sex, mingling the finer details of their scents. A growl startled me before I realized it was coming from my chest. I forced my inner omega to calm the hell down, breathing through my mouth as inconspicuously as possible. It wasn't uncommon for me to feel jealous of alphas giving attention to others, but jealousy this aggressive was new. Fucking omega quirks.

"Oh look," one of the females said in a fake hush. "An overexcited freshman already arrived."

There were some chuckles from the other females, and I was glad my first emotion was frustration. I clung to it, fanning the emotion because the last thing I wanted was to give them more ammunition with pinked cheeks and the scent of me embarrassed. I went with the "pretend I didn't hear" act and took another sip of my coffee. At least the males didn't laugh, which I hoped meant one of them was a professor and forced to act cordial to the newbies hanging out by their doors.

"Morning." The male in front didn't look at me as he pulled out a key to the door I was waiting in front of. Thank goodness. I would rather the disinterested male than the beta female. Screw designation loyalty, betas were basically taught to fight for their place in this world among 'perfect' alphas and 'chosen one' omegas, and if one managed to snag an alpha? Let's just say that betas living the good life tended to forget they once struggled too.

The other couples moved into the room, but the male I assumed was the professor—shit, what was the professor's name for this class? —crossed his arms over his chest, waiting for me to say something.

He dressed like a male that just left a photoshoot for the coming winter catalogue. Brown pants with faint yellow stripes showed off his muscular thighs, an off-white shirt paired with a darker brown tie, and even his jacket was over his forearm like he was posing. The stubble on his chin and cheeks, the sharp nose, and the thick eyebrows made his eyes seem harsh despite the neutral expression on his face.

That close, I had no choice but to inhale his scent. It reminded me of something fresh. Clean. Even if it was tainted with what I could only assume was the beta females sprayed on perfume based on the chemically floral scent.

"You look pretty young to be a professor." Genius Koda, insult the male in charge of your grades. But I wasn't wrong. He had to be only a few years older than me. Maybe twenty-five?

"I'm twenty-six with my master's degree. I assure you; I can teach Quantum Mechanics just fine. But if you want to verify my credentials, Miss..." He trailed off, obviously hoping I would insert my name into his verbal blank. Just his voice had my inner omega wanting to please him by telling him my name, but I managed to hold back that particular instinct.

"No, I'm good. Based on the tuition to attend, I'm

assured the Academy would only pay for the best." The young professor preened at the compliment, which meant it would have been the perfect place to stop, but I couldn't hold back the need to test him. "Then again, Academy chancellors and other board members would probably get a pay increase if they were able to hire cheap labor. Have you compared your salary to other professors? Preferably from a different school district to compare?"

There was a flicker of amusement in his scent, a moment where he stopped meeting my eyes and took in my cropped shirt and low-ride floral jeans, before his face returned to his look of indifference. In a stern voice that couldn't lead to anything good for me, he asked, "What's your name?"

"What's your name?" Ah yes, the five-year-old come back.

The male raised an eyebrow, alpha arrogance radiating from him, but right before I was about to give in, one of the males from inside the classroom came barreling out.

"Jen, what the fuck are you doing, man? Your girl is getting prissy. Oh hey, who's the side piece?"

The two males, most likely pack based on their familiarity, couldn't be farther apart in appearance. Professor Jenson—I remembered then—had his hair cut so close to his head I doubted I could've gotten a good grip on it while the newcomer had gorgeous long, blond hair with curls that just screamed 'surfer dude'. Where Professor Jenson was stoic, his body large and unmoving like he was eternally serious, the surfer-wannabe followed his stereotype looking laid back despite the black dress slacks and plain white button up t-shirt. He even had the first two buttons of his shirt undone, hinting at a bare chest. I would bet one of my favorite pillows

Professor Jenson had hair on his chest like the perfect counterpart to surfer dude.

Both of their scents together made a direct line to my core, somehow stroking an arousal I'd only felt in the safety of my nest when I was deep in my imagination hoping to find some sexual relief. My primal instincts forced my beta senses to the back, showing images in my mind of surfer dude underneath me, forcing my hips up and down while I straddled him. Professor Jenson behind me, whispering in my ear how good I was taking his packmate's cock while he forced my hands behind his head and played with my nipples. My tongue would beg Professor Jenson to mark me. He would pull my hair back in his grip, the intensity making me gasp and tighten my inner muscles around his packmate, while he left his claim on my skin...

The wet feeling in my panties pulled me out of my fantasy of the two packmates. Shit, okay, as long as they didn't smell me, it wouldn't be a problem. My natural odor might not be one of an omega, but any alpha would be more than able to tell my designation when I was turned on. It was how I learned I wasn't actually a beta, despite the claims otherwise. Usually, I was better at controlling myself around alpha pheromones, but diving into a sex fantasy was making it exponentially worse. They just smelled so good. Like freshly washed linen and a desert rainstorm.

I think the males were talking, but I was so focused on needing to get to the bathroom, I interrupted. "Okay, well, I'll be back in time for class."

In my mind, I managed to walk away normally, but in reality, I was squeezing my thighs together so tightly, I worried I looked like I literally had a stick up my ass.

JOSEPHINE LIGHT

Chapter Three

Just a normal first day of classes with me in the bathroom wiping away the excess slick on my panties. Okay, now I knew those two alphas together had me imagining sexy times, making them dangerous. But I'd made it through puberty in high school without getting outed as an omega. I wasn't getting caught now. Despite the lock, I kept glancing at the door, fear convincing my rational brain someone was about to burst through.

I looked down at the small slick stain on my underwear, maybe the size of a quarter, but I didn't know if it would be enough to attract an alpha's attention. Omegas might be better at smelling designations and emotions, but alphas could smell arousal from ... well, I didn't know about miles, but they could smell it in a crowded room.

Shit, like a classroom where an alpha was a professor, and all the students were either betas or alphas too.

I started pulling my jeans off, wincing as my cold fingers accidentally touched my skin. Sure, going without underwear would be uncomfortable, but I wasn't going to risk myself on the first day. Taking my underwear off, I shoved it in the trash bin that was technically meant for used tampons or pads but fuck it. All the more likely the janitor wouldn't notice.

Heading back to the classroom, the door was open with students already walking in. Everyone was talking like they were old friends, which I guess made sense if they'd all been attending the last two years at the academy together. Friends were hard to make when I was terrified of someone learning my secret. My lie. Designations bloomed with puberty, and I was a dandelion hiding in a field of wildflowers. Technically a weed but looking enough like a wildflower in passing.

Inside the classroom, the two males I imagined—no, I couldn't think of that—the professor and surfer dude were whispering aggressively while the third male in the probably-a-pack pack was standing nearby, looking toward the door as if his one wish in life was to walk through it. This pack member was the tallest of the group. There was an air around him making him look less approachable than his packmates—not that my inner omega cared. Part of it might have been because he wasn't quite as stunningly handsome. The scowl didn't make him look rugged, just aggressively annoyed with life. His hair was cut close on the side and long on the top with perfect curls that looked like they would bounce back if I pulled them. And damn, could I imagine his head between my legs, me with a fistful of his perfect hair. Maybe my grip was the only thing keeping him in place. Maybe he licked my clit slowly before circling it with his tongue—

No. That was the opposite of helpful in a room filled with alphas.

I took a seat in the back of the classroom where there were plenty of empty chairs still. The whole room was set up more like a stage with the teacher presenting at the front and the seats positioned so everyone had a view over the head in front of them. Little desks folded out on the chairs—those were cute—and I put my drink down, waiting for class to start, purposely keeping my attention away from the pack I apparently couldn't stop fantasizing about.

The beta females were gone, but my nose seemed to have a direct line to their lingering scents on the alphas.

As more students came and found seats, the whole

classroom filled up, but the professor was still talking. Several of the students were starting to wonder out loud about whether the class was going to start when the third male in the pack just grabbed surfer dude by the arm and pulled him out of the classroom mid argument. I was surprised there weren't any dominance fights, but surfer dude went quietly, winking at me as he passed since all I could do was stare at him.

Professor Jenson introduced himself and I did my best to pay attention. It was a little weird to sit without underwear on since the seams of my jeans felt like they were digging into unsavory parts, but I did my best to ignore it. Especially since moving around would draw more attention to me.

Professor Jenson didn't make us all introduce ourselves, but he did scan all the seats. His eyes met mine for a moment too long, and I reminded myself he didn't know I wasn't wearing underwear because I had an illicit fantasy about him dominating me. But when his eyes moved on, I refused to look up from my notes again for the rest of my class. This was going to be a long semester.

JOSEPHINE LIGHT

Chapter Four

One Month Later

I told the barista to make anything as long as it was caramel flavored. She didn't disappoint. Not that I was surprised. I managed to come here every weekend for a reason.

I wasn't sure where most of the student body spent their Friday nights, but I spent mine at a café, just off campus, but still within walking distance from the beta dorms. It had large, singular chairs and tables set around for studying, calming music that was always from some orchestral instrument, internet connection, and it served coffee. I could have lived here if classes didn't grade attendance. Without any classes to physically attend on Fridays, I usually found myself in this exact spot.

The place had a steady flow of customers, but most got their drinks and left. The two baristas had found a balance between talking and taking orders.

Despite the soft music, I still wore headphones with a specific playlist set up for each class. First, I was working on Professor Jenson's class, Quantum Mechanics. I'd covered most of the surface space of the table in my books, notes, and the rubric for creating the '2-state model for neutrino oscillations' project.

Getting good grades had always been important to me. It was how I earned and maintained my scholarships. But my inner omega was desperate to please my professor, which meant I put in more effort to his homework, more time dedicated to studying his lessons, and probably had the best notes on his lectures in the whole class. Hence why I was already starting a project that wasn't due for another month. I was even early to his class so my inner omega could get her perusal of the other two alphas in Professor Jenson's pack. Luckily, the group of beta females that drooled over our professor begged for his attention after class, so I could pretend like I wasn't as desperate as them since I drooled in the morning.

We hadn't spoken since that first day, but that didn't stop my thoughts manifesting him when attending to my ... sexual needs. I'd never had a quicker orgasm than when I imagined Jenson dominating me—except maybe when I imagined his packmates joining us.

At first, I tried convincing myself I was hooked on the sexy male because he was my professor, thus unattainable. But I had to admit, his teacher status never appeared in my fantasies. In my imagination, I was simply Jenson's good girl.

I'd barely started reviewing the rubric when three females basically threw themselves on the remaining chairs around the table, their sprayed on floral scents doing nothing to hide their beta designations. If I was a kinder person, I would have made space on the table so they could put whatever they bought down. But their scents were familiar in a way that had my inner omega wanting to attack them for the audacity of breathing my air. Luckily, my beta side was fully in charge.

I took one side of my headphones off, forcing a tight smile, before saying, "I hope you don't mind I've sort of taken up the table space. Studying."

Good job, Koda, like they didn't understand why you had books spread everywhere.

"Do you attend the nearby alpha and beta academy?" The blonde to my right asked.

I thought the blonde sitting on my left had to be her sister or some close relative. They both had the same face with only slight differences in eye color and nose size. The blonde in front of me wasn't related since her genetics were obviously passed down from two people with the sharpest bone structure I'd ever seen. She was dating Jenson, but I wasn't sure which of the other two were paired with which alpha.

"Yep." I popped the p, trying to politely show how not interested in the conversation I was, but no one got the hint.

Sharp bone structure blonde actually picked up the rubric for my assignment, showing it off to her pack, saying, "Look at this, she's in my boyfriend's class." Her Hispanic accent was strong, and I couldn't help but feel like her words grated on my skin for the sole fact her accent made her sexier. "Maybe I can put in a good word for you."

My inner omega hated the idea that this beta female thought she claimed the professor I'd brought myself to orgasm thinking about. It was more than just the fact of her designation but also that she didn't have a claiming mark. Not even a temporary hickey most alphas like to adorn their romantic partners with. Then again, the idea of the sundress wearing female in front of me, with her hair straightened and face painted to perfection having a bright red and purple hickey on her neck felt like a butt of a joke. My own outfit consisted of sweatpants, an oversized t-shit I won from a random lottery at a car show in a parking lot of a restaurant, and a sweater tied around my waist in case I got cold. But my outfit still felt more appropriate for an alpha bruise. Or maybe I was just that jealous, and it turned me into a judgmental bitch. I may never know.

"You are so sweet, Eloise," the blonde on my left said to her friend. "I would love it if Aidan would do something more with his life. He comes from such an urbane family, but he spends his time running bars as if he's content being a glorified bartender."

I was incredibly intrigued about which one Aidan was (maybe surfer wannabe), but my inner omega didn't care for these females and wanted to work on impressing Professor Jenson. Both of those meant returning my focus to my assignment. Which was hard to do since the females chose the chairs next to the only person working and not waiting in line to either order or get their drinks.

"I have no complaints about Lorenzo," the right blonde added, her voice the most chipper of her pack.

"Really, Amy? Not even him demanding to go by 'Enzo' as if he's some ill-bred? What kind of nickname is that?" the left blonde said. Her laugh wasn't joyous but more like she was a cackling villain at her friend's unhappiness.

"Come on now, girls," Eloise said. "We are gossiping without even knowing the name of our newest friend."

"I'm Koda." I managed an introduction. "And it's been really nice talking to you all—"

"Well, I'm Eloise." Sharp Lines introduced herself, cutting me off before I got to the 'but I really need to study' part of my sentence. "That's Amy." She pointed to my right. "And that's Laura." She then pointed to the one on my left. "Are you seeing anyone, Koda?"

I ignored the side look Eloise gave her friends when she said my name. "Um, no. I'm sort of just focusing on school."

"No interest in joining a pack? You should really consider otherwise. Betas have just as much a right to a pack as an omega. Oh, hold that thought." The girls got up, grabbing their drinks.

As much as I wanted to just put my headphone back on, social rules dictated it would be rude to start ignoring the pack. Even if I didn't want to engage in their conversation. In their own way, they were trying to be supportive, and it wasn't their fault I was actually an omega—and one pining after all three of their alphas. I went the next best route and turned my attention back toward the textbook in my lap, not comprehending anything I was reading but hoping to look distracted enough to be excluded from the conversation. Then I could low-key put my headphones back in.

My plan only worked long enough for all the females to take their first sips.

"Not as good as the Preppary," Eloise said, shaking her head in disappointment.

"Nothing is," Laura said in agreement.

"Our males asked us to meet them here," Amy said in my direction, voice hushed like she was telling me a secret.

"Speaking of which," Laura said, sounding giddy, "the males have arrived."

Well, that piqued my attention. Then reality came back when I heard Professor Jenson's voice.

"Shouldn't you be out partying on a Friday night?"

I looked up to find Professor Jenson standing next to me, looking over my shoulder. His packmates were across from me, staring at the two of us like they were trying to figure out how we knew each other. It was easy, then, to confirm Aidan with Laura—the friend cackler— and Lorenzo with Amy—who had the better sounding voice—since the girls were clinging to their arms in their own version of a public claim.

I wrinkled my nose at what I assumed was a joke but came out more like an insult. "Seems very hypocritical of you since we are literally in the same place."

Jenson was wearing a dark brown suit and dark

red tie but with his coat still on, drawing my attention up to his wide shoulders and broad chest. He looked the most elegant of his packmates, but I wasn't one to overlook Aidan's all black outfit containing a button up shirt with a loose collar or Lorenzo's black sweater with a deep V showing off the curls of hair on his chest that made me want to beg him to take his shirt off so I could see how far the trail of hair went.

Jenson didn't answer, but then I realized he was looking over my personal notes outlining the paper for his project. I slammed the book shut before thinking it through all the way and glanced up to see Jenson smirking at me.

"It's not like I'm going to cheat from you."

"Ha-ha. I just don't need you judging me on work that isn't completed yet."

A deep line appeared between his eyebrows. "The project isn't about judging you. It's about ensuring you're understanding the concepts enough to put them into a life-like practical use. Let me take a look. Who wouldn't want their teacher's opinion?"

"Like everyone at one of those Friday night parties," I muttered, but I still opened the textbook and showed Jenson the outline I had hidden away with different starting ideas. He made himself comfortable on the arm of my chair, pulling up his pants leg before almost straddling the fabric. Had a thigh ever been sexy before? Because I was pretty sure there was an unusual amount of muscle in this male's body, and I had the very real urge to squeeze his leg.

Jenson's scent was clouding around me. It was clean, like fresh linen.

I managed to catch myself as I inhaled a second time. Once might be excused since it wasn't unusual to scent others when meeting, but I didn't have any reason to continuously scent someone I knew. But his scent was calling to me to take more, and I hadn't realized how diluted my nose had become after breathing in coffee fumes, random strangers, and the chemical smell that came with new textbooks. It was like I could finally relax without all my senses being slammed.

"Jenson, dear." Eloise tapped Jenson's knee to grab his attention. "I think the young beta would like some peace and quiet so she can study. We've already been distracting her for too long."

Jenson sighed, like the entire conversation had gone on too long.

I didn't bother to agree or disagree with what Eloise said since it wasn't directed at me. She was barely older than me but managed to treat me like a child that thought she was one of the adults. But I wasn't playing dress up, and Eloise scented of jealousy, burning away Jenson's better scent.

"We came here to talk, Eloise," Jenson said, standing from his seated position and handing me my notebook back. I might have purposefully brushed my fingers along his. "Let's do that."

The three couples left without saying another word to me. I replaced my headphones, restarted my playlist, and got ready to make a more in-depth outline before I gave in to the temptation to peek a glance at the couples talking outside.

Eloise had her lips pinched as Jenson spoke with her. Never had Jenson looked more like a teacher rebuking the actions of a student than in that moment. Lorenzo was looking mighty awkward with the tearful Amy as she used the back of her hands to wipe away tears despite never letting go of her drink. Aidan looked like he was having to hold himself back from laughing as Laura appeared to be speaking rather aggressively with him.

It was obvious, even from an outsider's perspective, what was going on. It wasn't unusual for packmates to get into and out of relationships simultaneously. Without ever being in a pack, I wasn't sure if it was simply a biological thing or a code of loyalty, but either way, seeing as the three females that held the interest of this certain pack had formed their own pack, it would make sense for the males to give them all up if they weren't willing to mark one. Tensions could rise if only one female remained in the relationship, destroying that pack from the inside.

I glanced over at the quickly dwindling line of customers. Everyone who came in had at least one person they were talking with, and the baristas never glanced toward the commotion happening outside. No one was looking my way. Or bothering to watch the free show.

I accidently caught Aidan's attention. One side of his mouth turned upward in an incredibly sexy smirk like he knew I was desperately wishing I had the ability to read lips. Shrugging my shoulders, I pretended like getting caught wasn't embarrassing. Technically, it shouldn't be since they were doing this in a very public place but, again, social rules dictated I pretended not to see.

But then the way Aidan and I stared at each other changed. His eyes narrowed and took on a playful look that had my inner omega wanting to run so the big bad alpha would chase. Choosing a more beta reaction, I widened my eyes in my best mock-innocence appearance. I watched his tongue come out and lick his bottom lip, an ache appearing in between my legs. I shook my head and narrowed my eyes at him, doing my best to tell him to knock it off.

Aidan just laughed. The action suddenly cut off

when he turned all his attention back to Laura, who seemed to cower at whatever Aidan just said to her.

The next thing I knew, Aidan was making his way back into the coffee shop and dramatically throwing himself on the seat next to me.

JOSEPHINE LIGHT

Chapter Five

I refused to take my headphones off this time. Nope. I was going to start writing shit down—okay reread the rubric and then start writing shit down.

As soon as Aidan stopped staring at me.

I glanced up, finding his smirk had turned into a full-blown smile. Whatever game he was playing, I want not interested in joining. Ridiculously good looking and smelling better than any male had a right to was not incentive enough for me to lose my focus. And that was what this pack was, a test of my dedication to my studies. My infatuation with watching them in the mornings was a mild obsession, but there was no harm in looking. From a safe distance. Where their scent didn't tease me.

I crossed my legs under the textbook and pretended to skim the pages like I was looking for something. Yes, I got the irony of not actually doing work but honestly, who could study when someone was staring at them?

A feeling of closeness had me looking up to Aidan suddenly much closer. Apparently, the chairs weren't studded down because Aidan scooted his so the fabric of our chairs' arms were touching. I glared at the offending fabric, refusing to lose my temper and snap at him. Not even for doing anything wrong but for making me want him so much. The urge to throw off everything on my lap and jump into his was stronger than I expected, and my inner omega was beating against my beta instincts.

I took a deep breath to calm myself and immediately regretted it. His beautiful alpha scent, like a perfect rainstorm, was tainted with the female beta scent of Laura. My inner omega growled at the territorial gesture from the other female even as my logical side argued he wasn't mine.

Aidan's eyes widened, and I cut the sound off. It was a little like choking to hold back my instincts, but it was all about protecting my future.

"What do you want?" I snapped at him, yanking both earbuds out. I hoped the growl came off as annoyance and not aggressive jealousy.

"You're pretty riled up for a Friday night."

"What is everyone's obsession with the date? I get it, it's Friday and I'm lame because I'm studying. There's really no need to point it out, and on top of that, you're in the same place as me, so it's pretty hypocritical."

I didn't make a joke, so I was pretty shocked when Aidan started laughing. "Jenson was right. You are feisty."

I couldn't say I didn't get excited about the idea of Jenson talking about me with his pack. At least, my heart thought it was sweet and my pussy definitely thought it got a compliment, but my brain reminded me any attention was bad attention. And while flirting with an insanely hot male would be rewarding in its own way—something to remember when I took a vibrator into my makeshift nest—I couldn't risk my future on something so meaningless.

"Look, I'm not trying to be rude, but I really need to work on this project, and I don't know you."

I moved to put my headphones back on when he said, "Well, good thing I have time tonight. We can do two positions before I let you come."

I stared at Aidan. Truly trying to figure out what the hell he just said. In fact, I stared for so long he started laughing and clutching his stomach. I thought he might have just had a mini stroke, but his laugh sure did make my voice catch in my throat, stopping any questions or concerns from coming out.

"I'll let you off the hook this once, but if we're going to be spending time getting to know each other, then you better learn to figure these out yourself. Two positions before coming. It's like killing two birds with one stone but with less murder and more sex." Aidan wiggled his eyebrows in a way that was too sexy for such a funny gesture.

"And what two things do you supposedly think you're going to be doing?"

"Introducing myself and helping you with your project, of course. I'm sure my brothers will help too once they're done outside."

I glanced over to where Aidan gestured to his packmates. Both Jenson and Lorenzo were still dealing with the females, and it seemed like they were disputing the breakup. If my inner omega wasn't on the verge of walking over there and claiming two males she didn't know, I would have continued watching the whole thing like a comically bad show.

"I'm Aidan, by the way. And you are?"

"Oh, so Jenson can tell you I'm feisty but not my name?" I ignored the thrill that went down my spine at using my professor's name so casually.

"You're Koda Tucker. Probably twenty-one years old, depending on when your birthday is. Maybe twenty-two." Aidan paused, looking around like he was about to deliver a secret before he leaned in and whispered, "And I would bet after a couple orgasms, you'd easily take my knot."

Could hearts beat triple time? Because mine was pounding so fast, I could not only hear it, but it was making me light-headed. I'd literally been struck speechless, without a drop of moisture in my mouth to make any sort of rebuttal. Maybe because my body had sent all my blood and moisture to my pussy as it leaked and cried for attention. For the promise of this alpha's knot.

I imagined getting on my knees for Aidan while completely naked. He'd be fully dressed and barely lower his pants and underwear before pulling his cock out. He'd tell me to open my mouth and stick my tongue out. Slowly sliding his cock on my tongue, gripping my hair on the back of my head to hold me still so I couldn't move. Finally, he'd shove his cock all the way into my mouth, hitting the back of my throat while I fought the urge not to gag. And then he'd say the words I'd been looking for as he forced me to stay on his cock until I stopped gagging—good girl.

Or maybe he'd wait to tell me until I had a pussy full of his packmate's cock. I could be on top of one male, Aidan behind me, pushing my chest down to meet Jenson's. The alpha under me would just barely pull out, and Aidan would push his own fingers into my sopping pussy, collecting my wetness before slathering his cock with it. I wanted Jenson, pushing back in, holding my shoulders tight, Aidan holding my hips from behind, shoving his cock up my ass, and Lorenzo kneeling in front of me, holding my jaw tenderly in his large hands before having me swallow his cock. And with all three alpha cocks finally moving inside me, forcing me to feel pleasure as they use my body for themselves, I would finally get the two words I craved.

"Betas can't take knots." I managed to croak the statement out, but there was no strength behind the words. My grip on my textbook was tight as I pushed it against my lap, simultaneously hoping it would cover any scent of my slick but also giving me a modicum of pain to balance out the threat of intense pleasure.

"Knot or not," Aidan said with a chuckle, "sex

always feels good. Now, tell me when your birthday is and then about your project."

I chose to ignore the first two things before giving him the basic speech Jenson told us about the project and then abruptly shoved the book in his direction. "Why don't you just look this over? The rubric is on the table. I'm going to the bathroom. Excuse me."

Since I managed to keep my wits about me, I didn't sprint to the bathroom like I really wanted. Instead, I calmly walked there, locked the door, and then wiped the slick off my thighs, tossing my underwear in the trash bin.

JOSEPHINE LIGHT

Chapter Six

I'd lost more pairs of underwear since being at college than in the four years of high school when I started noticing alpha pheromones. Alphas never paid me much attention as a beta and when they did, they always assumed I would jump at the chance to fuck them. They assumed a beta would feel lucky at being picked by an alpha. What they hadn't counted on was my inner omega side, which was completely unimpressed. Plus, none of the alphas had half as delicious a scent as Jenson. Or even Aidan. There wasn't anything similar about Jenson's clean laundry scent and Aidan's desert-after-a-big-rainstorm scent, but both had my body craving more.

Maybe it was a good thing all three males broke up with their betas. If they were going to be in close proximity to me, at least they wouldn't smell like the gossipy betas. That should calm down my omega's territorial instincts. Although, I had to admit, I was curious as to what Lorenzo smelled like. Would his scent call to me like a perfect match for this pack? Or would his scent be enough to turn my omega's interests to another pack?

Alphas and betas tended to sit with their own designation which meant most of the time the scents of betas were the only thing I inhaled. Of course, that didn't matter the first time Professor Jenson was running late, partly sweaty from his jog to make it to class. I could smell him from the back of the room, and I had to fake being sick, leaving the class almost as soon as he had arrived because there was no way I could have restrained myself for two hours in an enclosed space with my inner omega demanding I claim the alpha.

At least the lack of underwear wasn't as

uncomfortable in sweatpants. The pants were basically a size too big, which meant I had to tie the strings as tight as they went and roll the top a few times so they wouldn't fall. But it also meant the inseam didn't bug me.

I wished I had brought my headphones in the bathroom with me. There was something less vulnerable about leaving the sanctuary of a public bathroom to head back to my seat where a minimum of one, but potentially three alphas, were waiting for me. Or maybe I'd gotten lucky and they'd left.

Ha, yeah right. This pack of alphas had taken a certain interest in me. And I was apparently a masochist because I hadn't told them to leave me the hell alone.

Taking a deep breath, mostly to calm my nerves, but also to inhale the lemony tang of the bathroom cleaner, I hoped to calm my inner omega before dealing with whatever feminine scents were attached to the males.

I walked with all the confidence of one of those girls in a teenage drama show after she took off her glasses and was suddenly hot—but without subconsciously insulting people who wore glasses—and found three alphas sitting around the table I had occupied with my classwork.

Bypassing Aidan without a glance, I sat down in my chair and looked up to three set of eyes staring at me. I was used to staring at Jenson's brown eyes, but Lorenzo's blue ones and Aidan's green eyes were giving my body the wrong ideas. The undivided attention of three alphas was heady for an omega.

"Can I have my book back?" I was pretending my voice came out confident and unaffected by lust.

Aidan leaned over and set the book in my lap. The backs of his fingers brushed the tops of my thighs and—dammit—I couldn't hold back the gasp of pleasure that came from the simple touch. I hide my embarrassment by refusing to look up and throwing myself into restarting my playlist—again—and then trying to refamiliarize myself with my notes. Losing sight of the males, however, caused my other instincts to kick in, and I found myself sniffing the air for their scents.

Jenson's scent had the most beta interference, which meant Eloise had likely touched him several times. Luckily, I was able to hold back the territorial growl, though the strain of pushing my instincts away had my back molars grinding together. Before I could push my omega instincts to the back, I caught a whiff of Lorenzo—floral beta with an alpha's wild pine scent—and that pushed my inner omega over the limit. She had a crush on these males and wanted to make her interest known. That meant sending a whole lot of slick to my pussy so the alphas could scent it and choose me.

And that was my cue to start packing shit up. I closed books, not caring where papers were, and started shoving them into my backpack.

Brown fingers wrapped around my wrist, stopping me from my shoving escapade. Not even the desperate beta scent could block the refreshing pine tree scent that was Lorenzo.

"You want to tell us what has you panicking right now?" His voice had a slight accent to it that didn't help in cooling my growing desire.

I refused to look up into the owner of brown finger's eyes or use my voice that I knew would be more lust than intelligible, so I just shook my head. The fingers didn't let go, and I didn't look up, effectively forcing us into a stalemate. However, I had the short end of the stick because Lorenzo's grip affected me more than I affected him.

I could feel the calluses on his fingers, and I

wanted to feel his hands in more sensitive spots. I knew his grip would feel amazing squeezing my breasts. Maybe he would slide then down my stomach until—

No.

I was making this whole situation worse. I couldn't seem to be around these males without my thoughts turning sexual and making me wet. The worst part was, I couldn't even blame them. Maybe if I kept them talking, they wouldn't inhale deeply enough to notice my obvious arousal, and I could pull my wrist away from Lorenzo's grip.

"Don't you guys have somewhere to be on a Friday night?" Good, that sounded normal.

"I think we pretty much finished our plans for tonight," Aidan said.

"You planned to break up with those betas?"

"The females always knew they wouldn't last," Jenson said. But the way he said it left it open for me to ask questions. Like he wanted me to.

I stopped trying to pull my wrist from Lorenzo's grip, hoping it came off like I was simply calming down instead of being fully committed to the answer, as I asked, "And how did they know that?"

"We told them," Lorenzo said.

I'd be lying if I said it wasn't hot the way I was having one conversation but with all three of them. These males were obviously very close and had been packmates a long time if they deferred to each other. I always thought alphas preferred a hierarchy system, but that didn't seem to be the case with this pack. Just another thing I would've known if I'd attended the Omega Compound.

"Very kind of you." I rolled my eyes despite the fact my head was still down, and no one could see. "You told the betas you started dating they weren't endgame.

Why ever didn't the relationships work out?"

It was a rhetorical question, but Aidan answered anyway. "It has nothing to do with them being betas. But they're a pack. And we want to share a female."

I think all the muscles in my body simply froze. One moment I was making a joke and the next, I didn't even risk breathing. My muscles locked up. My brain simply overloaded with the idea of not one, not two, but three alphas pleasuring me. I would get to make a nest large enough for four. There would be enough people in the relationship where I wouldn't have to worry about smothering one in my need for constant attention. Three alphas in my bed, filling all my holes, and telling me what a good girl I was. Of course, I fantasized about it, but that didn't take into account what the males wanted. And now the possibility just became too real.

My lungs burned from holding my breath. I gasped, pulling in more and more air but also pulling in more and more smells. With every breath, I could taste the three males. In my rapidly aroused state, my inner omega wanted to touch all three, strip them of their clothing, and mark them as mine.

"Please let go." A whisper was all I could manage, but Lorenzo listened, dropping his hold so quickly I couldn't catch my inner omega's whimper before it got out.

I grabbed everything in my arms and didn't bother zipping my backpack before half running out of the coffee shop. I refused to look back as slick ran down my thighs and hoped they hadn't caught a whiff. My legs carried me all the way to my dorm, before collapsing of exhaustion in my nest.

JOSEPHINE LIGHT

Chapter Seven

It wasn't just embarrassment that kept me from arriving to Professor Jenson's class early on Monday. It was also the fact that Aidan and Lorenzo were outside the door, leaning against the wall and talking like they had all the time in the world.

A part of me felt conceited to think the two super attractive males were waiting outside my first class to speak with me. Logically, their packmate was the professor inside the classroom, so I knew they had plenty of reasons to be here. Not to mention they weren't really a unique site. Plenty of the females flirted with all three members of the pack—even Professor Jenson during class. Some females walking by to get to other classes would flirt with the males if they were outside. To my knowledge, I was the only one that knew they were recently single. Unless they found someone to share in the two days since I'd seen them.

My fists clenched in frustration at the idea of Aidan and Lorenzo sharing a new female. Which made no sense considering I was staring at them only talking to each other and ignoring all the passing students. Of course, common sense meant nothing to omega instincts.

And that was the root of all my problems: my inner omega.

It wasn't enough she'd grown territorial over three males I'd barely spoken with, but I also had to deal with the fact that my crush on the pack needed to stay hidden. Unlike the actual betas that attended the university, they wouldn't get expelled if they slept with the males. Or any males, really, because they weren't hiding their real perfume behind a mask of indifference to a whole designation. But if I were to give in and fuck one of these males, they would know my true designation and my time at the academy would be record short.

My whole life I'd been grateful for my beta-like scent, and I wasn't going to throw away my chance on a career for an hour in bed with three alphas. Ah, who was I kidding? I wanted a night in bed with the alphas.

Aidan and Lorenzo could potentially be convinced into silence, but I doubted Jenson would ignore the school guidelines and not turn me in. And there was really no way to guarantee Aidan or Lorenzo wouldn't do the same. That any alpha wouldn't do the same.

Even a beta might be able to figure out I was an omega when in bed, so it was better I didn't sleep with anyone and stayed away from males altogether.

And for any males that didn't get the picture, I hoped the extra sweet perfume I sprayed on this morning would push them away.

With that confident thought, I headed toward my classroom, choosing to ignore Aidan and Lorenzo altogether. That confidence wavered when I get closer, however. Now that I knew their scents, it was like my nose was more sensitive to it, picking them up easier. Not even keeping my coffee right under my nose stopped their scents from reaching me. A feeling of calmness worked its way to my muscles, making me feel relaxed and a little like I could nap.

I didn't stop when I passed Aidan and Lorenzo, my coffee weaker than their scents of desert rainstorm and a pine tree forest, and made my way to my undesignated, designated seat. There was a feeling of disappointment that neither of the males my omega desired paid me any attention, but I told my stupid heart that it was a good thing. Plus, I willingly whiffed their scents, so some hard rejection was probably a good reminder.

My seat felt more comfortable than usual as I got my notebook and pen out. Usually, I liked getting to class early to ensure I had the same seat each time—which I refused to acknowledge as an omega trait of claiming. But I was glad my delay outside didn't result in someone taking my spot.

"Do you smell that?" the beta on my right asked. His nose—which was already naturally upturned—half lifted into the air like he was scenting me.

Despite my calm mood vanishing and my hackles rising at the blatant scenting, I managed to calmly ask, "Smell what?"

Was my inner omega finally perfuming properly? Panic quickly set in as my thoughts spiraled to all the things I hadn't done yet and all the things I'd refused to do in case I was outed. I could have taken my classes quicker and done summer schooling—fuck the unending loans. If I knew my time as a hidden omega was limited, I would have had sex.

The beta sniffed in my direction again before sneezing four times in a row and gaining a lot of students turning around to look at him.

"I think it's your perfume," he said when he finally stopped sneezing, but his words were mumbled by the hands still over his nose and mouth. "You smell like chalky chocolate."

I took a deep breath, but it did nothing to return my previous calm mood. He wasn't talking about my natural omega perfume—which I knew smelled like burnt marshmallows—or else I would have already gained the attention of the alphas in the class. With my nerves on edge, I gritted out, "Then sit somewhere else."

The beta huffed like he was the one that had been offended but moved to sit a couple aisles behind me. I tried taking some calming breathes, but I couldn't get my heartbeat to calm back down. There was this thing I read once, on the back of a heart healthy cereal box, that said the reason it takes a body so long to calm down after experiencing fear was because adrenaline moved through the blood stream instead of electrically through your nerves, so it took longer for your brain to get the message to calm the hell down. But I'd been deep breathing for at least a minute now and my heart was still working overtime.

Fists clenched and muscles tight, I tried taking in another deep breath, finding this one easier. At least until words distracted me.

"Yeah, I need to sit there, so why don't you part like a female's thighs." Aidan. He was the only person in the world that talked like that, and he was kicking the kid on my left out of his seat.

"What the hell do you think you're doing?" I whisper yelled at him.

The beta, to my dismay, left, and Aidan had to step over the back of the chair in order to take the seat in my row. After sitting down, he had the audacity to look at me with innocent eyes. "What? Enzo's on your other side."

I looked over at Enzo, who had made himself comfortable in the seat I had just kicked the beta out of.

He shrugged his shoulder when I looked at him, crossing his arms over his chest like he was daring me to say something to kick him out.

"Well, Lorenzo didn't force a student out of his chair. You did."

"Koda, I'm going to make an exception and explain this for you." Aidan leaned over the thin arm separating our chairs and pushed his face so close to mine all I could see were his eyes. Dark green eyes framed by the lightest of blond eyelashes. "I'm not going anywhere. You can complain all you want, but then you're going to miss Jens' lesson. Of course, then I might feel bad for distracting you and convince Jen we have to invite you over so he can give you a private lesson. Is that your goal, sweet girl? Are you trying to get us to invite you to our house because I can think of plenty of other ways for you to get that invite without hurting your education."

My throat dried up so I couldn't respond. Every one of my instincts told me to mark Aidan—scratch him or bite him or something to mark him as mine. Omegas weren't stronger than alphas, but I would challenge any alpha to try and tell his or her omega 'no' to something they wanted. It was an omega's version of power, and I wanted that over Aidan.

I dug my fingernails into my own palm, hoping my marking instinct would calm down even if it was my skin. Aidan and I were in a staring contest that felt slightly like a battle of dominance. Warm fingers wrap around my hand and forcibly uncurled my own fingers. Without looking, I knew the rough hand belonged to Lorenzo.

"Enough you two. Jen is starting." When neither of us looked away, Lorenzo added an alpha command into his tone. "Koda, look away."

My eyes instinctively followed the command although I did throw out a snort so both males knew I wasn't happy. And just to be extra petty, I planned to ignore them for the rest of the class.

JOSEPHINE LIGHT

Chapter Eight

The plan was mildly successful. And by that, I meant successful because I ignored them but only mildly because I was constantly aware of both Lorenzo and Aidan. I had tried to make myself small to ensure I didn't accidentally rub my arms against either of theirs. There was a good chance I was overreacting to physical contact but also a slight chance I would get wet at their touch—especially after the whole dominance thing with Aidan—and I was not going to risk my future on a quickie.

It was like emotional whiplash. The scent of both alphas next to me was calming, even if I didn't want it to be. I knew I shouldn't have been comfortable next to them. One wayward touch had the potential to expose me, and I tried my best to care about that fact while inhaling their delicious scents.

And even though my first plan wasn't great, I decided to make another: with class over, I was going to figure out what the hell had gotten into these males.

I packed my stuff up as slowly as I could, continuing to ignore the two alphas on either side of me. Professor Jenson didn't have another class until later, but he usually waited around after his lectures to talk to any students that needed it. Typically, that time was used up by flirting females and this time was no different. I could almost laugh at their desperation if I didn't understand the lure that was wanting Professor Jenson.

There were seven women hovering around the professor's desk as he organized something on it. He wasn't even looking up as he listened to one of them speak, nodding his head along, even as his eyes never strayed from his hands. Regardless of his apparent lack of interest, the first inkling of jealousy blotted in my stomach.

I glared at the offending females. Anger of their annoying presence fought my jealousy that he was actually listening to them. They obviously weren't paying attention to the lesson if they already had questions they couldn't have asked in front of the class. And that was why I was angry. Mostly.

"You're starting to growl, sweet girl." I turned my glare at Aidan but cut off the near-silent sound emanating from me. "No reason to look at me like a momma bear denied both types of honey-goodness. Go get your alpha."

I snorted at Aidan's words—already getting used to the way he spoke—but didn't dignify it with a response. When I looked back toward Professor Jenson, he was sitting in his chair, leaning his elbows on the desk and listening to whoever was talking to him. Did it bother me that the females were directly at boob height and all he has to do was flick his eyes straight ahead to look at them?

Yes.

Was I going to do anything about it?

"Koda, how can I help you?" Professor Jenson asked me after I had basically run down the stairs to get to his desk, unaware of having given my feet the command to move. There was something about the look he gave me that made me think he totally watched me speed the hell down here and shove the female in front of him directly out of the way. Of course, I was basically working on fumes, so I hadn't concocted a very good plan on what was going to happen once I had his attention.

"Actually, Professor Jenson, I really need to speak to you about a private matter."

"Then you should schedule time with him," some

brunette said. I didn't recognize her, which probably meant she hadn't answered a single question during class. Or it meant the class had a lot of students, but I liked my previous thought better. Her shirt was a deep cut V with some design of eyes in the proximity of where her boobs were, and if I wasn't so bothered by her presence, I would think she looked hot. "I was in the middle of speaking with Professor Jenson, and there's actually a line of us that was here before you showed up." In a move I thought was supposed to tell me she meant business, the brunette crossed her arms and popped out a hip.

Keeping my eyeroll internal was borderline impossible. I wouldn't be surprised if I actually did roll my eyes a little. At least my omega side wasn't butting in yet. My inner omega might have wanted to handle the whole situation with more attitude, but as far as she was concerned, I was taking the first steps into claiming Jenson, so she was content letting me control the situation. And it was a situation because I had created one all to get away from his two other packmates.

"Perfect." I set my backpack on the floor and pushed some of Professor Jenson's papers out of my way before sitting my ass down on his desk like I fucking owned it. Crossing one leg over the other, I made myself comfortable.

"What are you doing?" a dark-skinned girl next to me asked. Her tone was more confused than angry, but I still needed her to leave.

"Just waiting my turn."

"Are you going to let her sit on your desk, Professor Jenson," brunette complained.

I looked over my shoulder at Jenson, who was already staring in my direction. The heat in his eyes wasn't from anger. But I could still smell the beta females tainting his clean scent. Turning my attention back to the females, I gave them my best 'you need to walk away' look. It was a mixture of anger, disregard, and straight-up hope they would simply obey. If I let my inner omega out a little, they would've known to back off, not only on instinct, but with ingrained reactions all betas had to leaving an omega alone. It was a simple consequence of being a beta in a society that preferred omega. Which was why I made sure to keep her reigned in.

"We have a pack meeting," Lorenzo said beside me. What should have shocked me from the proximity of his voice only made me feel more confident in my claim that these females needed to leave. "You all need to leave."

An exasperated sigh came from behind me, but Jenson didn't dispute his packmate. The females made their way away from the desk and when the last one—the brunette who I would bet my morning coffee on had never answered questions in class—walked past me, I hopped off the desk to grab my bag. Newest plan: arrive early for our next class together and then demand answers from this pack. For now, I'd respect the privacy of the pack meeting. Especially since the other females were gone.

"You stay." Lorenzo blocked my way past him with his body. With his height, my head just reached his pectorals. I wanted to reach out and touch his chest, rake my nails down him to mark him. But I forced my eyes away from the deliciously hidden muscles and looked up. His blue eyes stared right at me, but all I could think about was the distance still between our lips. I could only imagine the strain on his neck if he were to try and kiss me without lifting me up first.

"I don't want to intrude on your pack meeting." I

took a step back so my nose was no longer only inches from Lorenzo's scent but bumped into Aidan. Lorenzo's eyes were calm—if a little wild—to my own panicked ones.

Aidan's chest pressed against my back, making me feel every rise and fall of his breath. I shifted my weight toward my toes so I wasn't leaning against Aidan. But his hands came up and wrapped around my hips, holding me to him. His body wasn't soft. The hard pressure against my ass had my core clenching, becoming slick in anticipation of being filled. Fingers around my hips tightened, my body leaning against the inviting warmth of Aidan, and I couldn't stop the little moan as my body asked for pleasure without words.

The calming scents of Aidan and Lorenzo had an extra flavor to them that was driving my omega wild. It was more than just knowing the males were turned on. It was knowing that I was the cause for it. My heartbeat was going wild. I was prey caught between these two predators. And frozen. I was not running away like I should have.

Lorenzo took another step forward, pressing against my front. I felt a small amount of slick leaking from my pussy, my body's signal to itself that I wanted to fuck these alphas, but not even that convinced me to move away. And then the softest purr I'd ever heard started from behind me, pressing into my head, until I couldn't even hold my head up anymore. I rested completely against Aidan's body, feeling the strength in his hands and chest, closing my eyes to enjoy the sound.

I was barely coherent enough to hold back my omega's purr, but I managed it.

The room was so silent, I imagined if I could focus on anything besides reigning in my omega instincts, I would be able to hear a pin drop. As it was, only our collective breathing broke the silence, and it somehow only increased my arousal.

I was nearing the point where I had to admit defeat. I wouldn't be able to say no to these alphas without a little help. I looked to my left to try and implore Jenson to help me find reason, but he was leaning back in his chair, watching the whole scene between me and his packmates without any hint of wanting to put a stop to it. His tongue came out, licking his bottom lip, and I whined my need for these males.

The sound must have reached Lorenzo because he leaned down, grabbing my jaw and forcing my head in his direction before pressing his lips against mine in a harsh kiss. I knew I should have pushed him away, but I blamed my poor judgement on all the pheromones. I swayed into Lorenzo, my feet fighting for purchase as I reached up on my tip toes, wanting to feel his body completely against mine. His lips parted as his tongue traced against my bottom lip. My head wanted to fall back, to enjoy the moment, but Lorenzo's grip along my jaw held me steady for him to explore my mouth.

"Wrap your legs around him, sweet girl."

The words momentarily cut into the purr, but I listened without hesitating. Using my hands, I pulled myself up, climbing Lorenzo like a tree, exploring and learning my way around his body. My ankles didn't reach around, so I squeezed my thighs together tightly as if they could hold me up. While one pair of hands grabbed my ass and held me tight to Lorenzo's body, the other got a grip of my hair and pulled my head away from Lorenzo's.

He growled, obviously angry at losing my kiss, and my omega was about to do the same when a new pair of lips touched my neck and my whole body froze. I was panting more than breathing as I waited to feel if those lips would go where I wanted them.

I felt a kiss, and then another, and then the light sting of a bite that didn't break the skin but marked temporary approval from an alpha. My fingers grabbed onto Lorenzo's hair, pulling his head back toward mine for another kiss. This time, it was more than just the meshing of lips. This time, I opened my mouth and let my tongue explore Lorenzo's mouth, demanding more, and took control of the kiss.

The groan came from both sides, vibrating my body in all its feel-good places, but it was a growl that pulled me out of the moment. I was slow, like my senses needed a moment to come back to me after my brain registered the sound. Pulling my lips away from Lorenzo's, I released the tight grip I had on him and set myself back down on the floor.

I heard the deep breathing of everyone around me as I stared down at the floor like it would magically provide me with the answers. Maybe starting with what the hell I was doing?

The scent of a perfumed omega was in the air and clinging to Lorenzo where I had ground myself against him. This room would easily turn into an alpha frenzy for Jenson's next class if it didn't get aired out in time.

But more importantly, Jenson, Aidan, and Lorenzo knew my secret.

My heart rate was rising again—but not in the pleasurable way. I needed to get out of here. I needed to separate myself from this room and the scent.

"How is this possible?" Jenson asked. Well, he demanded, but since I wasn't going to tell him, it was a question.

"I don't know what you're talking about." The first rule of lying: deny, deny, deny. I'd been doing it since the day I found out I wasn't truly a beta, but a broken omega, and I was going to continue to do it until I was done with needing to hide behind my beta status. I was going to graduate and get a job. Even if I decided I wanted to stay home and be a typical omega, I wanted that option. At the Omega Compound, I'd be forced into it.

I grabbed my backpack and shoved past Lorenzo—who I knew only moved aside because he was polite. The man was built like a tree, as I could attest to—since I'd climbed him.

"It smells bad in here." I said to nobody in particular. "You better light a candle."

I only made it as far as the door before Jenson said, "I wouldn't go out there if you're trying to keep your secret."

"And why's that?" I didn't turn around, but I also couldn't get my damn legs to walk out the door.

"You smell like an omega."

"I don't know what you're—"

"Talking about." Aidan finished for me. "Jenson's right. You smell like an omega."

"I'll take a shower in my room," I said through a clenched jaw.

"And walk across campus? Walk into your dorms?" I didn't hear him, but I scented Lorenzo closer than before. It was like he was distracting me with words in order to get closer. Of all the males, his accented voice was my favorite. Deep and rumbly, almost as if he was permanently upset, but when he tried to come across as gentle, it made my heart jump. "The betas may not notice but the alphas? They won't buy that you were merely around an aroused omega. Omegas don't perfume like you do around betas."

"You don't know that." I'd heard of betas in alpha packs sharing an omega. It was rare since betas and alphas usually only worked without an omega, but it was possible.

"Are you willing to stake your future on that?"

My body spun around before I'd even acknowledged how angry I'd gotten. The longer I stayed here amidst my mistake, the more frustration and guilt I felt. How could I have fallen so easily into making out with these males? Sure, they smelled good, and looked good, but I was an adult. Not a hormone angst teenager who couldn't handle her emotions. Especially lust.

Boys used to hit on me all the time in high school and when I was sitting by myself at restaurants and apparently 'looking like I could do with some company'. They tried to turn me on with their words, catch my attention with their scents, but it never worked. In fact, it was always a turn off when I had to swallow my food quicker in order to politely ask a stranger to leave me alone. And I'd scented alpha pheromones I'd found pleasing, but none—besides this pack apparently—had such a direct effect on my libido. I never feared I would perfume just by grazing arms with some alpha stranger. If that was the case, I wouldn't have managed to stay hidden for so long in mixed classes.

"What do you want from me, Lorenzo? I can't just stay here until Jenson's next class." I did my best to look into Lorenzo's blue eyes, but I could barely hold his stare for long before I had to avert my gaze to his jaw.

"Call me Enzo."

I felt the rage in my veins like it was fucking tangible. I was point two seconds away from exploding when Enzo wrapped me up in a bear hug so quickly and tightly that I had trouble breathing. I tried squirming away, but his grip didn't loosen at all. It was like the fight just flowed out of me. For the second time in an hour, I leaned my head against a male's chest. My ear didn't reach Enzo's heart, but I could hear the inner workings of his body as I breathed. Or tried to breathe.

"Jenson has a car close by. We'll take you to our place so you can shower, and we can change without causing a frenzy." The words come from Aidan, but I didn't acknowledge them. That would mean coming back to reality, and I was perfectly content burrowing into Lorenzo's chest. In fact, I was so content, I leaned all my weight on him until my own legs didn't hold me up anymore and he was forced to grab me. His grip around my back and arms didn't waiver, but I knew he was carrying me since my head rested in the perfect spot along his shoulder, next to his neck.

"What the hell did you do to her?" Jenson whisper shouted as he led the way to his car, his clean laundry scent tainted with worry. He constantly glanced over at Enzo carrying me, checking around us like he was worried about getting caught, but I didn't have any worries.

Enzo's body had a steady rhythm I was entranced by. Even considering how cold it was outside, he only wore a single t-shirt as a layer. Alphas. If I had had the energy to roll my eyes, I would have.

"Talk about it later," Enzo said. The bastard didn't even sound winded. In fact … if I hadn't known better, I would have said he sounded giddy.

When that thought threatened to bring the anger back, I decided to close my eyes and concentrate solely on Enzo. His pine tree scent was everywhere, calming me with every breath, the wind wiping away any trace of arousal clinging to our clothes. I breathed deeply and tried to hold on to this fleeting moment because when I got my wits back, I needed to separate myself from this pack.

Chapter Nine

My head felt light. Not in a bad way, like I would fall down if I stood and had my eyes open. More like a lifetime worth of stress that had subconsciously weighed me down was gone. Also wet. I definitely felt wet.

The rush of panic almost made me open my eyes, but I managed to squeeze them shut before they opened on instinct. Gently, and slowly, I stretched my fingers, feeling around for any clues on where I was. They touch something smooth, and when I trailed my fingers up, they broke the surface of the water. The small movement rippled the water, making the temperature cooler than I realized. Like a tub that had been sitting for too long without refreshing the water.

Memories came back with each ripple of the water: kissing Lorenzo, yelling at him before being lulled into a calm state, and then falling asleep. I wasn't sure how he knew how to do that, but it was a neat trick. Although their expertise in caring for me went out the window when they left me unconscious in a tub. At least, I had better be in a tub, because if they had put me in a pool, then I would have argued attempted manslaughter.

"If the number of ripples in the water is equal to the number of thoughts running through your mind, you must think faster than a male comes touching himself for the first time."

Aidan.

I guessed if I wasn't alone, it was time to officially wake up.

Opening my eyes was easier than I thought it would be. Instead of bright lights, the room was dark with small, unscented candles for the only illumination. Aidan was sitting next to me, on the ground, his back to the tub making it impossible for me to figure out how he knew I was awake. I might want to be annoyed Aidan was here, but unfortunately, I found it comforting. At least they hadn't left me alone to drown.

"The water's cold." I sat up and leaned against the back of the tub, careful to move slowly so I didn't push any water out. The tub was wider and longer than anything I'd ever used before. In fact, I was pretty sure I had this exact tub pinned on my phone as a future omega-nest-want. Tubs didn't belong in the nest, but a bathroom near a nest felt important so I'd taken to imagining how I would decorate the space. The exact nest building ran completely on instinct, but the bathroom allowed for me to make decisions on what I actually liked.

"You've been in there a while." Aidan turned his head to look at me. I knew he couldn't see much in the dark, but I still felt my cheeks blush at his gaze. He could most likely see at least the tops of my breasts and my necklace holding my room key. It wasn't more than what I would show off in a cute top, but it was blatantly obvious I was naked. Speaking of which…

"Who undressed me? Why did you undress me?" I pressed my finger to Aidan's cheek, pretending like I hadn't lingered, before pushing his head to look away from me.

"Enzo had the honors of undressing you. He's very smug about it despite the fact he claims he didn't look. Something about not wanting to be a perv. I, on the other hand, had no issue with perving."

My cheeks were as red as they could get, but I didn't interrupt him. Arguing naked wasn't on my list of things to do with a basic stranger, even if he didn't feel like one.

"And as to the question of why. We promised to get the stink off you and that meant washing your clothes as well as you."

I was low-key grateful he called it stink, even if his voice faltered over the word.

"Where is Enzo?"

There was a bit of silence before, Aidan said, "Well, he's already jerked off twice since you've been in here, but I imagine he's doing it again."

I couldn't stop the gasp from escaping even though I begged my lips not to release the sound. If I could get words out, I would have begged Aidan to stop too.

"I bet he's taking his shirt your pussy rubbed against and fucking inhaling your scent as he takes his cock in his hand and imagines it's you. Maybe your hand, your mouth, your pussy. Any part of you. If he's anything like me, then he just needs a single fucking thought about you before he threatens to lose his load. That makes him grip his cock even harder to try to put off the ending, but it won't work. And when he's finished, it won't help. He'll just feel unsatisfied."

I didn't have any words. Actually, that was a lie. I had lots of words like "kiss me" or "fuck me" or "touch me in any way that will make the sudden appearance of the wetness in my pussy go away". But I wasn't going to get sucked in again. Saying no to one was easy. Easier. Still nearly impossible but necessary. I chanted the word over and over again: necessary.

"Do you have any soaps?" The tub was set up in the middle of the room without any lip for products. It was mostly meant for relaxing, not cleaning. Totally posh but it wasn't mine. Might as well indulge.

"Now that you're awake, I'll let you get washed. There's stuff Enzo picked out for you on the floor over here. I can turn the light on, on the way out. You'll see a towel and a robe hanging on the wall near your feet."

Aidan left, turning on the lights while I managed a whispered thank you and lots of blinking and eye covering to deal with the sudden brightness. Note to self: in my bathroom next to my future nest, I wanted dimming lights.

I picked up the soaps Aidan mentioned and nearly dropped the first bottle in the water. It was a fancy brand I'd never even heard of before but that wasn't what stopped me. Three incomes could easily afford the special non-scented soap. What rekindled the warm specks of jealousy I thought had extinguished were three words on the bottle in pretty cursive: Recommended for Omegas.

Was it irrational to be upset that the sexually active alphas had soap for the willing sexual partners they brought back to their house? Yes. But that knowledge didn't help.

I turned down the route of petty. If I was going to clean with the fancy soaps, I might need two or three washes. You know, just to ensure my true scent was really gone. I squeezed the bottle hard, but nothing came out. I hit the bottom of the bottle like it was one of those old style non-squeezable ketchup bottles. Still nothing.

Twisting off the cap, I found the source of the blockage. The stupid silver cover that meant the bottle was unopened was still intact. Did the males just hand these bottles out to their omega guests? I guessed that made sense. Like some sort of weird gift for their sexual encounters.

Oh goodness. Was that what I was? Just one of the many females who had made out with Lorenzo. Hell, I even met his ex. Who, come to think of it, was a beta.

What did that mean for the omega soaps? Sure, non-omegas could buy and use it, but other brands had options for alpha and beta pheromones. Why this omega specific product?

It took a few tries with my wet hands to get the protective cover off, and even longer to get the others off too. But I finally managed it and washed up in the cold water, letting my mind race. I ignored the water waving over the sides as I reached for bottles my inner omega preened at using. By the time I finished and reached for the towel while the tub drained, I worried more water was out of the tub than went down the drain.

Since my clothes were being washed—hopefully done now so I could make a quick escape—it left me with only the robe Aidan mentioned. It was softer than I anticipated and a white that reminded me of sheep's wool. I laid down the towel in an attempt to mop up the water before I carefully set it over the side of the tub to let it dry out.

A knock on the door came before I heard Jenson's voice asking if he could come in.

I wrapped the robe tight across my body and made sure to tie the belt to hold it in place. The robe had pockets, so I shoved my hands into them and told Jenson to come in. No longer in his work clothes, the alpha still looked elegant even in the comfort of his own home. Brown pants with a light orange shirt that unbuttoned down to his pectoral muscles. And damn, was I right before when I guessed—no, hoped—he had hair on his chest. Professor Jenson did not lack in the chest hair department and was it weird I wanted to run my fingers through it?

His eyes immediately went to the towel on the tub and a small smile formed on his lips before he glanced back at me, a serious look overcoming whatever inside joke.

"How was your bath?"

"Good." I internally cringed at the bitter tone, so I

tried again. "I love this tub." When Jenson didn't say anything to fill the silence my mouth kept talking without permission. "And the new bottles of unscented soaps were a nice touch. For omegas."

Jenson nodded like I asked a question. "Aidan was excited to finally use the stuff he picked out for our future omega. He goes on trips a lot and always comes back with something new."

Wait, Aidan picked all this out? I looked back at the soaps, clearly remembering Aidan telling me Enzo picked it out for me.

"Early on, Aidan would always show us what he found. Explain how our omega would like it for this reason or that. But over the years, he's started hiding away his finds."

They'd been a pack for years? Sure, Jenson might be a professor at the university, but he had to be new based on how young he was. I always thought of him as early twenties with his dark hair and model-like clothing. The male knew how to put outfits together better than a stereotypical gay character whose sole purpose in a TV show was to make their female best friend hot. And I guessed imagining him younger helped my conscious deal with how attractive I had found him. Who was I kidding? I couldn't put my crush in the past tense. It was very real, and very much threatening to arouse me again if I didn't distract myself on menial thing.

"How old are you?" I asked.

If Jenson was shocked by the change in topic, he didn't show it. "Twenty-six. I'm the oldest in the pack but only by a couple days."

"Who's next?"

"Aidan."

"And Lorenzo?"

"Enzo is a year younger than us, but he skipped a

grade when he first came here. We've all known each other since middle school."

I nodded, but I didn't have anything else to say.

"C'mon. I cancelled classes for the rest of the day, so I have time to look over the progress of your project for my class."

"Really? You'd do that?"

There was a look in Jenson's eyes I didn't like. It wasn't unattractive, but it made me feel like I was missing some vital information. I tightened the robe around me in a pseudo-protective layer.

He stood off to the side and gestured for me to actually leave the bathroom. "I'll take care of you," he said. His voice was so quiet, I wondered if he meant for me to hear it.

JOSEPHINE LIGHT

Chapter Ten

The rest of the house wasn't as elegant as the bathroom. And I hated to admit it, but I liked it. Damn whoever they hired for an interior designer because he or she or they were spot on. The flooring looked like wood but was actually tile. Hallways were large enough for two people to walk side by side, even alphas. Windows were floor to ceiling and appeared to be solid panes of glass. The doors to whatever rooms were twice as wide as I was used to and almost twice as tall. Photos of all three pack members doing different sports, hanging out, or with their blood families decorated walls.

It might scream cozy, but it was still a mansion. I was used to standing in a room and being able to see the whole space. This house had multiple hallways. The first had several doors that Jenson pointed out as three different studies and even an empty room for a nest— right next to where the bathroom was located. Another hallway contained the resident bedrooms and the final one held the garage, laundry room, and gym. The hallways all extended from a center space surrounding the kitchen and living room.

I found my backpack on the floor next to the couch in the living room. Jenson made himself comfortable on one of the single seater couches, and I joined him, careful not to flash too much leg. He already got a show earlier today when I made out with his packmate.

Holy hell, I didn't want to imagine what Jenson thought of me. It hadn't occurred to me until now that it was Jenson's annoyed growl that pulled me out of the cloud of lust with his packmates. I wasn't any better than all the other females clawing at him after his classes—

worse because I hadn't even kissed him—but he still had to watch me be sexually trapped between Aidan and Enzo.

"What are you thinking about?" Jenson's suddenly gruff voice didn't pull me out of the fantasy like it should've.

I needed a distraction. Something that wasn't sexual in any way before I was forced to take another bath because my pussy leaked, demanding attention.

But what?

My project.

I lunged for my backpack, which probably looked more dramatic than was necessary, and ripped open my folders and notebook before shoving it all toward Jenson. He didn't grab the papers, and I realized it was because he was staring at me. Or more like glaring. If glaring was sexy.

"Will you please look that over?" I asked, meeting his dark brown eyes.

Jenson continued staring at me, and I simply stared back, breathing harder than I should've considering I was sitting on the couch, not doing anything. I couldn't stay in this house much longer, no matter how much my inner omega loved it here. All three alpha scents covered everything. Every hallway, all the seats, even the air. Pine trees, fresh laundry, desert rainstorm. There was nothing sexy about the scents, but apparently my desperate female parts didn't care.

I wasn't sure what attracted an omega to certain scents, something I was sure the Omega Compound covered, and couldn't wait to learn about one day.

The longer I sat, the more their scents would cling to me. Hell, I bet my clothes were going to smell like them, and there would be no fighting my instincts on shoving those clothes into my nest when I got back to my room.

My nest sounded like paradise at that moment. Some place dark and comforting to hide away from the arousing smells and unfamiliar feelings. I could get my thoughts together without the quirks Jenson was obviously noticing even if he wasn't directly looking at me. My leg wouldn't stop bouncing, my fingers were wringing together, and I was biting the insides of my cheek. I worried I might make it bleed if I kept going. Fighting my instincts was harder than I thought. And right then, my instincts not only wanted Jenson sexually, but the stress of fighting them led me to wanting him for comfort.

Without anything to do, I stared at Jenson while he looked over my project. No, it was more than just staring. I memorized everything about him. His sharp jaw lines with the stubbled beard just dark and thick enough to cover his skin but not enough to grab—although the tingling sensation in my fingers wanted me to try. He was staring intently at the mess of papers in his laps, his brows low over his eyes and pulled together so tightly a crease formed between them. I knew what it was like to be on the receiving end of his brown eyes, to hold that intense gaze while he lectured.

Damn, was I actually jealous of my papers?

"Okay," Jenson said. He set the papers down on the coffee table, grabbed my hand, and pulled me up.

"You read it all that quickly? Wait. Where are we going?"

I was focused more on Jenson's grip on my hand than the direction he led me. His grip was firm, his hands larger than mine but steady in their hold. I could feel where every one of my fingers was holding on to Jenson. Not in any romantic way but more like a stressful, am I holding too tight, not tight enough, should I pull away even if I don't want to kind of way. It was my first time holding someone's hand, and it was more nerve racking than I imagined.

Keeping my designation a secret had always been my first priority. Which meant no dates. No crushes. No sexual desires except the ones I hid in my private thoughts deep in the safety of my nest. When I covered myself in blankets and pillows, it was like I could fantasize about anything—or anyone—without having to worry about my scent. It was my safe place.

Except I had let myself be lulled into sexual desire—into safety—in a public classroom, by not one but three alphas.

"Here." Jenson stopped in front of a random door down the same hallway as the bathroom I woke up in but didn't let go of my hand.

"Are you going to tell me what's on the other side of the door or am I supposed to guess?"

Jenson's lips quirked as if he was going to smile. "Just open the door and find out."

I reached for the handle but stopped myself from turning it. "If something or someone jumps out at me, I'm leaving. I will walk out of this mansion in a robe."

That earned a full laugh from Jenson, but I waited to hear confirmation before I risked following through with my words and walking outside basically naked. "Nothing will jump out at you, Koda. I promise."

With that reassurance, I opened the door. The first thing that caught my attention was how dark it was. There weren't any windows in the room to even hint at the time. I assumed Jenson found the switch because the lights finally came on in a dim setting, just barely illuminating the whole room. There was a ledge, at floor level with the rest of the house, that wrapped around the entire room. The middle of the room was about two feet lower than the ledge but a set of stairs in front of the door, just a step away, invited me to make the descent. Without any decorations, the room looked bland, but I could see its potential. Maybe with some blankets and pillows it could be…

"A nest?"

Jenson nodded. "An empty one. It's never been used, actually. I know we come in here sometimes to talk. Or if we want to be alone. At least, I used to come in here."

"Used to?"

"I still do, just less frequently. But I figured you could use the space." The confusion must have read on my face because Jenson added, "Koda, you're bouncing off the walls. You can't hold still. Sit in here, take a nap, whatever you need to feel like you again."

"But a nest? That's for an omega." And one inside a house is meant for a pack omega, not a guest.

I didn't meet Jenson's gaze, but I felt it on me like he was trying to see into my thoughts. My soul. Into my truth.

"Then I guess you don't want any blankets or pillows," Jenson said.

The thought of decorating this space for my nest intrigued me, any lie otherwise would be obvious. But what would happen when I left? When I walked out the front door and demanded these alphas left me alone? They would find a new omega. One that perfumed properly and wanted this room for his or her perfect nest. If they didn't get this room cleaned properly, an omega might smell me. Even if I did smell like a beta, it would still be my scent on the omega's blankets, pillows, and soaked into the walls.

And why does that idea excite me?

"If you tell me where to find the blankets and

pillows, I wouldn't object."

The look of surprise on Jen's face made me laugh, but he recovered quickly, telling me I could go into any room and just pull covers, sheets, and pillows off beds and couches. Seemed strange to me, but my inner omega loved the idea of taking things that would smell like these males. Better than clean towels and such that were locked in a musty closet. He headed back toward the living room, and I made my way from room to room to scavenge some nest materials.

My beta side was effectively pushed to the back as my inner omega went hunting.

Chapter Eleven

The hallway that held all the bedrooms was on the opposite side of the living room, closer to the kitchen. There were several doors down the hallway but without any decorations along the way there was no way to tell which room was whose. Without any consideration, I chose the first room on the left, closest to the kitchen. With a bed, a desk, and two doors on the one side that most likely led to a bathroom and closet, the scent of all three alphas was weaker here than in the hallway. Most likely meant this was a guest room. The thought of using these materials in my nest didn't excite me. Of course, I could've asked any one of the males to rub their scent all over it, but that felt too close to admitting the truth.

And yes, I knew they already knew, but it was their word against mine in any situation where they told the administration. As long as I didn't perfume in public or actually admit to being an omega—I was safe with my beta scent.

Not really a lie, even if it wasn't the full truth.

Now I just have to get my clothes and then convince these alphas to not bring this up again. To anyone.

I couldn't imagine Jenson would be willing to look over my project if he was just going to get me kicked out. Aidan wasn't angry when he flirted with me in the bathroom. And assuming Aidan was telling the truth, Lorenzo didn't seem to hate my scent. But would he hate that I'd sort of but not really lied to him?

I shook my head, wanting the serious and negative thoughts to magically fly out. Jenson was right, I was stressed, and a nest would help. A good one, not one with bad scents that would just make me more agitated.

So I left the room, closed the door behind me, and crossed the hallway, refusing to be intimated by my truth.

Barely opening the door, the scent of Jenson leaked out. My excitement felt palpable as I squeezed my way inside, trying to keep the scent in the room as much as possible. The head of the bed was pushed against the opposite wall. Large bookshelves lined the wall to the right. A door, opened slightly to the closet, on the left side of the room had a mirror installed on it. Farther along the same wall was a set of dressers, a desk that didn't look used, and another door that was closed (most likely leading to a bathroom). The windows were up high on the same wall as the head of the bed. They took up the whole length of the wall but were only about a foot down from the ceiling so Jensen could get undressed in this room without worrying about someone looking in or needing curtains.

Several framed pictures on the desk caught my attention but looking at them felt wrong. I was only supposed to get pillows and blankets. Ignoring my curiosity was unnatural, like an itch I was trying to power through instead of scratching, but I managed it. Sort of. I threw the pillows at my feet—at least I was clean—and started undressing the bed. I took everything off the bed. All the way down to the fitted sheet. I rolled them all up and headed back to the nest room.

Jenson wasn't in the living room anymore, but considering my backpack was missing, I assumed he was in one of the at-home offices he pointed out.

It took two trips before I had all of Jenson's bed—minus the actual bed—in the nest room. But I didn't stop there. Maybe for the nest in my dorm, this would have been enough, but not for a nest of this size. I needed more.

I went to the door next to the guest room and,

without thinking, slipped inside.

And froze.

In the room was a half-naked Lorenzo, a towel wrapped around his waist as he rifled through what I could only assume to be his underwear drawer.

He looked up at me, but I couldn't get my mouth to move. My lips were opened in a silent gasp as the memory of clinging to Lorenzo played over and over again in my mind. I remembered how soft and firm his lips were. How tight he held me against him, his moans, his touch. His rough demand for me to call him Enzo.

Being able to see his body was like the greatest temptation. His skin was darker than his packmates', and he had more hair on his chest and stomach than Jenson. I wanted to explore every inch of him with my hands. My lips. I wanted to run my fingers along his body and tug on his body hair to make sure he was only thinking about me while I took in my fill of his skin.

A groan that didn't come from Enzo, but near him, pulled my attention down his arms and to his death-like grip on the dresser drawer.

"I'm sorry," I managed to whisper. Whether or not he heard me, he didn't respond to my apology, but the veins in his forearms were somehow standing out. It was only concern for Enzo's health that helped me break out of my trance. "I should go."

"Why?" It was less of a question and more of a demand for an answer. "Why did you come in here?"

"I'm sorry. I didn't know it was your room. I should have knocked."

"Whose room did you think it was?" Talking didn't seem to help Enzo relax his grip. The color was leaving his knuckles as he held onto the drawer.

"No one's. Jenson said I could collect some blankets and pillows, so I'm going room to room. I wasn't really thinking." I felt my cheeks heat with a blush. Enzo's attention flickering from my own, down to my cheeks, only turned them a darker shade.

"For a nest?" I was about to deny it, to explain it wasn't really a nest, when he said, "Take it. Take anything you want that's mine, Koda."

The rasp in his voice almost brought me to my knees, but somehow, I convinced myself to walk to his bed. Instead of pushed back against the wall to the back of the house, Enzo's bed was on the far-left side, the head of the bed sharing the same wall as the guest. My eyes never strayed from his as I stripped the bed. He only had one pillow and I made sure to grab that as well.

Enzo watched me as I turned everything into a big ball to carry. Before I got the chance to say "thanks" and get the hell out of his room, Enzo crossed the space in just a few steps, stopping in front of me with only the ball of Enzo-smelling-sheets between us.

With all the alphas in this house, I had to tilt my head up to see them, but with Enzo so close, and the tallest in the pack, his proximity felt overwhelming. I remembered what it was like to have my legs wrapped around his body. To rub myself against him, trying to scent him and get myself off at the same time. He was so different from Jenson; I couldn't help but wonder how I'd attracted two opposites.

Enzo's blue eyes were bright even if they weren't as intelligent as Jenson's. His face was shaved but not smooth, like his hair was already growing back. I knew if I ran my fingers along his jaw, I would feel the bite of his stubble. And my fingers ached to reach out and touch him.

There was something with Enzo I didn't feel with the others. A comfortable silence. Like I could've dropped what I was holding, threw myself at him, and

Enzo would hold me. No questions ask.

I also knew Enzo would be a good alpha to his omega. But I was not that omega. Because I wasn't a true omega, and these males deserved the best.

"Thank you." I barely got the words out before I flew out of the room, throwing myself into the nest. Instead of focusing on the aching feeling that started the moment I was in Enzo's presence, I spread out the sheets that smelled of him and mixed them into Jenson's.

Every instinct in my body told me to go find Aidan's room and get his scent too, but I ignored it. I didn't know if I'd survive another run-in without dropping to my knees and begging to be rutted. I'd never had sex, but my body was definitely telling me that my pussy was too empty. I needed to be filled, and any one of the alphas in this house would do.

Making the nest with only two scents, however, quickly grated on my nerves. The more I created, the more I hated it until the nest was done and I tore it down again. Frustrated, I held onto that emotion and marched myself back out of the nest to find Aidan's room.

This time, I made sure to knock.

"Come in."

I would have just peeked my head in, but I didn't want to let his scent out. Weird but necessary. Unlike Enzo, Aidan was fully dressed when I came into his room. His bed was a single mattress in the middle of the room which somehow did and did not surprise me. Pillows were on and off the bed, the covers thrown around. Aidan's room was the messiest but also had the most decorations. Photos lined walls instead of just being displayed on desks like Jenson's room. Along the back wall was windows—like Jenson's—with light, orange-colored curtains covering them. Clothes of all type decorated the floor and basically any available surface.

If my dorm room wasn't also this messy, I might have made fun of Aidan. But alas, hypocrisy wasn't in the books for now.

I'd also realized I hadn't gotten a good look at Enzo's room, and it made me sadder than it should've.

I found Aidan sitting on the floor, leaning his back against the bed, while typing away on his phone. He looked up, his smile blinding when he noticed me. Or maybe blinding wasn't the right word. His smile was contagious because my bad mood at not seeing Enzo's room and not having Aidan's scent quickly disappeared. I matched Aidan's smile with one of my own.

"What can I do for you, Koda bear?"

My heart jumped at the nickname. "I was hoping to collect your sheets and pillows."

"Oh yeah, what for?"

I knew what he wanted me to say—it was the same thing Enzo guessed but hadn't made me confirm. "I'm making a fort."

"A fort."

"Yep."

"Can I help then? Since it's for a fort."

"Absolutely. I was hoping for bed supplies from you. That's helping."

Aidan's laugh was full. I watched him throw his head back with the beautiful sound. There were some people that giggled at small comments and then there were people like Aidan who threw their whole body and soul into everything they did. All their love and joy. It was amazing to watch.

When Aidan finally calmed down, he stood and started stripping his bed. "You need pillows too?"

I nodded.

"And pray, tell, where are you making this definitely-not-a-nest fort?"

"In an empty room Jen showed me."

"Jen?"

It took me a moment to realize why Aidan sounded confused. And then I realized I'd used Jenson's nickname. My inner omega liked the familiarity, but my beta side was worried I had crossed an intimate line I had no plans to remain on. I started picking up all of Aidan's pillows off the ground, pretending like I wasn't emotionally conflicted.

"I wish I had a nickname," Aidan said.

His melancholy tone caught my attention. I tried to meet his gaze, but he remained solely focused on stripping his bed. It felt like more than a simple wanting of a nickname. As if I had walked onto a sore spot for Aidan.

With the bed stripped and Aidan still holding some blankets, he nodded toward the door. "After you, Koda bear."

I led the way to the nest, carefully opening the door and setting everything down before a ball of blankets hit me, almost knocking me over. I gaped at Aidan, who'd obviously thrown the blankets at me.

He laughed at his own actions, hunching over as he wiped the tears that spilled onto his cheeks.

My omega side soaked in his laughter like the sound was made specifically for her.

"I figured you wouldn't want me to come in," Aidan finally said. "To your fort building space, that is."

A part of me wanted to tell him it was fine, but the other part—the one that came from pure instinct— hated the idea of an alpha in an unfished nest. I hadn't realized until he said it that I would have freaked out if Aidan had walked in without permission. Despite my claims this wasn't even a real nest. It looked like I was the only one believing that lie, but I was thankful for it.

"Thank you, Addie," I said without looking up. My inner omega couldn't stand the slight scent of Aidan's sadness clinging to him. If he wanted a nickname so he felt just as intimate with me as Jen was, I easily obliged. After all, pleasing alphas was my inner omega's sole purpose.

Turning, I started immediately on my nest, completely satisfied with all the scents. When I didn't hear the door close, I added without looking up, "Don't let the door hit you on the way out."

Addie's laugh was the last thing I heard before the soft click.

Chapter Twelve

By the time I finished the nest, I was breathing hard and sweating. It was hard work to organize and decorate and create a comfortable nest with this large of a space. My inner omega demanded all the ground, sides, and even the overhead to be covered in alpha scent which made the nest look like a very big sleeping bag. Or a fort.

Most of the time my nests were burrow shaped. I got in by digging myself under the pillows and blankets. But this time I was able to make a pseudo roof because the space had the proper bottomed-out flooring. It worked more for comfort but for sex, the roof would have to come down. I could sit up when inside but standing or too much maneuvering would ruin it.

But I shouldn't have been thinking of that.

Ideally, I would've had even more blankets and pillows to fill up the space, but my inner omega was content enough to let me rest.

Jenson was right. I felt calmer now than I had in … ever. The alpha pheromones didn't smell of arousal, which meant I could take as many deep breaths as I wanted without getting turned on. Of course, I could've accidentally turned myself on by imagining or remembering. But I refused to do that.

Instead, I took my robe off, climbed in, and napped.

****

An annoying knocking sound forced me to wake up, but, gratefully, it finally stopped so I could fall back asleep.

"She's not answering," Aidan said, his voice muffled.

"She's probably sleeping," Jenson said. His voice

was just as muffled but slightly annoyed.

"Yeah, with her face down and liable to suffocation."

Aidan's petulant tone had me smiling, attempting to shake off the last remains of sleep. It took only a moment to realize the males weren't nearby and to remember where I was—in a nest, in an alpha pack's house.

"Aidan, she's an adult and an omega," Jenson said. "She's not going to suffocate in her own nest."

There was a soft snorting sound. "She called it a fort. Which means we can just walk in and check on her."

Enzo finally entered the conversation. "We all know it's more than a fort. Don't do something that will push her away just to play with her boundaries."

I knew I should've stopped eavesdropping and told them all I was fine. Especially Aidan. But my nest was comfortable. I couldn't convince myself to disturb the silence with so much as a grunt. It didn't help that the alphas' voices lulled me into feeling safe, making the idea of leaving the nest feel even more unnecessary.

"Koda bear," Aidan shouted through the door. "You have thirty seconds to make some sort of noise to tell me you're okay or I'm coming into your nest."

"Absolutely not," Enzo growled.

"Enzo, calm down. Aidan, you need to relax. And Koda, if you're awake, stop adding to the drama and speak up." Jenson's frustration was evident even through the door. And it was enough to catch my inner omega's attention. Tempers were rising, and she was pushing me to soothe the alphas. Fucking instincts.

I stretched in the nest and finally crawled my way back out. It took a few seconds, but I finally orientated myself to the entrance, only to stretch again when I got out. My robe was on the stairs leading up to the edge where the door was. I put it on, making sure nothing inappropriate was exposed, and cracked open the door.

Three sets of eyes all turned to look at me, but I yawned before I could get out so much as a "hi". And it was one of those long yawns too, requiring my jaw to stretch for several seconds before I could finally close my mouth again. I felt even more tired than I did before I took a nap. My body swayed slightly before I lifted my arms up in front of me, waiting. The lights in the hallway were brighter than in the nest room, and I kept my eyes closed.

I wiggled my fingers, demanding without words. And when I finally felt someone grab me around the waist and lift me up, I took a deep breath of pine forest. I wrapped myself around Enzo, resting my head on his shoulder, my inner omega purring from the combination of safety and comfort.

"Do you want something to eat, Koda bear?"

The question had me open one eye.

Aidan smiled at me, but there was a look in his eyes that I recognized from staring in my own mirrors. Loneliness. It was the same emption I'd scented on him earlier. Even as he was surrounded by his packmates.

"What are you making, Addie?" My voice was still croaky from sleeping, but the use of his nickname made the sadness disappear. Even if it was temporary.

"Anything you want, Koda bear."

"Need. Coffee."

"I don't know. Sleepy Koda seems more pliable." The humor in Jenson's voice made me huff.

I closed my eye again when Enzo started walking. His rhythmic pace made it hard to keep my legs wrapped around his large frame when I was too tired to work my muscles.

Enzo seemed to get this because he set his arms,

like bars, under my thighs, and held me up. A more aware Koda would've complained, but I was really more asleep than awake.

Eventually, the rhythm stopped and something hard—harder than simply Enzo's thigh—pressed against the side of my calves. I remembered I was in a robe, but my inner omega didn't seem to sense an issue with that. I stayed leaning against Enzo until his hand started rubbing circles on my back, startling me. The quick dose of adrenaline helped open my eyes for a moment, but all I saw was the empty living room.

"Coffee is on the counter," Jenson said. I would have ignored the words altogether in favor of more sleep, but I could smell the coffee. And I loved coffee.

Pushing against Enzo's chest, I turned my head around, looking for the delicious smell. My inner omega was loving all the attention.

"Mine." I wiggled my fingers again, my sights zeroed in on the mug, even as most of my body stayed draped over Enzo.

Aidan reached for the mug, a plain white one with the words *8 to the Bar* written in blue cursive, and handed it to me. "Don't spill on Enzo. He might put up with a lot, but I think hot coffee on him will make him angry."

A soft purr underneath me begged to differ. That purr said I could spill all the cups of coffee and Enzo would continue to let me lay on him. But I didn't want to do that. I took extra care to ensure I had a good grip on the cup and slowly brought it to my lips.

The first sip was delicious. There was a small amount of caramel in it, hinting at added syrup. The idea any of the alphas might have noticed the kind of coffee I drank when they came to the coffee shop or stared long enough at my cups in Jenson's classroom made my omega preen.

With every sip, my mind became clearer. By the time I was halfway done with my cup, I managed to push back against blatant omega instincts. And then I realized I was still straddling Enzo. If I could die from embarrassment, the guys would've needed to start CPR. But alas, I was stuck flushing bright red and sweating through my palms. Carefully, I switched hands on the mug and untangled myself from the alpha. His hands slid against my thighs as I pushed off him, but I put all my focus on not tipping my mug.

There was an awkward silence when I got in my own bar stool. I refused to look up from my mug as I took sip after sip until it was all gone and I was stuck staring at the bottom, still refusing to look up.

The sound of footsteps spiked my curiosity. Jenson walked down the hallway toward us—although I hadn't noticed when he walked away—with folded clothes in his hands. My clothes. He must have used de-scenters since the fresh laundry scent was only tinged with a natural alpha male scent from Jen. A part of me hoped his natural scent clung to the clothes, and I had to physically shake my head to rid it of that thought.

"Do you remember the way to the bathroom you used earlier?" Jenson asked.

I took the clothes and nodded, all without looking at him, careful to not graze his fingers. Then I hurried from the room, ignoring the pain building in my chest.

Entering the bathroom, I found the candles blown out, their lids securely placed. Several switches were by the door, working the lighting in different areas of the room. I stared at my dream tub, wishing I could've taken it with me when I left.

The counter space was covered in numerous products, almost like they had been strategically laid out. In fact, despite the drying towel I had used earlier for my body, the sink, floor, and tub looked clean to the point that there weren't even water stains. If all the males had bathrooms in their bedrooms, who used this one?

After I put on my normal clothes, I stood in the middle of the bathroom, holding the robe and only slightly panicking over what to do with it. Did I bring it out into the living room so they could clean it? Did I just leave it the way I found it, marking it as mine for another omega to notice? I stared at myself in the mirror above the sink, knowing if any of the alphas barged in, I would've looked crazy.

I could admit, in another lifetime, I would have enjoyed being the omega to these alphas. The tub I'd always wanted in a bathroom just for me, a nest full of pleasurable scents and large enough for all four of us, even the delicious coffee with the attentive males who knew how to make it. Addie with his lightness, Enzo with his comfort, and Jen with his encouragement.

And I wanted to cling to it. I wanted to ask them to wait a little bit longer—until I graduated or maybe worked for a few years. Then I could be their omega.

But to ask them to put their lives on hold for me? I wasn't that selfish.

No matter how much I wanted them, I was still keeping my inner omega hidden, living as the part of myself that identified as a beta. Maybe I could've taken on one alpha, especially since this pack had a history of dating betas, but there was no way I could've chosen between the three. Omegas got packs—not betas.

This pack wanted to share a female—an omega. They might want me temporarily, but just like the other female betas, I wasn't endgame. Not while I was still a beta.

I needed to leave. I needed to focus on school, on graduating and living my life as a typical beta. Maybe even make a friend. The only person that said "hi" to me regularly was Knox, and she had to say hi to everyone who lived in our dorm.

Taking a deep breath, I left the robe draped over the tub, so it wasn't on the floor but would still be washed, and braced myself to say goodbye to the alphas. I told myself over and over again that I wanted this.

I found the alphas sitting in the living room. Despite their relaxed postures, the air was full of melancholy and silence. All three males looked my way when I entered, but they didn't look happy to see me. They looked more … resigned.

"Thank you for washing my clothes." Just those words felt impossible to get out.

"Of course, Koda." Jenson never took his eyes from mine, blatantly ignoring Aidan glaring at him.

"I have to leave," I said.

"We'll drive you home," Aidan said, finally tearing his gaze away from Jenson to look at me. It was the blond alpha I was most worried about convincing me to stay. While Jenson was an alpha to always support me and Enzo was an alpha to put my wants above his, Addie was an alpha unable to hide his emotions. His sadness. His longing.

"I think it's better if we part ways here. Now." I ignored the swelling feeling in the back of my throat and the pain in my heart as I said the words. But now that I'd started, I couldn't seem to get them to stop. "Whatever you think happened earlier in the classroom didn't. My natural scent is the scent I claim, and every designation test I've ever took says beta. So that's what I am."

"Koda—" Lorenzo called my name, trying to interrupt me, but I kept going, ignoring the burn that had moved from my throat to the back of my eyes.

"Please, you can't tell anyone. I'm so close to

graduating. I know it's against the rules, but technically I am beta. Like a half-beta and there aren't rules against that."

All I could do was wait, holding my breath until my lungs burned. It was terrifying that my future solely relied on these males. My whole body was shaking with nerves, and I clung to that instead of my sadness. I had no back-up plan if I was kicked out of the academy. My heart wouldn't be able to take the loss of this pack with the loss of school. I didn't know what was so different about this pack, what called me to them, and them to me. But I knew my omega had decided they were hers. And losing too much might've destroyed me.

All three males finally broke the deafening silence, agreeing to keep my secret.

I refused to let the relief fill my body, although I did finally take a breath, gasping for air. I stared extra hard at Jenson, pleading with my eyes.

Finally, he said, "I promise Koda. I won't tell anyone. You can keep going to school."

I felt like I could breathe easier knowing my secret was safe, even if it did nothing to block out the pain in my heart. My inner omega didn't care about my education. She was focused on the scents coming from the alphas, wanting to console them. Aidan's sadness. Jenson's frustration. Lorenzo's anger. But I fought it.

"I need my backpack and phone please."

Aidan stood, walking off toward the hallway with his bedroom. It took me until the door slammed to realize he wasn't planning to get my stuff.

"I'll get it," Jen said, his words feeling quiet even in the silence.

Then it was just me and Enzo. Not even my beta side was immune to wanting to comfort him. I wanted to run my fingers through his hair before I lost that right.

But I never had it. They wanted an omega, and I wasn't ready to be one. My choices were pack or school. Alphas or a career. I wanted to explain that, but I didn't know how. I didn't know how to get my tongue to move, how to get the words out, how to make his pain go away. "Enzo—

"Here you go, Koda." Jenson came back into the room holding my stuff. Enzo left without a goodbye, and all I could do was watch. "I ordered a car service to come get you."

"Thank you."

A tear slipped out, and Jenson reached up to wipe it away. But I knew the moment I let him comfort me, I'd change my mind about leaving. I took a step back, letting his arm fall between us.

"I think I'll wait outside."

JOSEPHINE LIGHT

Chapter Thirteen

I was fine.

After eleven days of continuing to live without the alphas my inner omega wanted to claim, I knew the pain wouldn't kill me. It was just lowering my appetite, increasing my stress, fucking with my sleeping, and making me irrationally horny to the point I'd given myself an orgasm two or three times a day but found no relief.

None of the alphas had argued with me—for me—when I left their house. It had been the last time I saw Lorenzo and Aidan, since neither had showed up to any of Jenson's classes.

And it wasn't the caffeine—from the two cups of regular and iced coffee I'd had—or the heartbreak, that had me shaking. It was the possessive instinct from my inner omega demanding that I went back to their house and claimed those alphas. I hadn't even realized how hard it would be to leave them until I'd gotten in the back of the car Jenson had ordered for me.

Since then, I'd relived my time in that house over and over. Why hadn't I spent more time with the alphas while my clothes were being washed? If that was my last chance to kiss and taste them, *I should've taken it.*

I was a mess.

I couldn't even convince myself to get ready and go to the coffee shop like I usually did on Fridays. In fact, I hadn't done a lot of work this week. I'd ensured the bare minimum in homework was finished, not managing to stay ahead in anything which, consequently, was the only reason I had survived on minimal work this week. The world was mumbling, and I couldn't focus enough to understand what was being said even if I did manage to take notes. I knew if I didn't get my shit together, my classes would only get harder.

This wasn't safe. Not for my health; and not for my stay at the academy.

My inner omega had basically taken control of my life, pouting that she was without her alphas. I spent every available moment in my dorm's makeshift nest, trying and failing to find comfort without the alphas' pheromones.

Something had to change, but without any friends, I had no one to confide in. I'd spent my entire life so focused on my goals, so focused on my own routine, I'd never had to deal with the unknown before. How did anyone handle heart ache? A crush? Who should I have talked to?

In a moment of pure desperation, I forced myself out of the dorm and down to room 101. Because desperate people would do anything. Even talk to over-preppy RAs.

I had barely knocked on the door before it flew open, revealing an overly cheery Knox. Her pepper alpha scent beat at my nose. "Hey, Knox, can I talk to you?"

"Oh goodness, yes, yes, yes." She laughed at something, maybe her own excitement, but stopped quickly when I didn't join her. I tried giving her a reassuring smile, but that was like a trigger for tears, so I wiped that emotion from my face. "Why don't you come back into my office, Koda? We can talk more privately there about anything."

Her "office" was really a desk with two chairs in her dorm room. All of her walls were covered in posters about joining bands or events on campus and photos of her with family and friends. Bright colors were everywhere on the bed sheets, blinds, and blankets, but at least it was clean. It was slightly nauseating being in an alpha's space with such strong pheromones. My inner omega had gone from tolerating Knox to hating the female simply because she wasn't one of 'my' alphas. But the beta part of me needed change, so I forced myself to remain seated as I tried not to choke on her scent. How had I ever tolerated her pepper scent before?

Knox made herself comfortable on one chair, sitting on the pillow that was on it while I held the other pillow in my lap and sat across from her. She played with the ends of her two braids, obviously trying to be patient with me since I had reached out to her. She made it all of a minute.

"You seem like something is bothering you," she said, shoving a pen and paper in my direction. "And I want to help. I am, however, obligated to let you know I must report any crimes we talk about. If it's something you did or something done to you, you are welcome to talk to me about it, but I can't guarantee you I won't have to seek out help. If you can just sign this which says I went over everything I just told you, then we can get started."

The purple pen had a little pom-pom on it, but I grabbed it and signed my name, wondering if I'd made a huge mistake coming here. Explaining why I couldn't be with this pack all came back to me hiding my inner omega. Knowledge—I'd just signed—that Knox would have to alert administration about. I wasn't particularly sure what I had thought to accomplish by coming down here, but Knox was the only person I knew to reach out to. And now I was about to spew lies to my only pseudo-friend.

"It's nothing bad," I said, pushing the paper and pen back in her direction. "I was just looking for something to do this evening. Somewhere to go to get out of the dorm."

Knox pursed her lips. "Are you sure that's all? You seem … stressed, to put it gently."

"I am." Maybe that would explain my knees' inability to stop bouncing, my fingers attempting to pop knuckles I'd already popped, and the constant attention my eyes showed the door.

"School stress or relationship stress or familial stress?"

I gave her a look that asked why it mattered.

"Trust me, I know everything happening around campus," Knox said. "Different stress calls for different remedies. Home sickness calls for a theme night that helps remind you of back home. We have plenty of those, but you may have to wait for a certain day or week. School stress can be more low-key. Something to get your mind off classes and homework but should probably be around others so you can be fully distracted and maybe even make friends to help with studying. But relationship stress requires forgetting how to even use your mind, usually by means of getting drunk, albeit safely. So, which is it?"

"I guess it's a mix between relationship and school." Even more so if I considered the complication that was Professor Jenson.

The pity coming from Knox's scent was strong to the point where my fingers tightened into a death-grip on the pillow. It was like she sprayed a perfume bottle right under my nose—and the smell wasn't good.

"There are several clubs open, but the best options are on Kappa Street. Do you know where that is?"

I nodded.

"Okay, if you're looking for low-key, there's the 'Burpin' Frog' which is going to have all sorts of games you can play. Billiards, darts, that sort of thing. Games where you can drink but not necessarily drinking games.

There's also a jazz club with a live band, a karaoke bar I would only suggest going to if you're brave, and a drag bar if that's your thing. Just know a lot of these places are going to be filled with alphas or at least run by them."

I nodded. My inner omega hated the idea, but I needed to get her back to the point where she was tolerating alphas again. Maybe this would help.

"If you want drinking games, then you should head to a sorority party. Those are on Grace Boulevard—which isn't too far from Kappa. Luckily, it's Friday, so you've got plenty of options. Do not go to a fraternity party without a friend or letting someone know—even me. I'm part of the Gamma Kappa Phi Sorority and we know any female—especially a beta—walking in by herself automatically gets a pledge-shadow from GKP for the night for protection. But only the sororities do this."

My inner omega snarled, her limit of being in Knox's presence, inhaling the alpha's scent, and tolerating the headache forming from every color of the rainbow being represented, reached. "I think I'll try the jazz club. Live music and a low-key environment sound perfect. Thanks, Knox."

I stood, but she continued, "Of course. Do you have a ride there? A way to get back?"

"I'll walk. Kappa Street isn't far. But I have the campus transportation app on my phone if I need that."

"Stellar. And if you ever want to talk about anything else. Serious or not, hit me up. You know where to find me." She laughed at her own joke.

I thanked her and—no offense to how nice Knox was—got the hell out of that room before I couldn't hold my gag back anymore. Back in my room, I got undressed. I really, really just wanted to throw my clothes in the dirty hamper, but I found myself tossing them in my little trash can, unable to keep the pepper drenched clothes. I wished the clothes the alphas had washed contained their scents, so I could've cleansed my nose and calmed my omega.

My inner omega had wanted me to put every article of clothing my alphas had ever touched or saw me in, in the nest, since I didn't have their scents to decorate it. I already had to give up the nicer nest and the pack, the least I could do was give in to my private guilty pleasures. And so, my nest was now also my closet. And my bed. And my desk.

I took a quick shower, washing off any of Knox's lingering scent, before heading into my nest. There were a few hours before it was socially acceptable to go out, and I needed the time to prepare myself.

Being in my nest was my attempt to ease my inner omega. She was becoming more and more in control. I needed her calm, my instincts under control.

Chapter Fourteen

Kappa Street was much farther on foot than it looked on the little blue line of my phone's map. Although it was near campus dorms, those dorms were the alpha ones and were all the way on the other side of campus. I had no doubt a campus map—likely something I would have received at the first-year orientation—would have been helpful.

Everyone walking around was dressed like they couldn't feel the cold night air, and I was pretty sure they were running the risk of hypothermia. I was glad for my layers. I wore dark tights under my flair skirt, matched with a top that looked like it was two layers with one long sleeve and the other a tank top but was really a single item of clothing. My necklace key was hidden under my shirt. In all, I thought I found a way to look good while staying warm.

I had no idea if alphas and betas ran hotter than omegas and that was why everyone walking around acted like winter hadn't started, or if they'd rather just dress how they wanted and gave a big, 'fuck you' to weather. I blamed my delicate omega sensibilities for the fact that I liked to be comfortable at all times. That meant warm.

Plus, I was going to the jazz bar not the frat house parties like the group of a dozen students that passed by. They were loud and already drunk, talking about which house to visit first when they got to Grace Boulevard.

I fought the urge to mindlessly look at my phone while I walked. Not because I was against using it as a way to tell strangers to fuck off. But I was pretty sure I would've pulled up the college ride share app to take me back to my dorm. Despite the urge to do that, I knew I needed to power through. This was a good idea. I'd handled being around alphas my whole life. I couldn't stop now because I had a stupid crush on stupid good smelling alphas. If I ever hoped to get a job, I needed to be around alphas without my inner omega snarling and demanding my nest.

I hadn't been this worried about handling my inner omega since I first learned she existed.

As I got close to the entrance, a buzzing neon blue light let me know I'd found the right place. A large number eight was all I could make out of the sign. A single memory was trying to push its way to the front of my thoughts, but an argument between a small female and two large males distracted me. Just the sight of the three bodies in a heated discussion had me slowing my steps, not sure if I should make myself known.

Alphas surrounding a beta, unfortunately, was not a unique sight. Omegas were the only designations that could take an alpha's knot, but that had never stopped certain alphas from trying it on betas. It was rare to see omegas in such a position since they went to the Omega Compound the day they perfumed and were only allowed outside with the presence of their mated alpha.

Slowly, I opened up my phone's camera, taking a picture of what was happening. You know, in case I went into a coffee shop and saw a flyer for a familiar looking female gone missing.

"You can't be serious," the female demanded. She was obviously not intimidated by the two males blocking her way into the club, which could've been a good thing, meaning she wasn't in danger. Or she could've been stupid-brave. Her hands pushed through her dark purple hair with enough aggression I wouldn't doubt she pulled out a few strands.

"Look, we've already told you twice. No omegas allowed in without a packmate," the male closest to me said. He looked over at the other guard as if waiting for his approval, finally getting it in a single head nod.

This was just another reason why I hid my status. Unmated omegas weren't allowed away from the compound and mated omegas were always supposed to have a member of their pack with them. Apparently, a claiming bite could be faked or put into a place that was hidden so it wasn't considered enough proof an omega had a pack. The laws were said to be for omegas' protection, and yet, we were the ones with the restrictions.

I watched the omega as she became more frustrated. She had a good sense of style going by her outfit tonight: black boots with heels and studs on them, shorts that looked like skin-tight leather, and a top with sleeves covering her arms but cut off at the shoulders. That didn't even take into account her perfectly curled purple hair. Everything about the girl screamed sexy, confident.

"I already told you my pack is inside," she said through gritted teeth.

"That's what they all say, doll," the other guard who hadn't spoken yet said. "And boss man wouldn't like the compound on his ass because we made an exception. Even for a fine piece like you."

The woman pulled out her phone, aggressively putting it to her ear as she murmured under her breath. "Look, no one is answering their phone, but if you just walk in there with me, I can prove most of my pack is inside."

"Not going to happen, sweetheart," Guard One said. The two males wore identical black outfits, but they were easy to tell apart. Guard One, as I'd nicknamed him, had a hunch to his shoulders. Not like he was trying to seem unthreatening but as if he was incapable of looking down without his chest concaving. Guard Two stood normally. By their size, and attitude, it was easy to tell they were alphas before I'd even scented them.

The omega growled, and I decided that was my cue to help. If she actually had a pack, they would've come running at sensing her agitation, but I had no problem acting like I was with this female. She shouldn't be faulted for her designation. And it wasn't really lying. Just acting.

"Hey, babe, what are you still doing out here? The pack's inside." I threw my arm around the omega's shoulder and gave her a quick kiss on the side of her head, demonstrating a propriety ownership I didn't actually have. Her lavender scent was mingled with annoyance, but she didn't have a trace of fear. With her tall heels and my baby ones, we were just about the same size.

The other omega smiled wide when she looked at me, picking up on my intent quickly.

She squeezed her arms around my side tightly, and I couldn't help the pride invading my chest that I was able to help her. Since my inner omega had set her sights on Jenson's pack, she had no problem with protecting this already mated omega. And she was already mated—I could scent her claiming bites this close, not that I admitted it.

"These males wouldn't let me in." She added a little pout, which definitely worked in our favor.

"Well, it won't be a problem now, right?" I asked.

Both males scented the air, but I knew even if I was part of her pack, they wouldn't scent me on her unless we'd touched recently. Alphas could bond with both omegas and betas, but betas and omegas couldn't directly bond together. They had to be connected through an alpha. I was hoping the omega's flowery lavender scent was potent enough to block out the lack of scent markers on me.

"You have a beta in your pack?" Guard One asked the omega, obviously not liking that idea. Despite not actually being a beta, I rolled my eyes. Typical alphas. All they cared about were omegas and knotting them. And maybe their pack, if they had one.

"Yep," the omega said cheerfully.

Guard Two looked between us before he addressed me. "Omegas can't be out without a pack member. You'd be wise to remember that. Some males not as nice as us might have called her in to the Omega Compound by now. Your whole pack would have to be evaluated to see if you were caring for this little omega properly."

I wanted to roll my eyes again at the guard referring to himself as 'nice', but I managed to stop myself so I didn't anger the alpha. The omega next to me didn't have the same concern, considering she huffed like what Guard Two said was idiotic. But it made sense—I doubted the omega had gone through yearly mandatory beta relations classes explaining how to appear unthreatening to an omega and how to ensure you didn't anger an alpha. I had attended one since the year I was tested and my natural perfume had officially deemed me a beta.

The guards slowly parted ways and let us in. But before the door closed behind us Guard Two grabbed my arm, holding me back. His alpha scent reminded me of leather, making my skin feel just as tight and uncomfortable as if the material was constricting me and not his pheromones.

The omega stopped when I did, but I said, "Go find the rest of the pack, babe."

She marched off, a determined glint in her eyes,

and I gave my attention—and glare—to the hand on my arm.

The male released me as Guard One let the door shut, crowding me against his friend. His own alpha scent was like petrol leaking at a gas station. With both alphas close, I scented their distaste for my presumed designation.

Even with my inner omega sending me strong warnings to get the hell away from these alphas, I would've called my outing a success. I'd met an omega, like me, that didn't care about societal rules.

My inner omega demanded to be released so it could attack the threatening alphas. I might not have been strong enough to physically fight them off, but I was sure the element of surprise—mixed with running the hell away while they were supposed to be working—would be enough.

"What's a beta like you doing in a pack with an omega?" Guard Two asked. Or demanded.

"I don't see how that's any of your business." I tried stepping away from the males, but both moved with me, continuing to keep me trapped between them. My inner omega bristled at these males' attempts to … well, to exist near me.

"I doubt they give you any attention at all in that pack. They have an omega, what do they need you for?" Guard One asked.

"But we could help you with that. I bet you're already forgotten now that the little omega is here," Guard Two said.

There were a million ways for me to say 'no' and 'ew', but I was saved by the door to the club flying open. A large male, another alpha, loomed at the entrance with the purple haired omega clinging to him.

He was tall, strongly built, with dark black skin

and a shaved head. He dressed in more casual clothes than his omega and looked like he should be at a sports bar, not a jazz club, but who was I to judge?

"C'mon, babe," the omega whined like she was waiting for me. "I want to get drinks before the band starts."

"As you can see," I said to the guards, "I'm not easily forgettable."

The guards didn't move, but they let me walk away.

I smiled at the omega bouncing up and down on her heels like she enjoyed this little game.

She stretched her hand out to me and I took it, cause why the hell not.

Her alpha glared at the guards but followed behind us as the omega brought me to her table. There were already two alphas sitting in a booth, and luckily, it was a rather large booth. Obviously, this place understood pack dynamics.

One look and I assumed the other two males were alphas. When I scented the air, their alpha designations were confirmed. It was hard to dissect which scent belonged to who as all the smells mingled together, but they all had one thing in common: they reminded me of fruits.

The omega pulled me to sit with her while the alpha that helped rescue me took a seat on the other end of the U-shaped table.

"I'm Hannah," the omega said, introducing herself. "That's Jackson." She pointed to the alpha that had come with her. "Next to him is Han." The alpha was some kind of Asian descent, which was really broad, but that was all I grasped from his olive toned skin and the tilt of his eyes. He had the strongest bone structure of anyone at this table, but the sharp lines didn't make him look harsh. Just handsome. "And next to me is Zeke." He was the smallest of her alphas, with dark brown skin and some design shaved into the side of his head.

"Nice to meet you all. I'm Koda."

"Well, Koda, you totally saved my butt out there. I was ready to go down—you know, fists flying and the whole thing, but my nails live to see another day. Let me buy you a drink as a thanks." I knew Hannah most likely didn't have her own money, but I didn't point it out like a bitch would.

"Sure, that would be great. Thanks."

"And while we're waiting for drinks," Han said. "Hannah here can explain why she isn't with Seb and needed a stranger to help her. No offense, Koda."

"None taken," I said honestly and then looked to Hannah, curious myself on whether the omega was brave or foolish.

The blush on Hannah's cheeks made her already pink skin become darker.

"That's my other alpha," Hannah said, ignoring Han's question.

"And the alpha she should be with right now," Zeke said.

Jackson hadn't said anything, but he also hadn't stopped staring at me since I sat down. And not in the way that made me feel attractive. More like I was sitting next to his omega, and he was ready to break me in half if I moved too quickly.

I stopped myself from breathing through my mouth, like I wanted. It would have helped limit all the scents, but I was pretty sure Jackson would've noticed.

"He got a call about something private. I told him I would just meet you all here," Hannah said.

"You told Seb you were going to come to the club by yourself? And he let you?" Han didn't sound pissed off. More like he simply didn't believe her.

I wanted to stand up for Hannah, to tell the alphas that the rules keeping omegas from going out alone were dumb. An omega's perfume might catch attention, but it was alphas making it aggressive. But I didn't say anything. This wasn't my pack, and one of the many things my beta relations classes had taught me was that packs didn't want a beta's advice.

"Well," Hannah said. "I might have made it seem like I was coming with Zeke."

Zeke chuckled. "He's going to spank your ass."

"Guys, you're embarrassing me in front of my new friend," Hannah said. It was obvious these males loved their omega—and spoiled her—since drinks arrived at that point, and they all dropped the topic.

"I've never had a beta friend before," Hannah said, turning so she was almost directly facing me.

"How come?" Hannah and I had the same drink, something delicious, green, and apple flavored. I tried pacing myself but was becoming increasingly unsuccessful with each sip.

She shrugged one shoulder. "Lots of reasons. Mainly because betas don't typically like me, but we rarely hang out in the same groups. Even now, I have my online college classes that I know have betas in them, but I never interact with any of them."

I tried not to sound too curious, or shocked, but I took another sip and couldn't help myself. "You take college classes?"

Without actually attending the Omega Compound, I didn't know much about it. But I—along with like, everyone else that had never attended—always heard classes at the compound were based on raising a family and better understanding your designation. Taking classes online, for a degree, was unheard of for an omega.

Actually, it wasn't even allowed at most schools.

"Oh yeah, you're looking at a proud college student. It's only two classes, for now. I'm still trying to figure out what I want to do."

"That's amazing," I said. "I didn't know the Omega Compound lets you take college classes."

"They don't."

"But how—"

"It's all about who you know," Han said.

"And my pack is in the know." Hannah flashed me a conspiratorial wink before giving her packmates the 'gimme hands', indicating she wanted to try all their drinks.

"What do you do, Koda?" The voice shocked me. It was deep and basically a growl, and absolutely belonged to Jackson.

I took a sip to wet my mouth, and maybe gain a little liquid courage. "I attend Braker Academy."

"The male who owns this bar? His family founded the academy. And I think he has a packmate that teaches there," Han said. "I can't remember the professor's name though. Some old guy name, I remember that. The other packmate is in the band that's playing tonight."

"I have a Professor Bert Stockfield," I said, thinking of the first 'old guy' name to come to mind. Stockfield was a professor at the academy before it allowed betas in, and he'd made his opinion on the change very clear: he didn't support the designations mingling. "But he's older than I would expect for someone who has a packmate owning a club like this. Although a pack mate that plays jazz, I could see that."

Han shook his head. "No, that doesn't sound right. I hope Seb shows up before they make their rounds. He's the one that's friends with the bar owner."

I took another sip of my drink before realizing I

needed another. And why not? I was forgetting and moving on … and not driving. And I'd made a friend. Definitely a cause for celebration.

JOSEPHINE LIGHT

Chapter Fifteen

Hannah bounced in her seat, wanting to greet her alpha, but was too polite to tell me to get the hell out of the way. I grabbed my drink and got up, letting Hannah fly to the man I assumed to be Sebastian—or Seb as they seemed to prefer to call him. She wrapped her arms around his neck and kissed her fourth mate like she hadn't seen him in years instead of hours.

"Seb, you made it!" Hannah squealed loud enough that I heard her over the crowd and music.

"Hey, princess. How's the club?" Sebastian moved to sit down in what had been my spot, and I took that as my cue to leave this pack alone.

I headed to the bar along the right side of the wall, finally taking in the actual club. The space was made up of a large sitting area, a stage, and the bar. Lights were dimmed to an orange hue, the large U-shaped seats were black satin, and the tables had a thin film over them for easy clean up in case of spills. Speakers were strung up alone the top of all the walls like the greatest surround sound of all time. Two feet off the ground was the raised platform with bright lights shinning down in various empty spots. The background played jazz music that must be from a radio or a playlist, but it was still good as the deep female voice sung about her love of an unnamed woman.

There weren't any stools to sit at the bar, forcing me to stand and wait while the bartender took a bunch of orders—mine included—and started mixing. When I finally got my refill, I looked around for an empty place to sit. I glanced back at Hannah's table and happened to catch her eyes. She waved me over, still wanting me to sit with her and her pack, and my body decided it was the perfect time to be nervous.

Her kindness toward me could've easily been excused as her thanking me for helping her, but now she wanted to get to know me. Potentially be friends. And my experience with meeting new people started and ended when teachers forced their students to introduce themselves.

"She wants you to sit with her, you sit with her," a deep voice growled beside me.

I looked up, finding none other than Jackson, his hands somehow balancing four drinks. He had big hands. But I would've guessed that just based on how wide his shoulders were.

I shrugged, having no objections to sitting with Hannah, although I felt better about my decision being taken away by Jackson's demand. The truth was, Hannah fascinated me. An omega who had found an alpha pack who not only cared for her but 'let' her go to college. There wasn't any question in my mind if Guard One or Two had an omega, they wouldn't let him or her attend college. But these alphas did. Even if it was online, she was still doing something unheard of in the omega community.

I had to admit, it made me wonder about my own potential alphas. They knew about my inner omega and promised to stay silent so I could continue my education. But would they still say the same thing if they'd claimed me as a proper omega?

When I sat down next to Sebastian, he didn't even stop telling his story to introduce himself, which was fine by me, but had Hannah rolling her eyes, making me smile.

"Did you ask him if the omega would be willing to at least meet you?" Zeke asked Sebastian.

He shook his head in response, taking a long sip

of the dark drink Jackson handed him. "I did. He said the omega was alpha shy. Which makes sense. Hiding in plain sight, completely alone without anyone to explain what's going on? I wouldn't be too quick to trust either. But I'll ask again when he shows up here to make the rounds."

I must have look confused, because Hannah leaned around Sebastian, giving me the short version of his story. "Sebastian's friend, the alpha that owns this bar, has been asking him for help. Apparently, he found an omega who presents like a beta. And get this, the omega isn't registered at the Omega Compound either."

My breath caught in my lungs, forcing me to choke on my drink. The more I tried to hide my coughing fit, the sharper the pain came in my throat until I simply had to hack away like I was dying.

An omega that smelled like a beta? I had never considered anyone else being like me. My entire life, it had been a weird mix of being around others but always being alone. Always having to keep my secret to ensure I could have the future I wanted. Everything I'd ever done had been about ensuring the decision I made years ago to go to school. But if there was someone else like me, unable to enjoy their life because they were too scared of being close to alphas, I could help them. They could help me.

I couldn't wipe the shocked look from my face. My eyebrows couldn't go higher up my forehead, and my eyes couldn't widen any more. Being alone was something I'd always taken on. But the possibility I could share my secret with someone without worrying about my future? That had my heart beating in overdrive and my tongue turning to lead.

I finally opened my mouth to say something— although I wasn't truly sure what—but any sound was cut off from the words spoken behind me.

"Hello, Koda bear."

Even if I hadn't recognized his voice, I would've known that nickname anywhere. It was so brand-new I could've listed the number of times it had been used on one hand.

Everyone at the table was looking at either me, or Aidan behind me. Their questioning gazes made me blush. Some shuffling was done, and then I was pushed over to sit between Sebastian and Aidan.

"What? No hello for me?" Aidan asked, his voice filled with amusement.

I glanced up, Aidan's eyes immediately meeting mine. Of all three alphas that had recently entered my life, his eyes were the most expressive. Like now, despite the amusement I heard in his voice, I saw a flash of possessiveness in his eyes.

Pulling my eyes away from his green ones, I gave his outfit a cursory glance but couldn't make out much in the dim lighting besides the fact he was in a fancy suit that was matte black. His hair was down, brushing the tops of his shoulders, and his blond locks were perfectly, imperfectly curled. Aidan was always eye candy, but when he put the effort in, he was probably the best looking in his pack. Not that it was a competition, just something to note.

"Hi, Addie," I said, my voice barely a whisper. My inner omega was beyond ecstatic that he was here, ready to be bent over the table from a single word from him. And my beta side wasn't far behind.

I sniffed the air, wanting to draw Aidan's scent into my lungs. It was easy to filter through all the other alpha scents and alcohol to find his desert rainstorm scent, especially when he was so close. But just one smell wasn't enough. My body rebelled against common sense, pressing my nose against his neck to inhale his scent directly from his skin.

A rumbling sound brought me out of my own inner need: his purr. Perfectly content for the first time in what felt like forever, I rested my head on his shoulders and took another sip of my drink.

"You look beautiful," Aidan said.

I blushed at the small compliment. "You, too."

Everything about Aidan was beautiful, but when he smiled, pure happiness shone through. I wished I could've bottled up his image, saved his smiles and kind words for later. Maybe even saved his lips for kissing and his tongue for more delicious things. With that inappropriate thought, I tried distracting myself, taking a long sip of my drink, only to stop short with it halfway to my lips when I noticed all eyes on us.

Sitting up straight, I put my drink down, suddenly wishing I had something stronger in order to get through what was about to happen.

"Um, this is Aidan," I said to the table.

Sebastian looked between Aidan and me sitting together, his nostrils flaring as he scented the air, taking me in again. Or I guess the first time since he hadn't really noticed me when I arrived.

My eyes widened, matching my rising worry, as Sebastian looked between Aidan and I like he was trying to solve a puzzle.

"How do you know Aidan?" Hannah asked, breaking the silence that had fallen over the table. She smiled cheerfully, but there was a new look in her eyes that hadn't been there a drink and a half ago. Was she upset because she thought we were together? It wouldn't have been the first time an omega scorned an alpha-beta relationship, but it would be the first time that I was on the receiving end.

"We don't really." I cringed at my ingenious response.

Hannah raised a single eyebrow at me. "You know, if anyone, beta or not, greeted one of my alphas like you did with Aidan, I'd bite the bitch's head off."

I blamed the drink and a half because there was no other reason I growled at Hannah. "Well, he's not yours."

Somewhere in the back of my mind I acknowledged she wasn't threatening me or my place with Aidan, but I couldn't tear my eyes away from Hannah. My inner omega felt challenged, and I couldn't reign her back in.

The purr behind me got stronger, and I was lifted off the seat onto Aidan's lap. There wasn't enough room for me to cross my legs, so I had to sit with my back pressed tightly to his front, straddling one of his legs.

But the fact Aidan was so close, touching me, purring for me throughout an omega dominance fight, had me purring in response, finally looking away from Hannah. Aidan shifted under me, his muscular thigh pressing up, into my core. The thought of riding his leg quickly came to an end when I remembered I couldn't perfume here. I was an unmated omega in public. Perfuming was not a good idea. That meant no getting turned on by sexy alphas forcing their leg between my thighs and vibrating against my back like the best sex toy on the market.

I adjusted myself to sit on Aidan's other side instead of on his lap, forcing him closer to Seb and giving me an easy get away if necessary. Looking up, I caught a flash of disappointment in his eyes before it was gone, and I wondered if I'd imagined it.

He grabbed my hand and gave it a slight squeeze.

At first, I thought he was just comforting me, but

when he did it again, I realized he was trying to catch my attention.

"I'm sorry, what?" I looked around for someone to clue me in on what I'd missed.

"Sebastian asked what you're studying at Braker," Aidan said.

I almost sighed in relief at the topic change. "Astrophysics." After finishing off my glass in several huge gulps, I said, "I want to study black holes after graduation."

Han whistled. "How did you get into that?"

"I just um—" I couldn't find the words to explain my reasoning since I didn't have one. Astrophysics wasn't my dream. Black holes weren't my passion. School was. My scholarship required me to be in a degree plan, and Astrophysics sounded cool. "I just picked it one day."

"I was thinking about getting an English degree," Hannah said, saving me from wherever my tongue was taking that topic. "Right now, I'm just taking some random classes. I want to get my degree, but then I look at the all the hours of credits needed, and it just feels like too much. Too long."

"It has been a long time. I did two years at the community college before I started this semester at Braker. And I still can't see the finish line." For my education or my secret.

"What does your packmate teach?" Zeke asked Aidan.

"Jenson? He's a professor of quantum mechanics."

I nodded along as if agreeing to this information, but before anyone could ask if I was a part of that class, I motioned to my glass, and got up for a refill. While I stood, wait for the bartender's attention, again, some of the band started trickling onto the stage, setting up. I wasn't an expert in instruments, but I saw a trombone, trumpet, and some other large instrument that had a big hole on the top but wound down for the player to blow into. Either I was starting to get tipsy or that instrument was fake.

When my drink appeared, I took a sip of the familiar apple flavor, wondering if this drink was weaker than the others since I couldn't even taste the alcohol. It was probably my last one anyway. There was no way I'd get up when the band started, and I didn't have any plans to stay after. Being out and getting to know Hannah was fun, but now with Aidan, my control over my omega was fading.

With more and more people entering the club, I scented the air, trying to hide the obvious action since most betas didn't scent a lot. Alphas filled most of the space, covering up any inkling of a beta scent and even overwhelming the alcohol. Hannah's omega scent was growing stronger, but I doubted any alphas actually scented her besides her own.

Sudden warmth at my back let me know I'd been crowded in. I tried moving away from the body at my back, but hands wrapped around my waist, holding me still. Usually, I would've had better control over my instincts, but it was either my inner omega having mixed with alcohol or the comfort I felt being near Aidan, but it made me instantly territorial.

I set down my drink, grabbing the fingers touching me, and tried prying them off my body, growling at the owner, baring my teeth as if I was trying to appear stronger than I actually was. The male, probably a beta based on the fact he touched me without allowing me to scent approve him first, seemed shocked by my reaction, which allowed me to break his grip and shove him away. Turning around, I made sure my back wasn't to him anymore, but my inner omega was on edge, frantically looking around to make sure I wasn't touched again.

The shove must have set his thoughts back on track, because the beta recovered and replaced his shock with anger and arrogance. "What the hell's your problem, babe?"

His words hit me like adding oxygen to a fire. My inner omega felt like she already had an alpha—three to be specific—and being touched by another male not only made her angry but disappointed that her alphas hadn't protected her. I could almost hear her pettiness saying if I wore their mark, this wouldn't have happened, as if a mark would've done anything to ward off assholes.

The complexity of emotions mixed with alcohol had me ready to fight the beta. On a normal day, I'd probably lose, but with my current rage level, all inhibitions went out the door, and the bet was on.

I'd never actually been in a fight before, but I lunged for the beta, arms stretched out to claw at his face with my stressed, bitten down nails. Before I made contact, a new pair of arms banded around my stomach. Only this time my inner omega didn't give the newcomer any attention. My sights had zeroed in on the beta who dared to touch me without permission. Who insulted me. Who called me 'babe' as if I belonged to him.

Ignoring whoever held me back, I clawed at the air, trying to reach the beta. When the male stepped back, my inner omega smirked at her display of aggression. At least until the aggressive rumbling against my back reminded me I wasn't alone in my attack.

Whatever. Win was a win.

"She's not your babe," a familiar accent growled.

I looked down at the brown hands, verifying the

owner of the Italian accent. If I could've, I'd have roll my eyes at my inner omega. No wonder she didn't feel restrained by Lorenzo holding me back—she liked him.

"I suggest you move along."

Agreeing with Lorenzo didn't bug me like I wanted it too, so I focused my attention on the male in front of me.

He looked angrier than I would expect in the face of an aggressive omega and alpha, but it wasn't uncommon for betas to lack an understanding of alpha-omega relations. When the beta looked at me like he wanted to say something else, Lorenzo spoke again, letting his alpha command infuse his tone.

"Leave." It came out like a grunt, as if he couldn't be bothered to form a full sentence for the beta. Lorenzo pulled me tighter to his body when I growled at the beta, but when the jerk finally decided to get lost, I was still being held.

"You can probably let go of me now," I grumbled. I watched the beta walk away with his friends before they left the club. I didn't think Lorenzo meant to kick the beta out of the club, but I wasn't going to correct the beta's assumption.

My attention was pulled to the side of my head where Lorenzo's lips grazed my ear. Holding my breath, I waited for him to say something, wondering how his breathing could be fucking erotic.

"Enzo?" Was that my breathless voice?

"Yes, Orsetta?"

"What?" I turn around in Enzo's arms, officially confused, but when I set my eyes on him, all my questions got stuck in my throat. Just like Aidan, Enzo was dressed up. His hair was slicked back on the top, making him hit his Italian stereotype hard. His suit was a light blue color with a black shirt underneath, which should've looked bad but somehow found the perfect mix of attractive and professional. It was hard to take him all in when we were so close, and I had to crane my neck to look up at him, but the neckache was totally worth it.

"What did you call me?" I asked.

Enzo didn't explain.

Instead, he looked in the direction the beta and his friends went before saying, "Let's find Aidan. I don't want you sitting alone."

I grabbed my drink as Lorenzo walked behind me. His hands wrapped around my waist as I led, his body so close I could almost feel every breath he took. "I'm not."

He stopped at my comment, forcing me to stop too, but didn't let me go. His grip tightened around me, and his lips lowered to my ear again. I shivered when he asked, "Who did you come with?"

I parted my lips to tell him I hadn't come with anyone, but Jenson popped up in front of me, distracting me. His face showed shock from seeing me, which meant he was probably looking for Enzo. Why did that disappoint me? At least once the shock wore off, he appeared happy to see me, even if he did give the way Enzo's hands wrapped around me a curious look.

Jenson was dressed just as nice as his packmates in a dark brown suit and a darker orange undershirt that should've looked tacky but didn't. Even though Jenson looked plenty attractive, I was familiar with his perfect style, so he didn't strike me dumb like Aidan and Lorenzo did.

"What are you doing here, Koda?" Jenson asked.

"I was trying to enjoy a night out," I said, and his already serious face seemed to darken.

"Aidan's here. You can sit with him."

"That's what Enzo said." I pointed in the direction of Hannah and her pack. "I was sitting with some people

I met, and Aidan showed up. Then Enzo, now you."

"Aidan owns the club," Jenson said like that explained all three of the alphas I was trying to get away from showing up.

"You were sitting with Sebastian's pack?" Enzo asked. His question sounded more aggressive than I associated with Enzo so I couldn't find the words to agree, feeling like I'd somehow disappointed him. It wasn't like I chose to sit with Sebastian—or his pack. I'd made a friend with Hannah.

I managed a nod. I scented the frustration and jealousy on Enzo as he looked in the direction of Hannah's table. Without thinking, I reached up and touched the side of Enzo's cheek with my hand, drawing his attention back to me. I wasn't sure why I did it, but it seemed to work in changing the anger to calm within Enzo, and in return, stopping my own mood from plummeting. I ignored the thought that if I'd gone to the Omega Compound I would've known why I did what I did and why it worked. Instead, I continued staring at Enzo, caressing his cheek and pretending it was only us.

Jenson finally spoke up, forcing me to break away from my Enzo-trance.

"Enzo, it's time for you to get on the stage." Neither alpha acknowledged how shocked I was to learn Enzo was in the band. I felt like I'd known, but also like the information was new? And after a long pause, where Enzo and Jenson had some sort of silent conversation with their eyes, Enzo brushed his lips along my cheek and disappeared.

I gently touched the spot where Enzo kissed, wanting to feel the warmth just a little bit longer.

"C'mon," Jenson said, guiding me toward Hannah's table. "I see Aidan."

Being near Jenson was different than the other

alphas. He had an inner working of my academic knowledge and that somehow left me more vulnerable than I expected. Like I was always in a state of having to prove myself. My inner omega loved Jen's intelligence, always wanting to push him to react emotionally.

Jenson was the reason I pulled away from Enzo last week. His growl had brought me back to the present, but was it a disgusted growl or an interested growl? Usually, I would've considered myself pretty good at interpreting alpha grunts and growls, but I had been so focused on Enzo—and Aidan—that Jenson's sound had barely registered. My inner omega just knew I had to stop. Jenson had wanted me to stop.

Did that mean he didn't want me? I knew Aidan and Enzo found me attractive, but did they just want to fuck me, or did they want me as their mate? And why did I even care if I wasn't willing to bond with them?

When we reached the table, the look in Aidan's eyes told me he very much liked seeing me approach with Jenson. He looked between us before standing up and buttoning his suit like he was about to go to a business meeting.

"Where are you going?" I whimpered.

"Aidan has to do some work in his office while we're here, but I can sit with you, if you don't mind," Jenson said.

I glanced over my shoulder, shocked to see Jenson looking unsure of himself.

His hands were tucked into his front pants pockets, arms locked and shoulders high, as if he was shy now that he didn't have a reason to touch me. I was so distracted by Jenson's appearance, I forgot to answer. "I think it'll make Enzo feel better to know I'm near you."

"You're always welcome to sit with me, Jen," I said honestly. Maybe too honestly, but I couldn't stand the thought of my alphas hurt or worried. I was rewarded with a soft look and Jenson taking a small step closer to my body like I had finally given him the permission he needed.

"You'll say goodbye, right?" I asked Aidan.

A softness appeared in his eyes, making me wonder what he was thinking. Aidan ran his fingers along the waistband of my skirt, forcing me to hold my breath, as if scared moving would draw his attention lower. I didn't know whether or not to be disappointed because he didn't linger before ducking his head, placing a quick kiss on my lips, and escaping in the direction I assumed his office was in. I stared after Aidan, lips slightly apart, wishing for another kiss and wishing he hadn't kissed me at all if he wasn't going to give me more.

This last week, I had tried convincing myself my memories were glorifying the actions and words from this pack. That I mistook kindness, and sexual tension, and turned it into some great romance in my mind. That when I did see the alphas again, they would have moved on from their interest in me after I made myself unavailable, and I would've been the only one heartbroken. But I was quickly realizing I hadn't imagined their interest in me. It was more than just heat in their gazes when they looked at me, more than slight touches and possessive gestures.

"Take a sip of your drink," Jenson whispered in my ear. "You look parched."

I unglued my eyes from the direction Aidan went and stared at Jenson, raising my drink and taking a sip. He gave me a smirk that said he knew exactly what I was thinking. Turning away from that look, I sat at Hannah's table.

Everyone shifted seats so we could fit. Jenson was last, then me, Hannah, Jackson, Han, Zeke, and Sebastian on the other end. I would've sworn Jackson was one sudden movement from switching positions with Hannah. I didn't need to scent the alpha to know he didn't trust me and was weary of another alpha at his table. It just proved the power an omega had over a protective alpha. Jackson might've wanted to bare his teeth at me and make me disappear, but he'd settle for overattentively guarding Hannah if it made her happy to have friends.

"So how little do you know Jenson?" Hannah asked, throwing my previous words back at me.

I blushed but was luckily saved from answering— or lying—when the band suddenly started playing. No introductions, just the stopping of the current song and the beginning of a beautiful, deep voice.

JOSEPHINE LIGHT

Chapter Sixteen

Enzo played guitar. Or bass. I wasn't really sure what the difference was or how to tell them apart, but I knew the instrument in Enzo's hands looked like a guitar with an extra-long … handle. I also knew I hadn't taken my eyes off Enzo for the entire time he played.

Watching Enzo with his head bowed, sitting on a stool with one knee propped up, while sitting close enough to Jen I could inhale his scent with every breath, was doing funny things to my body. I sipped on my third drink, or was it my fourth, while listening, my body leaning more and more on Jen the longer Enzo's band played. And if my inner omega wasn't missing Aidan, I could have relaxed perfectly.

An hour, and several songs later, Enzo's band finally finished. Hannah clapped her hands with the rest of us but quickly grabbed a hold of my arm and half-pushed, half-dragged me from the booth. She dragged me toward the rapidly approaching stage, her intent becoming clear.

"No way," I said, basically yelling at Hannah over the noise of people leaving and the background music coming back on.

"Yes way," she said without even turning her head around.

"How much have you had to drink?"

That got her attention. She turned her head to give me a mock glare. "We're friends now. Friends don't let friends dance alone on a stage."

"I'm pretty sure that friends don't let friends dance on a stage—period."

"Nope. You're wrong."

I sighed out loud, because Hannah was right.

Friends didn't let friends dance alone. And I really wanted to be friends with Hannah. Even Knox, helpful, kind, outgoing Knox, I didn't want to be friends with. But I wanted to get to know Hannah better so I could trust her with my secret, because I had this feeling she would be totally supportive.

Hannah bulldozed her way to the stage, pulling me in her wake, before somehow managing to dance to jazz. She should've looked crazy, dancing without a partner, but the deep voice singing about waiting at a bar matched perfectly. Dancing when the song didn't have instructions, was not my forte. I stared at Hannah, hoping I'd learn through osmosis.

"Here you go, ladies," a new voice said. It belonged to a male wearing a black, buttoned-up shirt and a little apron wrapped around his waist. He had dark skin, a close shaved head, and tattoos covering almost all his available skin, but there wasn't anything intimidating about him or his kind smile. "The males at the bar sent these for you. I poured them myself."

I searched the bar, expecting to see Jenson or Enzo, or hell even one of Hannah's alphas, but a group of four males had their bodies turned this way.

One of them, I think he was the drummer in the band, but I couldn't guarantee that, raised his own drink like he was accepting thanks.

Without hesitating, Hannah grabbed the small glass and threw back a clear colored alcohol in a single swallow. "Free is free," she said, shoving the remaining glass in my hand and guiding it to my mouth.

"Free is free," I said, before taking the shot—though not as eloquently as Hannah. The liquid burned the back of my throat, and I would've sworn the heat went all the way up my nose. I tried to hold back my coughing but was very unsuccessful.

We thanked the server who, even in the dim light, blushed. Hannah went straight back to dancing, but even with more liquor in my system, I couldn't make my body move beside a simple sway and foot tapping.

Taking pity on me, Hannah stepped close to me, gripping my hips in her small hands, and guiding them in an almost figure eight like movement. Her hips acted as a mirror to mine. Without any place to comfortably settle my arms, I placed my hands on Hannah's shoulders. She scrunched her neck like she was scared I would tickle her. I laughed until my stomach hurt. Dragging my hands to her biceps, she nodded, letting me know my hand position was better.

Just like that, we danced. Hannah occasionally twirled me and then held my hand in position while she twirled herself. I wasn't sure if this was sober or drunk Hannah, but she was fun either way. I never would've thought of dancing in this type of club, or to this type of music, but the stress of the day—of the week—just seemed to fall away. My only focus was on following Hannah's lead.

The shy server came back twice more, always assuring us he made the drinks, before offering it to us on behalf of the same group of four males.

When Hannah let go of my hips and ran her fingers through her dark purple hair, I wondered if I should dye my hair too.

"Do you think I'd look good with pink hair?" I didn't have to yell now that the crowd had mostly left or talked amongst themselves in their booths, but I struggled to regulate my own volume.

Hannah's eyes widened, her smile forcing two dimples to appear. "Oh goodness, you have to get pink hair. You'd look so hot." She stopped dancing and actually bounced up and down before reaching for my hair, looking at the ends. "I'll give you the number of my stylist."

Hannah patted down her body before realizing her phone wasn't on her. Out of thin air, Han appeared, telling Hannah something along the lines that if she couldn't remember where her phone was, she's had too much to drink. Hannah took one look at Han and jumped on him, dragging his face to hers so she could kiss and suck on his lips.

Deciding not to intrude on the moment, I made my way to end of the stage, staring down at the floor, wondering how the stage seemed to have risen since Hannah dragged me up here. It made sense that it would rise up and down so the people in the back of the club could see, but who would've moved it higher when people were dancing on it? And why didn't I feel it? Also, there should be stairs.

Without anything to hold on to, and not wanting to jump and risk breaking an ankle, I sat down and scooted to the edge of the stage. My feet settled on the floor, and I easily stood up. Huh, it must've been an optical illusion to look higher when on the stage.

"Where are you going, Koda?"

I smiled up at Jen, who obviously had too much to drink since he was swaying slightly. Grabbing a hold of his upper arm, I let him lean onto me.

"What are you doing, Koda?" Jen asked.

"Holding you up."

He laughed, taken over by the alcohol, but the sound was so infectious I joined him. I definitely thought his joke was funnier than he did based on our laughing volume. Wait. What was his joke? I'd already forgotten it, but I didn't want to admit it, so I tried to phase out the laughing.

"I think you've had too much to drink," I told Jen.

"But don't worry, I'll take care of you."

The stress Jen seemed to constantly wear on his face smoothed away, and he kissed me on the top of the head. I lost my balance slightly and couldn't help but be overcome with giggles.

"Take deep breathes, Koda," Jen said, but I could barely hear him over my own laughter.

He became blurry, and I realized I was crying, laughing so hard tears flooded my eyes but I couldn't remember the joke. Again. Jen was going to be upset with me if I kept forgetting his jokes. He might've thought I didn't like him as much as Aidan or Enzo. Just the thought of Jen worrying about that made me cry harder, but this time, without any joy.

Then my nose was pressed against something soft that smelled like warm laundry that had just been taken out of the dryer. It was so relaxing my entire body sagged as I continued taking deep breathes. I tried getting even closer to the amazing smell. My lips touched something warm. And soft. Whatever it was, I liked it.

Pressing my lips against it again, I took in a deep breath, finding the scent even stronger. And something else. Was that ... alpha arousal in my laundry? Hmm, I liked that. Taking another breath, I carefully licked where I found the scent, the slight salty taste mixing with arousal. A small vibration from whatever I licked added deliciousness.

My body responded to the arousal by pushing harder against where the smell was coming from. I could feel my legs already wrapped around something hard and wide and brought my dangling arms up until they found something spikey. Short hair, if I had to guess.

Another rumbling came from the warm feeling against my lips. I mixed in some kisses with the licks before attempting a small nibble, unable to stop the urge to bite. Every breath pulled heat into my veins, and I could taste the arousal getting stronger. There was so much heat turning around inside me I tighten my hold, locking my ankles and curling in my fingers. I ground down my hips, trying to relieve the tension.

"Koda," a voice rasped.

It sounds a lot like Jen's, and it only increased my arousal. I imagined it was Jen I was clinging to. That it was his arms tightening around me, his arousal scent making me ache for release. My kisses became more urgent, increasing in pressure until I thought of claiming my imaginary Jenson. I sucked on the skin, encouraged by the possessive growl rumbling against me.

Wanting to see if I really did leave a mark, I opened my eyes, happy with the slightly red skin.

"Happy now that you've marked me up, little bear?"

Weird. I figured once I opened my eyes, I would stop imagining Jenson. But I missed my alpha and the pain of his absence had tears coming to my eyes. Great, I was crying, and the arousal scent was leaving.

"Little bear, what's wrong?" The panic from my imagination version of Jenson sounded very accurate and that just seemed to turn the tears on high.

"I want Jen," I managed to get out through the coming sobs.

"What the hell?" That new angry voice sounded like Enzo, and that didn't make me happy like I thought it would. I missed Enzo too, but I really wanted Jen right now. I wondered what they were doing. Did they see me dancing at the club? Did they want to take me home?

"Why is she crying?" Enzo's angry voice asked.

"I'm trying to figure that out," Jen's voice said, never losing the softness, but still sounding worried. "Tell me what's going on, little bear."

"She had too much to drink."

"That's not helpful, Enzo."

"None of this is helpful. She's still crying."

"I want Jen," I repeated. The alpha might've made me nervous, but that didn't mean I wanted him any less than the others. He might not beat someone up like I suspected Enzo would if someone looked at me wrong or make me laugh quite like Aidan would, but Jenson had a consistency about him that was comforting. He was my calm, and I desperately needed that.

There was a swaying motion and I held on tighter, to the point of fusing myself to my imaginary Jen and squeezing my eyes shut. Imaginary Jen wasn't deterred by my grip. He continued to sway before falling suddenly. I screamed out quickly, but the fall was short, and I hadn't felt any pain. I tried wiggling my toes to make sure I was okay but couldn't feel them. That was good. If something was wrong, I would've felt pain.

"Koda, I want you to open your eyes. Can you do that for me?" I felt large hands cup my cheeks, and my head lolled as I gave my weight over to the grip. The hands tightened along my jaw, holding my head up. "Little bear, open your eyes and look at me."

It took a lot more effort than I expected, but I managed to get one eye open before using all my will power to open the second. Everything was a little blurry at first. I blinked a few times, and then my heart stopped. Like actually stopped beating before restarting so hard I could feel it pounding at my inner chest.

I threw my arms around Jen, shoving my head into the crook of his neck and ignoring the stretch I felt in my thighs from this awkward position.

"You're here," I whispered.

"Where do you think you are, Koda?" he asked, one of his hands massaging the back of my neck.

My mouth opened to tell him I was in my dorm room, but something about the way Jen asked had me hesitating. I lifted my head and looked around, finding us on a gross leather couch that reminded me of something someone interviewing for a porno should be sitting on. A large wooden desk behind me had two computer screens on top and so many papers scattered on it I was surprised the A/C hadn't blown them off. Two chairs were placed in front of the desk. The couch had the perfect view to watch someone at the desk yell at whoever sat in the chairs. Almost like it was a late addition.

Speaking of multiple people, hadn't I heard Enzo earlier? And where was Aidan? Was this his office?

"Orsetta?" The Italian word caught my attention, and I found Enzo sitting next to me on the couch. Well, kind of next to me. Was it considered 'next to' if I was sitting on a lap and not the actual couch?

I felt like I was supposed to be answering a question, but I couldn't remember, so I said, "Yes."

"Yes, what?" Jenson asked.

"Um, to whatever you asked?" That wasn't the right answer. I could tell right away from the look on Jenson's face. It was one I was familiar with from class, when he asked a review question and the student he called on got it wrong. I'd managed to not be on the receiving end of that look in class, so I needed a distraction. "Can I get another drink?"

"I think you've had plenty to drink tonight."

"Too much," Enzo added.

At that reminder, I realized I hadn't paid for any of my drinks. I needed to find my wallet and close my tab.

"Where are you trying to squirm off to?" Jen asked, his hands wrapping around my waist to keep me from getting off him.

"I didn't pay for my drinks." Worst case scenarios started running through my thoughts: What if the bartender told Aidan, and he thought less of me? What if the bartender told the police, and then they thought I was a thief and had to put me in jail? Then I had to tell everyone I was an omega because that scenario would be too dangerous to hide my designation. "I don't want to go to jail. I'll starve. The food is notoriously bad."

"Your bill is already settled, little bear. And no one is going to jail." Okay. If Jenson said it, it must be true. Enzo would have lied just to comfort me.

Although, food sounded like a splendid idea.

"I'm hungry."

"We'll get you some food once Aidan finishes his closing routine," Jen said.

Closing routine? "What time is it?" I didn't feel tired, but that would make sense if I had a little nap.

"It's not too late. Aidan kicked everyone out once you started—

"No," I half-shouted, trying to pull out of Jenson's grip. He tightened his hold on me, pressing our chests together so our noses were inches apart.

"Koda, what's wrong? Use your words."

"I didn't get a number from Hannah." I pushed against Jenson's chest, momentarily distracted by the hard muscles under my hand, before returning to my need to find Hannah.

"She's already gone, little bear. Now stop struggling to get away from me and maybe I'd tell you we gave Hannah your phone number so she can contact you later."

It took a couple more shoves against Jen before his words managed to make sense. Without any more complaints, I sort of just sat still, contemplating what to do next, but I couldn't get my thoughts to come into full ideas. Trying to focus on only one gave me a headache so I decided not to do that anymore.

"Are you tired, little bear? Why don't you lean against me and shut your eyes?" Jen asked.

I wasn't tired but I also wasn't going to pass up an opportunity to lean against Jenson. Touch was definitely the love language in this pack, and I had to admit, I was soaking up the attention.

Leaning my head on Jen's shoulder, I felt his hand press into my back like he wanted us to be closer than chest to chest, stomach to stomach. Obliging him was my pleasure. I used my hands, braced on his shoulders, to drag my knees up his thighs, wanting our hips to touch, but a bump stopped my hips from fully meeting his. A pained groan came from Jenson.

"Did I hurt you?" Embarrassment caused me to whisper.

"No, little bear," he said, his voice a whisper to match mine. "It felt good."

"Oh."

The idea of making Jen feel good was exciting. A vague memory tried pushing to the front of my mind, but I didn't want to deal with a headache while trying to work another groan from Jen. I strained my thighs, hovering slightly and rubbing my core over the slightly raised portion in Jenson's pants. My alpha groaned, but I only made two more passes before hands gripped my hips, stopping me from moving.

"What are you doing?" I asked, pouting my bottom lip.

"I could ask you the same question, little bear." Jenson's calm voice had a slight strain to it that made me smile. I inhaled deeply and caught his scent tinted with arousal. All signs pointed to Jen finding me attractive, and that knowledge had tingles appearing in my stomach.

"Let go, Jen." I slid my fingers down from his shoulders until they pressed against his hip bones. Slowly, I started rotating my hips again, watching his face closely to catch every reaction.

The hardness under me somehow got longer and harder, pressing perfectly against me. I put more pressure against him, loving the way he felt against my pussy. But I wanted more. I wanted the clothes between us to disappear so I could feel his cock rub against me. I wanted to feel the burn in my thighs as my muscles worked to ride Jen's cock. I moaned at the illicit ideas, my imagination provoking my lust.

My hands worked at the behest of my pussy. I grabbed Jen's wrists, pressing his hands against my breasts. His fingers immediately tightened, and I groaned at the sensation, grinding harder against him. He moved his hands, running his thumbs over my nipples, gentle tracing the hardening points over my shirt.

Every breath told me that Jen's arousal was getting stronger and stronger until every inhale—pant— was more of him than oxygen.

My hips were still moving of their own accord, but I needed something more—something I couldn't place until Jen pinched my nipples, twisting the hard peaks. The slight pain stole my breath and sent shocks of pleasure straight to my clit. My heart was beating aggressively along my whole body, making me fully aware of everywhere I was being touched. I could feel how wet my pussy was. My whole body throbbed with unreleased desire, and I needed something to help me over the edge. It was just out of reach but also so close if I could have just—

A hand came out of nowhere, pressing against the back of my head, forcing me to collide with Jenson. This kiss was so different than the one with Enzo but just as effective in curling my toes. Jen's tongue requested entrance to my mouth by licking over the seam of my lips and diving in when I gasped.

Was it weird to note that his tongue was warm? Because it was. And he pushed it into my mouth, playing with my own tongue. I think he groaned, or maybe that was me. Either way, the sexy noises were like a tickle against my lower stomach. I wanted to get closer, but there wasn't any closer with me already on his lap, pressed against his front. My fingers found where his shirt was tucked into his pants and started yanking on the fabric.

Jen pulled away, but only barely, kissing my cheek and making his way to my neck. I managed enough focus to get my hands under his shirt and rake my fingers against the lines of his skin, feeling the heat radiating toward my palms. If my nails weren't bitten down to their beds, I would have raked my nails against his stomach, wanting to feel his muscles tense. Instead, I continued tracing his body. I wanted to be able to identify my alpha by touch alone.

"Jenson, you need to knock this shit off, man. Wait until we get her home at least."

The beautiful voice saying the words sounded like he was in pain. I wanted him to be closer so I could ease the pain but even without looking, I knew he was too far away for me to reach. I whined for the other alpha, recognizing his pine forest scent even with it mostly overwhelmed by his arousal.

Was it neglectful to grind on one male while another was in the room? If it hadn't felt so good, I would've considered stopping, or maybe being embarrassed. But grinding against Jenson made my whole body feel alive—powerful.

My fingers dug into his shoulders, holding him

beneath me. My stomach and thighs started to burn from the exertion, but the feeling in my pussy encouraged me to keep going, keep moving. A tightness in my breasts I'd never felt before only felt marginally better when I leaned into Jen to rub them against his chest. What I really wanted was for him to grab each breast in his grip and squeeze.

Jen's hands were rubbing along my back in an almost erotic massage when I was suddenly pulled off his lap. My breath huffed out on a harsh exhale, my eyes flying wide to figure out what was going on.

There wasn't any panic, just confusion, as I looked around for some sort of attack or logical reason to deny me my immanent orgasm.

"Shit, Aidan, you scared Koda," Jen said, his arms still reaching out to me like he was ready to accept me back at any moment.

I looked over my shoulder and somehow still managed to be surprised Aidan was the one pulling me off Jenson. The move felt far too aggressive for the male I would've considered the most laid back out of the bunch, but I wasn't scared. Startled, more like, and a little dizzy, but even if I hadn't known it was Aidan, my body automatically trusted his scent.

"Is that true? Did I scare you, little bear?" Aidan didn't look at me when he asked, flaring his nostrils like he was trying to take calming breathes but inhaling the scents of everyone aroused. That would explain his tight jaw and eyebrows pulled together in a glare.

I shook my head no but said, "Yes. No, wait. No. That's my final answer."

Aidan glanced down at me, an amused look on his face.

"Did you bring me food? Jen said you were going to bring me food." I looked down at his hands wrapped around my stomach and felt the burn of incoming tears behind my eyes. Aidan didn't bring food, which meant there was none, and I was going to starve to death.

The alarm on Aidan's face was my first cue my tears had escaped their eyelid prison.

Aidan was quickly shoved to the side by a growling Enzo who took me from his packmate. I clung to Enzo like a bear climbing a tree, tucking my face into his neck as the tears fell faster.

"Don't worry, Orsetta. We will get you food."

And just like that, Enzo managed to shut my tears off. I pulled my face out of his grip and quickly wiped at my nose before demanding we leave for food. There was a moment where the alphas seemed shocked to take orders from me, but the three quickly gathered their things. Enzo put me down, and I found myself sandwiched between him and Aidan as Jen went to get the car they had arrived in.

"I'm thinking tacos. No, quesadillas. No, I definitely want tacos. Something spicy that makes my tongue burn." I could already feel the flavors making my mouth water.

The club seemed smaller with all the lights on. A back door was discreetly hidden behind the stage and was obviously set up so the band didn't have to drag their heavy instruments through the whole club.

A dark rumble came from Enzo that was just slightly more laughter than growl. I liked it. It was deep and somehow vibrated his whole body. I could imagine him hovering over me, his whole body over the length of mine, moving slowly to let me get acquainted with his size. And when I begged for more, for harder, for faster, with my whole body wrapped around him, he would laugh at my pleas. His laugh would shake his chest, rubbing against my peaked nipples, my hands would feel it along his back, and his cock would seem to somehow expand farther inside me, teasing his knot at my entrance. Not because he was merciless with my pleasure, but because he had warned me I would only get pleasure when he gave it to me. When I begged for it.

"Koda." Just like that. Enzo would half-growl my name like he was struggling to hold himself back even though he was the one trying to tease me.

"Koda bear, you're perfuming." Aidan was near too. Even better. Although I wasn't sure why he was shocked I was perfuming. I was hornier than I'd literally ever been in my life.

"Oh," I said, realization dawning. "You don't want those assholes to know I'm an omega."

"What assholes?" Aidan asked, his usually cheerful voice turning angry.

"The bouncing ones, outside."

"The bouncers?" Enzo asked.

Aidan gave Enzo a nod that Enzo returned with a glare. The two were sharing a private conversation I couldn't interpret. It was over my head. My omega instinct told me I needed to nip that habit in the butt.

Kinky.

"What are you guys talking about?" I asked, trying to sound as innocent as possible.

"Nothing important." Aidan broke his silent communication with Enzo, but his denial pissed me off.

I felt the growl more than I consciously used it, but the effect was the same. Aidan's eyes widened, and I watched him fight his own lips like he didn't want to show me he was amused.

Before I could get a straight answer out of Aidan, or turn my investigative skills to Enzo, a faint car horn honked twice in quick succession outside.

"Let's go, Koda bear," Aidan said. "You can

question us in the car."

"No wait. Where's Jenson?" I looked around frantically, hoping to find him appearing out of thin air.

"He's out in the car, Koda bear." Aidan didn't sound concerned over his missing pack mate, so I skeptically followed him, ready to turn back around if Jen wasn't there.

A surprisingly normal car, all black including the darkly tinted windows, was idling only a few feet from the back door. The night air was chilly, even with my alphas close, but I knew Aidan and Enzo were keeping the worst of the chill off. But just to be sure, I took a step back from the car, out of the little cocoon my alphas created. The cold breeze hit me, twisting my skirt and playing with my hair. The wind ran its cold fingers along my cheeks and nose, painting my skin a light red. Yep, their body heat had definitely been keeping me warm.

"Get in the car, little bear," Jenson demanded. He rolled down the back passenger window to watch me, and I smiled wide at him.

Rushing into the car, I leaned over the center console and planted a small kiss on his cheek. "I missed you, Jen."

The spot I kissed immediately turned red, and it took me a moment to realize it wasn't the wind, he was blushing. I liked that a lot, though I couldn't tell if it was from the kiss or my comment.

Aidan sat in the passenger seat and Enzo joined me in the back. Enzo pushed me into the seat behind Jen and even buckled my seat belt which I would've totally done if I hadn't forgotten.

I started to tell him this, but he cut me off, asking, "You want tacos, or no?"

"Tacos?" Jen asked.

"I know a place that will be open this late," Aidan

said.

For the first time in a week—no longer than that—since I first moved to this campus and met Jen and his pack, I felt happy. I didn't have to worry about keeping my secret because they already knew. Already promised to keep it. Now I just got to have fun.

A purr erupted from my chest, and I let the sound settle over the quiet in the car.

JOSEPHINE LIGHT

Chapter Seventeen

Aidan gave directions to a little taco truck that already had a line formed. I guessed the dark sky didn't necessarily mean it was late. The space was barely illuminated by the nearby streetlights, and the truck was set up in the middle of a parking lot for a grocery store already closed for the night.

I unbuckled my seatbelt—earning me a look from Enzo—and then a hand on my knee had me stopping from reaching for the door.

"You can't go out there, Koda bear," Aidan said, squeezing my knee in a comforting gesture. "You're perfuming, remember?"

I looked longingly at the taco truck and felt heat building behind my eyes again. That time, however, I tried holding back my tears. I really wanted the tacos, and being this close to them, while being denied, was the worst kind of heartbreak I could've imagined.

"Orsetta? Why are you crying?" Not even Enzo's nickname for me brightened my mood.

I snorted up my dripping nose, leaning my forehead against the window and letting the tears stain my cheeks as they slowly crawled their way down. "I want tacos."

A growl filled up the car and I knew instinctively it belonged to Enzo. I was surprised the sound was so aggressive, but my sadness over the tacos wasn't swayed by the momentary distraction.

"Koda, look at me." The firm voice belonged to Jenson. When I glanced in his direction, I found him turned almost completely around so he stared at me through the space between his and Aidan's seat. "No, don't look away. I want you to look at me. That's it. Now take a deep breath." He paused, waiting for me to follow his instructions before he continued. "Atta girl. Are you ready to listen?"

I narrowed my eyes at the condescending tone, ignoring the small chuckle from Aidan, and nodded.

"Good." With my sole focus on Jen, I felt the sadness at the loss of tacos diminishing. "Aidan is going to wait in line and get your tacos. You perfumed earlier, which means we all smell like an unclaimed omega, but your scent on Aidan is the lightest."

Aidan growled at that truth. I turned my head to look at him, but a tight grip on my chin forced my gaze back to Jen. My chest started purring at the show of dominance. Not only was he handling me, but he just set himself up as the lead alpha—or at least higher up the hierarchy than Aidan—and the simple realization of that truth meant we were solidifying pack dynamics. Not to mention, the blatant hold on my chin had me trembling at his touch.

I wasn't supposed to like that idea, but I couldn't remember why. Especially staring into Jen's eyes full of dominance and … something else. Desire?

"Are you listening to me, little bear?"

"Yes, alpha."

The hold on my chin tightened. Jen's scent flared, telling me how much he liked my submissive gesture.

"Very good, little bear. Now tell Aidan how many tacos you want."

Jen still hadn't let go of my chin so I could only see Aidan in my peripheral. "A lot, please."

"How many is a lot?" Aidan asked.

I raised my hands and held them only a few inches apart. "If they are this big, like six." A little farther apart. "This big maybe five." Pulling my hands even farther apart, I shrugged. "Let's just go with five. No six.

No, five is fine. Five, I've decided."

Aidan didn't hesitate. The slam of the car door made me jump, but Jen finally released me. A soft click let me know he'd locked the car doors. The only light in the car was provided by the touch screen console up front. Running my hand along the ceiling of the car—no wait. Roof. Running my hand along the roof of the car, I searched for lights. I found a little switch, slid it to the right, and filled the space with a dim orange glow.

Having leaned so far forward, my chest was only a few inches away from Jen's face. For the first time tonight, I blushed at our nearness. Jen didn't seem to notice, however, since he hadn't taken his gaze away from my breasts. I was small enough I didn't have to wear a bra unless I was going to be working out, walking around all day, or chose to give my breasts an extra oomph. And since Jenson had literally fondled my breasts like an hour ago, he knew I hadn't worn anything under my shirt. Alpha arousal grew stronger in the small space.

A tug on my hips pulled me away from Jen only to make me realize my previous position had placed my ass right in Enzo's face. But that time, the embarrassment didn't get a strong hold because my thoughts turned into how effective that position could've been. One male at my front, playing with my breasts, biting and kissing my collarbone, my neck, as his fingers played with my nipples. If I was lucky, he wouldn't be wearing any pants, and I'd be able to take his dick in my hands, licking his tip to get him ready for my mouth. And with another male behind me, he'd play with my clit until he eased a single finger inside me, dragging that digit along my inner walls to find the perfect spot. Adding a second finger and maybe a third until I was soaked enough for his dick to slide easily inside me. I felt the phantom pulses of my pussy clenching down on nothing.

"Orsetta." I turned my attention to Enzo and out of my own vivid imagination. He was much closer than I'd realized, although his scent wasn't as strong as Jen's.

"Yes?" I asked, my voice barely a whisper.

My mouth, throat, and tongue were so dry it was like I'd swallowed sand.

Enzo didn't get a chance to explain whatever he was going to say because a familiar scent of burnt marshmallows invaded my senses. For a moment, I'd forgotten where I knew the scent from, but one look at the males' straining muscles, labored breathing, and blown pupils reminded me.

My perfume.

A thrill of excitement washed over my other emotions, drowning them out until all I wanted was to take my clothes off so everything I'd imagined could finally come true. And even the parts I hadn't dared to dream about: an alpha's knot.

Just the thought of a knot was enough to flood my pussy in wetness, increasing my scent in the car. But even as the haze of horny potential wrapped itself around my thoughts, a nagging feeling gave me a headache—like a splinter you only felt when you rubbed your finger across it just right.

Aidan. I was missing Aidan.

I turned to look out the back window, searching the crowded line for familiar blond hair. For the male I needed in order to complete the pack and take my turn with them—and their knots.

"Fuck. We need to distract her," Jen said, but I was barely paying attention. I needed to get to Aidan.

Reaching for the door handle, I pulled it, but it didn't budge. I tried unlocking it, but the car seemed broken, because the button wouldn't click.

"What the hell?" I yanked on the handle again

before turning my attention to Jen. "Unlock it."

"We can't let you go out there, little bear."

Glaring at Jen, I hated his calm words that didn't give me what I wanted. "I want Aidan."

"I thought you wanted tacos?" Enzo asked.

My thoughts were at war, battling for control over what should take dominance. The tacos lost against my desperate core. If I couldn't get to Aidan, I'd bring him to me.

Reaching toward Enzo, I half crawled onto his lap, carelessly climbing over his thighs until I got into the position allowing me to straddle his hips. Sitting on Enzo's lap, his lips were still slightly too high for me to reach if I also want to rub myself against his hardness.

I tried spreading my knees wider so I could press myself down on him, but my left knee pressed against the door, stopping my descent. I growled at Enzo as if this inability was his fault. The slight scent of arousal and pine trees disappeared under the new scent of alpha anger.

One of his hands clasped the back of my neck, careless of the hair strands that got caught and pulled at my scalp. His grip was unrelenting—punishing. I was forced to look at Enzo's face, his dark blue eyes caged behind long eyelashes. My main instinct demanded I submit, while a different instinct demanded I get away from the angry alpha. I bucked and fought to get off his lap, but his hold kept me from being able to move away.

His dominance radiated around me, growing stronger, sharpening his pine tree scent, and demanding my submission. But my body wouldn't listen. The stronger his scent became, the more my body reacted in equal parts fear and arousal. His grip tightened until a whimper escaped my throat.

"Calm, Omega," Enzo growled, his voice laced

with an alpha tone I couldn't deny. My body stopped trying to grind on him, stopped trying to get away from him. I just froze and handed over complete control. "Good girl, Orsetta."

Even though I preened at the compliment, I wasn't feeling truly subdued. I wanted a knot. I wanted Aidan. An omega's secret weapon was their alpha's desire to please them.

"You smell delicious, Koda." He pulled my face closer to his. My heart jumped, anticipating feeling his lips on mine. Instead, I found my lips pressed against the space connecting his shoulder to his neck. When my body rose slightly, I realized it was Enzo inhaling deeply, scenting me. "How is this possible?"

I tried pushing away from the alpha, not sure if I was trying to answer him, go back to grinding on him, or reach for his lips now that I was closer than before. But his grip didn't loosen. I tried again before giving up and contenting myself to lean against him, inhaling his pine forest scent.

"I don't know," Jen said, although I wasn't sure to what. "Sebastian said he would need her to agree to give samples of her blood. But as far as he's learned, this hasn't happened before. He did warn that her body might have more beta influences than just her scent."

I growled at the mention of a male not in my pack. My brain struggled to understand the full implications of Jenson's words, but Enzo stiffened under me. Disliking the change in the alpha, I nipped at his neck, not to draw blood, but enough to get his attention and leave a small red mark. Liking the mark, no matter how temporary, I set my lips around it and sucked until I was sure the mark was bigger.

The purring told me Enzo liked my actions. Despite the pleasant vibrations being sent to the space between my legs, my body suddenly felt low on energy, so I contended myself to giving soft kisses around the dark red mark on his neck and zoned out the alphas' conversation, letting their words act like a kind of lullaby.

I must have fallen asleep, because the sound of a slamming door had me on high alert and a growl releasing before I could check myself. The amused look from Jenson told me I wasn't as scary as I thought, but I didn't pay much attention to him because the hurt look on Aidan's face made me regret the defensive action.

The cab of the car quickly filled with the aroma of tacos. Meat, spices, and—I sniffed the air again to double check—grilled vegetables. Not wanting to seem ungrateful (and fully intending to pull off any vegetables that had ruined my taco before I ate it) I ignored that particular scent.

Enzo easily lifted me off his lap, but instead of returning me to my previous seat, he set me down directly next to him.

"She can't sit there," Aidan said, my usually joyful alpha sounding grumpy.

Already reaching over me to buckle my seatbelt, Enzo stopped, turning his head over his shoulder to look at Aidan. "Why not?"

"Middle seat is too dangerous."

Jenson turned around too, before nodding in agreement with Aidan. Enzo pushed me over back to my original seat, buckled me in, and sat in the middle seat himself.

"I thought the middle was dangerous?" I directed my question to Aidan since he seemed to have the most knowledge on car seating placements and safety.

"The safest place for you is behind the driver."

"But Enzo is in the middle seat."

"That's safer for you too," Jenson said.

I wanted to argue some more, but it would've taken too much energy to focus my thoughts and then get those thoughts to my tongue, so I didn't bother. Leaning against Enzo as Jen started the drive home, only the smell of tacos managed to keep me awake. Until even then, I was lulled to sleep by the cruising rhythm of the car.

Chapter Eighteen

A beautiful accent tried convincing me to wake up, saying, "Come on, Orsetta. We have to get some food into you."

I moved to roll away, to hide from the voice and fall back asleep, but the bed was more like a cocoon, holding me in place. I didn't like it.

"Why don't we just let her sleep?" a different voice asked, whispering to keep his voice quiet.

"She needs to eat, or she'll feel like shit tomorrow," a third voice said. "Little bear, if you don't wake up soon, your tacos will go cold."

The reminder of tacos shot enough adrenaline into my body for me to open one eye. Only inches from my face was Jenson, squatting down so he was at my eye level and running a hand along my hair. There was definitely amusement in his scent, but it was mostly overshadowed by the sternness on his face.

I wiggled my toes and fingers, rolled my shoulders, but the amount of energy it took to actually sit up was too much. Exhaustion threatened to pull me back down, and I wasn't strong enough to fight it. Cold tacos weren't too bad, right?

"Fine, if you're not going to eat your tacos, Koda bear, I will."

That got me up. I shot into a sitting position, my sight going dark at the edges and my whole body swaying slightly. Lots of hands reached out to steady me, two on my hips holding on from behind me, and two on my cheeks as Jenson tried steadying my head. It took a couple deep breaths and lots of blinking, but my body finally returned to normal.

The first thing able to penetrate the fog that was

my thoughts, was that I wanted my tacos. Immediately after thinking that, my body became aware that two males were touching me. If I leaned forward, I would've been able to capture Jenson's lips with my own and taste my alpha. I could encourage him to finally sate the hunger that had temporarily tempered off but that I knew I could rise with the simple action of meeting his lips. If I leaned backward, I could wrap my fingers around the back of Enzo's head and—

"Do you smell that?" Jenson whispered. I watched his throat bob as he swallowed, my fingers itching to reach out and wrap gently around his neck. Not to cut off his breathing, but to simply hold him in place. To keep him near me.

"What are you thinking about, Orsetta?" The question was so quiet, I was almost shocked I'd heard it at all.

My tongue suddenly felt too dry to lift, so I wiped the tip of it along my lips, trying to get some of the moisture back in my mouth. I swallowed once, twice, and finally managed to say, "Nothing."

Jenson raised a single eyebrow, obviously not believing my blatant lie, but Enzo saved me, saying, "Come on, Orsetta. Let's get your tacos before Aidan eats them."

Looking around, I realized I was on a single-seat couch in the pack's living room—the same place where I'd said goodbye to them.

Aidan was in the connected kitchen, having already sorted all the tacos out in front of undesignated designated spots. When we walked into the kitchen, his eyes lit up when he saw me, and he patted the bar stool next to him for me to sit in. There were only two bar stools on this side of the counter, which meant Jenson and Enzo had to stand.

Whoever designed this house had considered the appearance over pack dynamics. The backsplash in the kitchen was black tile with gray caulking between the pieces. The top for the island and the rest of the kitchen counter space was marble with a black and white design. Cabinets didn't have any exterior handles and appeared flush against each other instead of standing out.

The kitchen made an "L" shape with a small window over a deep farmhouse style sink and a dishwasher nearest the living room wall. Going from left to right along the longer portion was a stainless-steel fridge and freezer set I was pretty sure had the ability to speak if it was the same one from the commercial, lots of counter space containing blenders, a coffee maker, an air fryer. Then there was the stove top, which was not connected to the oven (which I loved) and finally a door to the pantry near the entrance to the hallway for the males' bedrooms.

Everything about the area screamed stylish, not comfort. Actually, despite how nice the kitchen was, there were a lot of changes I would make if I lived here. Starting with different bar stools needing taller backings and ending with more splashes of color.

Unwrapping the taco in front of me, all thoughts of interior design vanished. The corn tortilla was steaming and filled with something looking like pulled pork but smelled different. It was topped with finely chopped cabbage, some sort of cilantro and onion mix, and if my nose was correct, lime. No unnecessary vegetables. My mouth watered just from the smells alone. It had cooled down to the perfect temperature to still be warm but not burning the roof of your mouth hot that I suspected they were when Aidan first bought them.

Aidan was already on his second taco, Enzo on his first, but Jenson was simply holding his, watching me to make sure I liked mine. I took a bite, and little red dots of the sauce fell onto the wrapper, but my main focus was on the delicious taste of my favorite taco. The spices, and whatever the meat was were the perfect mix between sweet and savory. I took another bite and then another until I was eating the taco so fast, I accidentally bit my finger.

His chuckle told me that Jenson saw it happen, but I didn't slow down. Unwrapping the next taco, I dug in.

****

I ate too much. Five tacos seemed like the perfect number, but now my stomach was bloated to the point of hurting. In addition, my headache may or may not have been related to overstuffing myself. Whatever—no regrets. Those tacos were the best thing I'd ever eaten.

When I went to lean back and stretch out my stomach, it dipped, telling me a moment too slowly I was about to fall backward. Luckily, I had three strong alphas that managed to catch me.

I erupted into giggles for so long that tears came to my eyes and my stomach ached from the workout it apparently received. As the laughter finally subsided, I wiped under my eyes. My body seemed to have exerted all my energy in eating, laughing, and staying awake, because I could feel it crashing. Eyelids growing heavy, I rested my forearms on the countertop, carefully cradling my head.

"Tired, Koda bear?" Aidan asked.

I nodded, too exhausted for words.

"Okay, c'mon. I'll carry you to bed. You have to stay with one of us so we can make sure you're okay throughout the night. Whose room do you want?"

Whose room? Like, I had to choose between my alphas? Was that what these males wanted, for me to pick? How could I explain that I wanted them all when I could barely lift my head off Addie's shoulder? And when did he pick me up?

Without thinking it through too much, I told Addie I wanted my nest. The swaying motion suddenly stopped. When I lifted my head to figure out what was going on, Addie's hand came up to the back of my head, gently pressing my head back down.

"Okay, Koda bear. I'll take you to your nest." With my head on his shoulder, and against his throat, I felt him swallow. It was a weird sensation and would've totally made me giggle if I had the energy. As it was, I barely managed a smile.

I didn't hear the door opening, but the strong scent of all three alphas was my indication that not only had my nest in their house not been aired out, but the alphas had left their pillows and blankets in the room.

"We hoped you would come back to us," Enzo said.

My chest started purring to show how much I liked that idea.

"Do you want me to carry you in, Koda bear?" The question came so quietly from Addie, I instinctively inhaled his scent.

Aidan's sadness almost completely drained out his desert rainstorm scent. The need to comfort him became my first priority, as if I could physically fight my tiredness to be present.

"Why are you sad, Addie?" A horrible thought hit me that maybe he didn't want me to stay here. Especially in a nest meant for his omega. My heart broke at the realization. But I wouldn't stay there if it meant upsetting my alpha.

Aidan gave me a small smile like he was trying to hide his sadness from me. "I was just hoping you would plan to sleep with one of us tonight."

Wait. What?

Aidan's cheeks turned pink, hitching my confusion higher. What did he have to be embarrassed about?

"It's okay if you're not ready for that, little bear." Jenson's voice startled me, reminding me that Aidan and I weren't alone. The house was soaked with all three of the alphas' scents, making it impossible to know whether they were nearby when I couldn't see them. "We're just happy you're comfortable enough to stay here, in your nest."

Speaking of which—I scrambled down from the Aidan, momentarily ignoring his pained scent increasing, so I could shut the door to my nest. Then I glared at all three alphas. "Don't open the door. The scents will come out." It was a ridiculous notion since the whole house smelled of the alphas, but my mind couldn't be swayed. People came into the house. Scents clung to clothes. All those scents could've ruined the sanctity of my nesting space.

All three alphas seemed shocked but nodded their agreement. Going from ninety percent asleep to fully awake and pissed off was giving me emotional whiplash.

"Now. You three need to go get your pajamas on and then meet me back here. Knock but make sure you close the door behind you."

My beta side was telling me this was a bad idea, but I didn't listen to her. These males were mine—I'd proved it when I offered them a place in my nest. But the longer they continued staring at me, the less confident I became. Why weren't they excited at the invitation to join me in my nest? Did they not know how to turn me down? Was my beta side, right?

"Are you sure, little bear?" Jenson asked. "You

know what it means to invite us into your sacred omega space?"

"Yes. It means we're pack." Even my beta side knew that. Although, she was adamant that I was forgetting something.

I scented the alphas excitement moments before all three disappeared without another word, leaving me alone in the hallway. Slipping into my nest room, I took a deep breath, feeling immediately calmed by the familiar—untainted—scents. Without their emotions to manipulate their scents, my nest simply felt safe. Plus, the huge pile of pillows and blankets helped.

Finding the entrance to my nest was easy, but I still hesitated. This wasn't right. It looked the same as I left it, but I had built that nest for myself, for comfort. Now my alphas were going to be joining me and the space was all wrong.

A door slamming jostled me out of my frozen state. I slid my skirt and tights off, tossing them into the middle of the nest for more fabrics to use. I considered leaving my key necklace on but decided to take it off, carefully putting it off to the side. The males might cuddle me, and they wouldn't want to wake up with a key imprint like I occasionally did. I'd never been embarrassed about having my nipples be noticeable when they turned into hard points and had shown through my shirt. But that was just normal, everyday boobs. Now my breasts felt sexy, and the hard points seemed to somehow grab more attention than usual. The thought of all three alphas joining me made my nipples hard, begging for attention, and my pussy grew wet like it was expecting a knot to just jam up in her at any moment.

A knock on the door distracted me from my clothing, and I turned to face it, expecting them to just walk in. Instead, there was a beat of silence. "Koda. It's

Jenson." Another slight pause. "Aidan and Enzo are here too. We're ready whenever you are."

Having alphas need permission to enter my nest was a first-time experience, and it made me feel heady with the power. And arousal.

Outside of this room, I bent to the will and strength of alphas. Not just mine but every alpha. In here, though, it was my sanctuary. It smelled how I wanted, was set up how I liked, and I had complete control over what did and didn't happen.

Which reminded me—I looked over at my nest. There was a vent above the door to the room, but it must not have been on since the alphas' scents still clung to the pillow and blankets enough to please me.

"If I let you in the room, you have to wait to enter the nest." Having a comfortable nest was important to me but almost as important was how my alphas liked my design.

"Yes, Omega," Jenson growled, disliking the order but deferring to me.

Opening the door, I peeked through as if I could've spied on the alphas. Three sets of eyes looked down at me. Taking in all the alphas raised my body's internal temperature up several degrees. Jenson's stomach was sharply defined, drawing my eyes to the space between his pectorals, down to the outline of his abdominals, and to each side that had the definition of a V. He was in a simple pair of gray sweats hanging low on his hips. My beta side was shocked at the realization her professor was ripped.

Aidan was also in sweats, but his were short, having been cut off above his knees. He was the thinnest of my alphas with the kind of body that looked like he could eat without gaining any weight. But that wasn't what surprised me the most. Ink decorated his body. His light skin tone made the perfect canvas for the colorful tattoos. Usually dressed in suits at the academy or even at his club, I had only seen Aidan's neck and forearms. But now. Images of animals, some wielding weapons, some attacking others, were drawn along his calves and thighs, covering almost every available inch of his legs.

Enzo was the most covered in his pajamas, and I wanted to demand he take the offending fabric off. He wore a black tank top that was tight on his body like a second skin and allowed the hair from his chest to peek through. The dark curls called to me, demanding I run my fingers over it. Instead of sweats like the other males, Enzo wore basketball sports and socks. The combination would've been humorous if he hadn't looked so good. He was my biggest alpha, his body built heavier. He might not have had a six pack, but that didn't stop him from looking like the strongest male in his pack.

"Do you plan to let us in?" Jenson teased, earning a glare from me. "Or are you planning to drool from behind the door all night?"

"I have to fix the nest still." I left the door open and focused all my attention on making the necessary adjustments to the nest. Every movement became more urgent as the fresh scents of my pack filled the area. This needed to be perfect. The concaved roof needed to be fixed—the whole nest needed a good fluff. I extended blankets, made sure the pillows were firm, and sorted through the best fabrics. I needed enough space for three large alphas and a single omega.

Adjusting and fluffing and spreading and all the little touch ups were like a little work-out routine. I hadn't noticed my heavy breathing until I finally sat in the middle of my nest, in a delicious sandwich of scents and blankets. I had actually forgotten about the males waiting for permission to join me. But without anything left to manage, I quickly remembered.

"Okay. You may enter. Just…"

"Just what, little bear?" Jenson asked.

"Don't ruin it." I stared at the small opening that was available for my males to enter. I'd made it as big as I could, but my fingers itched to try again. If they weren't on the edge of fatigue, I might've.

"We wouldn't think of it, little bear."

The first male to enter my nest was Jen, solidifying him as the head of this pack. He was just barely able to crawl in, but his elbows were still bent to ensure he didn't accidentally knock down the stretched blanket acting as a roof. My nerves settled when he made it all the way in.

Jenson scooted his way to the deepest portion of my nest and then Aidan's blond locks appeared as my second alpha crawled his way into the nest. He looked around, searching for a spot to claim for himself, but I couldn't help but scrutinize his gaze. Was he impressed with my nest? Did he think it was too small? I could probably fix the corners so they were even tighter, and he could push his head against the top to give himself more room … although I didn't do that originally because that meant the blanket would sort of sag. But maybe if Aidan preferred it—

"Wipe that look off your face, Koda." Aidan sat down beside me, but leaned in, grabbing my chin so I was forced to look directly at him. "Your nest is perfect."

Four simple words and I felt the tension leave my shoulders. I hadn't realized I was sitting up straight enough to sharpen a knife, but my muscles thanked me for a break in posture.

Last to enter was Enzo, who didn't hesitate when climbing into my nest and immediately made himself comfortable laying out. He bundled up the clothes I'd worn earlier to act as a pillow and didn't even acknowledge me until he was all laid out.

"I thought we were sleeping," Enzo said.

"We are. We are." I looked back and forth between Aidan and Jen. My instincts weren't as strong now, leaving room for other emotions to seep in—hence my nerves. "How are we going to do this?"

Aidan dragged me toward him, forcing my knees to straddle him. "Just relax, I'm getting comfortable." And that was exactly what he did. Somehow, half cradling me to his chest, he maneuvered around, and then proceeded to lay down with me on top of him. When he finally got comfortable and stopped fidgeting, I pushed my hands against his chest and sat up.

That put me in the perfect position, specifically over the bulge that pressed against the space between my thighs. It was exactly what I'd wanted in the car earlier. His arms were bent behind his head like he was trying to feign casual, but the strain in his muscles and the scent of his need gave him away.

I let my fingers wander where they wanted, tracing invisible circles over his warm skin, pressing against his ribs to feel him breathe, and scratching gentle white lines down his pecks. When his nipples tightened to points, I circled the light pink skin and gently pinched them.

The moan from Aidan moved through his whole body until I felt it along my thighs. Just the sound alone sent a rush of wetness to my core. The knowledge that I was somehow pleasuring Aidan—it was a heady thought that seemed to short circuit my remaining common sense.

"What are you waiting for, little bear?" Jenson rasped. Where Jen was barely breathing, my chest heaved with deep breaths. "Kiss him."

I didn't need any other encouragement. My lips

pressed against Aidan's. A hand came up to hold my head in place, as if I would've even considered putting any space between us. The kiss wasn't a gentle press of lips. No, it was more like hunger, as if we'd been starving and needed each other's lips in order to survive. He pushed his tongue into my mouth, demanding I felt him. Demanding a taste of me. My lower stomach tightened with arousal, my entire body clenching against the incoming pleasure.

His natural brewing storm scent grew stronger, mixing with his arousal, to the point he was the only scent I was breathing in. The tension in his body reminded me of the thunderstorm he smelled of. The thunder was his heart, beating so hard in his chest I felt each boom against my fingers. When his hips rolled against my body, the brilliant light flashing behind my eyes was the lightening. His scent, the desert rain, forcing the flowers to bloom so all I wanted was to take deep gulps of the smell.

Aidan's lips left mine to trail kisses down my jaw, but I still whimpered at the loss of his lips on mine. I ran my fingers through his hair, grabbing fistfuls of the long length and forcing his mouth back where I wanted it.

The growl didn't come from Addie, and it was my only warning before hands grabbed the hem of my shirt, yanking it over my head. My top was thrown blindly, but I didn't even care about the disorganization in my nest.

Two hands wrapped around me from behind and squeezed my breasts. With so much stimulation, I pulled my lips away from Aidan's to try and catch my breath, enjoying the feel of warm hands touching me. Even if I hadn't scented Enzo's nearness, his rough hands and slightly calloused fingertips clued me in on who was touching me. His tank top must have been in a pile with my own shirt, because I felt his chest, the hairs I had wanted to run my fingers through earlier, pressed against me. Free to kiss me wherever, Aidan returned his lips to my jaw and down my neck while Enzo's lips were on the opposite side.

Fresh pine battled with the desert storm, but neither was as strong as my own growing scent. My slick was drowning my underwear. The emptiness in my core was becoming almost painful. I wanted to be filled by one of my alphas, but I couldn't get the words out.

Hands moved to my hips, guiding them to rock back and forth over Aidan's cock in a way that helped relieve the ache but also made me more desperate.

"How are you doing, little bear?"

I turned my head slightly to look at Jen. His muscles were tense, his scent aroused even as he held himself back. I wanted to growl at the distance between us. All three of my alphas should've been touching me, but I didn't know how to ask without feeling as if I was forcing him.

"Good." I managed this single word between breaths.

Enzo pinched my nipples and I cried out from the sudden pain. Aidan sat up, taking the sore point into his mouth, tonguing one peak before moving to the other after Enzo pinched that one.

I threw my head back, not caring about anything but increasing my pleasure. I needed it. I needed more.

Reaching my hands out to Jen, I bent my fingers in the universal sign for him to get his ass closer to me.

The male didn't move, however. Instead, he kept watching me, his rising scent of fresh linen and arousal I wanted to grow until he couldn't stay away from me.

Enzo growled his frustration, bringing my attention back to the duo. I grabbed his hands, trying to gather my thoughts for a second—just a second—but

Aidan took up the vacancy with his own touch. He wrapped his whole hand around my breasts, squeezing as he cupped them from underneath, pushing them together. His grip was tight, and he went from teasing my nipples to biting the side of my breasts, leaving temporary marks.

Unceremoniously, I shoved Enzo's hands toward my dripping pussy, hoping he'd get the idea of what I wanted without me having to form words.

His chuckle shook his body, but he didn't disappoint, gliding his hands up the middle of my panties and shoving the top down enough to reveal the curls there to anyone who looked.

I glanced over at Jen, watching his gaze flutter back and forth between Aidan and Enzo's hands.

A frustrated growl came from him.

There was something intriguing about having Jen watch but that was for another time. For my first time, I wanted all three of them to touch me. To choose me.

Enzo ran his fingers through the curls, moving lower until he could feel the wetness leaking from me. I wasn't even embarrassed when he pulled my underwear away from my body and gently fingered my outer lips. The light touch was too much like a tease, so I rolled my hips toward his hand, encouraging more. Begging for more without words.

"What do you say, Orsetta?" Enzo whispered.

I closed my eyes, unable to handle all the stimulation now that words were being thrown into the ring. "Please."

"Please, what?"

I gasped for breath. "Please, more."

Jenson groaned like my pleas hurt him, and my eyes opened to watch the sound leave his lips. He still hadn't moved to touch me yet. The small kernel of hurt I hadn't let myself acknowledge before grew without permission. Why didn't my arousal pull him in? Did he not like the scent of my slick? And, even if my scent hadn't pleased him, shouldn't just the notion of his packmates pleasuring a single female have made him jealous enough to want to join in? Not that I wanted him simply out of jealousy, but I was starting to feel desperate.

My internal worries were trying to distract me. Whether or not Enzo noticed didn't seem to matter because he was still stroking my slit, refusing to push his finger exactly where I wanted him. He gathered the wetness pouring out of me, pressing harder on my clit. My hips bucked wildly. Enzo did it again and again, circling my clit and pressing down harder with each turn as my hands searched for purchase on something—anything.

I'd never been this aroused in my entire life, and I hadn't even reached my own climax yet. I knew I wouldn't until all three alphas were touching me. It wasn't about being coy or having the strength to deny my orgasm. Every instinct in my body refused to climax until I was touched by all members of this pack. But the knowledge didn't help cool off the heat scorching my every nerve. On the contrary, it was like my very molecules rioted at the understanding, ratcheting up my arousal, trying to force Jenson into joining us. Into touching me.

Enzo finally stopped playing with my clit and shoved a finger inside me. My entire focus went to that single intrusion, my inner walls tightening, trying to keep him in there, but my body screamed that I needed more. Something bigger, stronger, and longer. I was gasping for air, struggling to breathe, but the need to come was more important than inhaling oxygen.

"Cazzo," Enzo growled. "She's sucking me in."

He barely pulled his first finger out before shoving in another. My back bowed from the tension, sweat dripping down my forehead. I felt like screaming in frustration. It was all too much. With Enzo's fingers still inside me, the heel of his hand pressed into my swollen clit, I couldn't hold back my scream.

"Frustrated, Koda bear?" Aidan taunted before licking up the center between my breasts.

"Are you doing this on purpose?" I asked between breaths. My body felt like I'd run a marathon, but there was still no finish line in sight.

When I glanced over at Jenson, he had his hand on his crotch, squeezing his dick through his sweats like he was trying to hold himself off. I growled at him, hoping to get his attention and demand his response. Keeping himself away from me wasn't just breaking my heart, it was forcing my climax higher and higher to the point of nearing pain.

Jenson immediately growled back, his voice full of possessiveness and arousal but so much dominance. All it did was flood my pussy with more slick. I hadn't known I could produce so much—especially from a single growl—in a single sexual experience.

"Please, I can't—" My words were cut off in my throat like someone turned the tap off the sink when Jenson finally moved closer. I watched him over Aidan's head, as the blond alpha bit and sucked his claims all over my chest. "Jen. I need you. Please."

My legs were shaking with tension around Aidan, my back slipping along Enzo with sweat, my core trying to get satisfaction from only two fingers, but it was just out of reach.

But Jen moved closer, pulling my hands away from their grip on Enzo's forearms. He took one hand and shoved my middle finger into his mouth. He let his tongue run over the pad of my finger and gently bit the tip. If my core was a bonfire, Jen would be gasoline thrown on. I didn't know if I was screaming in frustration, pleasure, or pain. Jen's fresh scent allowed me to take a clean breath—for what seemed like the first time—in the midst of chaos.

Taking my finger out of his mouth, he blew cool air on the wetness, and my core tightened to the point of pain around Enzo's fingers. I wasn't sure if there were two or three inside me, but I knew it wasn't enough.

"Are you paying attention, Koda?"

The words drew my attention even as the touches refused to stop. Jen. Jen was talking to me.

I couldn't get words out, but I managed a simple shake of my head—no.

"Listen carefully. I'm going to take the pain away. I'm going to touch you, Koda, but I need you to do something for me first. Are you listening?"

I nodded. Anything. Yes.

"I want to claim you, Koda. We all do. And we know it's too soon for all three of us, so I'll be first. We already know you're the omega we want. Hell, before we knew you were an omega, we wanted you. But I need to claim you. I won't be able to touch you without doing so."

The relentless touches were too much of a distraction to get my thoughts in order. All I could focus on was a promise of his touch and surely, if I didn't get it soon, I'd die. Or burst. Or cry hysterically.

I nodded. "Please, alpha."

But still, Jenson denied me release. Shaking his head, he said, "I need you to say it, Koda. I need the words, and then I will make you come. I promise. You held yourself back from us before because you didn't want to admit you're an omega. Because you were intent on denying a side of yourself. But we want to convince you to let us be alphas to both your beta and omega side. We don't care how you perfume. We'll share your beta side just as we will your omega."

My beta side was conflicted. She had spent our life in control, but the pheromones were too strong for even her to fight. Now was my turn for control, and I was going to get us a pack. A family.

I did my best to speak, to try and explain, but Enzo moved his fingers in such a way that distracted me. My mouth was open, but no sound seemed to come out.

Hands cupped my cheeks and then I was staring into brown eyes so dark the division between the brown and black was almost imperceptible. Jen's forehead pressed against mine and I closed my eyes. I could feel how close his lips were with his every breath. And then his nearness was gone. His lips pressed against my neck in a gentle kiss, and then again near my collarbone.

"How about here, Koda? Should I bite you here?"

My hands moved of their own volition, holding the alpha where he'd promised a bite. "Claim me, alpha."

There was no hesitation. Jenson bit down around my collarbone painfully, making me cry out, my body tensing. I tried shoving him off, but his teeth clamped down and too many sets of arms were holding me. My entire body went into overdrive. There was nothing small about the orgasm that made its way through me. My core tightened, and I was sure Enzo couldn't have pulled his fingers out if he tried. Muscles shook from the exertion, toes curled, and my mouth fell open like I wanted to scream but couldn't find the volume.

And then the world went blissfully dark.

Chapter Nineteen

I dreamt of a beautiful nest. One large enough for all my alphas, filled with their different but delicious scents, and decorated to perfection, exactly how I liked. Nests were the ultimate symbol of control. I chose who went in, where things went, what it smelled like. And my dream nest had three alphas in it, filling it with their scents and wrapping me up in their limbs so if anyone peered in, they wouldn't know whose arms were whose and whose legs were whose. I dreamt of a perfect morning in my perfect nest.

The gentle rise and fall of my mattress was nice at first, but the out of sync rhythm with my own breathing quickly became annoying. I tried cracking an eye open but immediately realized it was too bright and shut it again.

When I tried to roll off, I extended my leg, which had apparently been bent all night, and it didn't take too kindly to the quick movement. A cramp in my thigh all the way to my right ass cheek woke me up, however. I tried rolling over onto my opposite side to rub my ass, but something stopped me. No. Someone.

"Koda, what's wrong?" Jenson's voice finally resonated with my sleep-filled and pain induced mind.

"Cramp. Cramp. Ow." I tried massaging the ass cheek, but Jenson's fingers moved mine out of the way and dug in deeper. It hurt more at first and I tried to move away from his prying fingers, but Jenson didn't relent. Finally, the knot seemed to work its way out until I could bend and straighten my leg without pain.

But just as soon as the pain disappeared, the memories came back from last night. The club. The drinks. The car ride with the subsequent tacos. My orgasm. Being claimed.

I covered my breasts, but Jen pulled my arms away, dragging me toward his chest. His purr was immediate, loud, and strong, pulling all of my attention and washing away my worry.

We sat there for a few minutes, my head pressed against his chest, and his hands rubbing up and down my spine. When his hands rubbed along my shoulders and down toward my collarbone, a dull prickling sensation spread from his fingers, feeling like the spot on my collarbone had been rubbed raw. I definitely needed a bandage to cover the bite wound.

And then the realization really hit me. I remember being claimed, remember Jenson demanding I ask for it, and then begging for his bite. More than just facts—I was bound to this alpha, to this pack. As a half-beta, half-omega, I had an alpha mate. When Monday came around, I'd be a mated half-beta, half-omega student.

Jen inhaled deeply, as if he was enjoying my plain beta scent. "Don't be scared, little bear. Everything will work out just fine."

"You can hear my thoughts?" I squeaked. I wasn't aware the bond was that … intrusive.

"Not exactly. But the bond lets me feel every emotion you have, and I can piece the puzzle together. For instance," he said, lowering his voice and trailing his lips in an up and down pattern along my neck, "I can feel how happy you are. Your excitement over being pack. But that's mainly overshadowed by your fear. I can feel your anxiety about the future and your doubt that your scent calls to me even if you aren't perfuming."

At least I knew he couldn't read my thoughts, because that was way more eloquent than what I was actually thinking. But completely true.

"And what are you thinking now?" I discreetly

scented my alpha—my official alpha—but didn't pick up any anger or jealousy or anything setting off my omega's instincts.

"I'm thinking I need to feed you. I can also feel your hunger."

A warning growl started in my throat before I could cut it off. Jen knew exactly what I meant, and the unusual smirk on his lips was proof. It seemed bonding with my usually serious alpha turned him into quite the jokester. And it was way too early for jokes.

"No, Omega, I'm not upset about what we did last night. And I like your scent whether it denotes you as a beta or an omega."

"It's more than how my perfume presents. I like the privileges that come with being a beta."

"So be one. Claim that designation. It doesn't matter to me or my pack."

My eyes widened to an almost comical amount at Jen's inclusion of his packmates. The stereotype surrounding alphas—especially newly bonded alphas—wasn't one of sharing. Plenty of horror movies had centered around a possessive alpha who could only be controlled through his kidnapped bonded omega. Usually, the villain needs the alpha to steal something of importance or else the omega would be killed. But my alpha was already including me with his packmates less than twelve hours after bonding me. Did it have to do with my natural beta scent making him less possessive? Maybe it didn't pull at an alpha's protective heartstrings like an omega?

"Come on, it'll all make more sense once we find the others." The calm tone of Jen's voice, and his comforting scent, temporarily soothed my nerves. I might have been confused, but I knew one fact: I was now a part of the pack. It was a hard concept to accept when I'd convinced myself it was impossible. I needed time to get my thoughts under control, but it seemed impossible without my morning coffee. What I really wanted was some space from the distracting scents and the delicious alpha who knew how intimately I was feeling in order to rebuild my emotional walls, but the mere thought of being outside of Jen's line of view made me panic. And it would forever be impossible to hide how I felt from my alpha. I'd barely acknowledged the bond between us, but it already felt like an intrinsic part of who I was.

"Need coffee." My sleepy voice was nowhere near as sexy as Jen's considering he sounded like a gruff male, and I sounded like a toad who'd smoked a pack a day for the last twenty years.

"You're in luck. Enzo and Aidan have been awake for some time so there's at least a cup ready for you."

I felt bad admitting—even to myself—that I hadn't noticed the other two alphas weren't present. Yep, I definitely needed coffee if I was going to start thinking clearly. I was pretty sure Jen mentioned the other alphas weren't even in the room earlier, but my mind didn't seem capable of grasping facts.

"And which one turned all the lights on?"

Jen chuckled. "I'll make sure they keep the lights dimmer for you, in the future."

Despite the need for caffeine crying in my veins, my body wouldn't move.

"I don't want to leave," I admitted, clinging to Jen tighter.

If my declaration shocked him, he didn't show it. He lowered his head, placing chaste kisses on my neck until he reaches my collarbone, and then my entire body melted, my muscles no longer able to hold me up. There was still a slight intimidation in the back of my mind when it came to Jen, but it was dramatically lessening with each passing moment. He chose me. There was proof of it with every breath I took stretching the tender skin around my claiming bite. And it did help that he wasn't impeccably dressed, like always. Somehow being naked with Jen was like an even playing field. I might've even had the upper hand based on the way Jen couldn't stop looking at me and touching me, his scent giving away his innocent gaze.

"Alpha," I purred, begging for more of his attention despite his focus already being solely on me.

"Omega." Jen gently nipped at my collarbone before asking, "Do you mind?"

"Mind?"

"Being called 'omega'?"

I shrugged. "It doesn't sound wrong, if that's what you're asking. I've always considered myself both an omega and a beta."

"Hm."

"Coffee," I demanded when it seemed like Jen was going to get stuck thinking on nomenclatures.

Jen laughed and tapped my exposed bottom. "Get up then. I'll be right behind you."

With the promise of caffeine, I crawled out of the nest, stretching every muscle in my body and admiring the imprints of Jen's body as red lines on my own. It definitely looked like I'd slept well last night, but I guessed an orgasm like the one I had would do that. There was a neat pile of clothes by the door to the nest room, which I immediately recognized as Jen's by the smell.

"They're for you," he said, stretching just like I did. Watching his arms and stomach flex had me almost drooling. When he clasped his hands above his head and swayed from side to side, my core clenched as if she was unsatisfied with being empty this early in the morning.

Jen's nostrils flared, immediately taking in the change in my scent, so I blurted out the only thing I thought of to distract him.

"How are you so fit?"

Jen raised an eyebrow while I distracted myself with putting on the clothes left for me. Basically, it was a long shirt and boxer shorts, but it would work for around the pack house. I didn't remember taking my underwear off last night, but it was probably soaked with my slick. My necklace was placed nicely next to the laid-out clothes, and I decided to put it on, needing the feel of normalcy that came with wearing it.

"I work out," Jen said.

I whipped my head up and glared at him. My alpha had jokes this morning. "Why are you so fit?"

"You don't like my body?"

I huffed out my annoyance, ignoring the warm, fuzzy feeling at our banter.

Jen was completely unfazed by my pseudo-frustration. Laughing, he finally gave me an answer. "Despite what it may look like from the outside of our pack, I'm actually the one with the most free time. Aidan runs multiple business and Enzo has his band. The two of them also have to deal with their families. I only teach a couple days a week and before that I was in graduate school. Working out keeps me busy. Or at least it did. I have a feeling you're going to be a handful, little bear."

I blushed at the insinuation but didn't disagree with him. There was a lot that Jen and I needed to discuss, but not now. Later. Like, after coffee.

****

Leaving the room with my nest was harder than I expected. Every step felt like a tether connecting me to my nest grew tauter. I felt skittish, like something bad could've happened to me if I wasn't under my pile of pillows and blankets. Just another omega quirk.

Before we entered the kitchen, Jen stopped me. I thought I was acting strange, but even Jen seemed to have grown just as agitated as me.

"Are you okay, Jen?"

"I'll be fine, little bear. Just stay near me, okay?"

I nodded and Jen placed a hand on my lower back, half like he was lending me his confidence and half in a possessive gesture.

Aidan and Enzo were sitting in the living room, talking quietly until they notice us. Their eyes took in my clothes. Their noses lifted slightly to scent me.

Behind me, Jen growled a warning to the other males, who quickly looked away and returned to whatever they were talking about before.

I couldn't lie and say my heart didn't hurt at being ignored by the other males, but the display of jealousy was enough of a comfort. My beta side wanted the attention of all three alphas and my omega side wanted Jen to assert his claim of me over his pack. He mentioned trusting me with his alphas, but now he was all growls and irritation. The last thing I wanted to do was create a rift between packmates—how had Hannah bonded with four alphas? Maybe I could schedule a meet up with her and get some advice.

"Here, little bear." Jen pulled me along to the kitchen, filling up a cup of coffee with the caramel syrup I liked.

"Thanks."

There was only enough for a single cup, so Jen started another pot for himself. I sat on the counter, not caring about the numerous health code violations, and stared toward the living room while Jen occasionally touched my knee, shoulder, or hair in a reassuring gesture. It felt slightly obsessive, as if he wasn't consciously doing it.

I enjoyed the clarity that came with drinking coffee, taking the time to officially wake up. By the time the pot was done for Jen, I was ready for my second cup, which he quickly filled up for me before starting his own. With an adequate amount of caffeine in my system, I could finally think through all my emotions. Of course, being this close to Jen, my number one emotion was an abundance of happiness. Which wasn't a bad thing but didn't help with making decisions. Space might've helped—even if the idea of being away from Jen made me want to dig my nails into his chest until I drew blood to ensure he didn't step too far away.

Aggressive? Yes.

But I was civilized, so I didn't do that.

Enzo was the first to break the silence of the morning with a strong declaration. "I think we should talk. All of us. Things were done last night in the heat of the moment—" Jen growled but Enzo continued talking like he hadn't heard him. "But more big decisions still need to be made."

Aidan nodded along in agreement.

I had plenty I needed to say, answers to their questions only I had, so I agreed.

Jen shrugged, still glaring at Enzo for his remark about the claiming but not disagreeing with his packmate.

Instead of sitting in the nice living room in the comfy chairs, Aidan and Enzo came to Jen and me in the kitchen. They sat on the bar stools we had dinner on last night, while I sat on the counter near the coffee pot. Jen stood next me, not so casually touching me.

My finger tapped anxiously along my coffee cup. I'd never done anything but deny my omega side before, which meant actually acknowledging it felt … not wrong but taboo. Like if I admitted the truth out loud, the males would laugh and admit this whole thing was a hoax and I had to leave the academy. But my beta side had always been more logical whereas my omega ran on instinct. A claiming bite, for example, told my omega that the alpha was to be trusted. And since that decision had already been made—by me—I was going to have to trust that instinct. Trust my omega side.

"What first?" I asked.

"Might as well get the hard stuff out of the way," Aidan said. "You're an omega."

It wasn't a question, but I nodded.

"You don't smell like one. In fact, you smell like a beta unless you're turned on. Then you smell like … like burnt marshmallows."

I took a long sip of my coffee, wondering how I was going to explain this to them since I didn't really know how to describe it myself. The best I could do was give them the limited information I had.

"I don't know much about my parents. But I do know when I was old enough to go to school, they shipped me off to a year-round academy, and I haven't seen them since."

Jen squeezed my thigh, no doubt feeling my pain at being abandoned through our bond.

"The school accepts all students and then once their designation is known, they either continue their education there or get sent to the Omega Compound. It's very standard procedure. I know some get tested when they're younger if they present some characteristics of a designation early on, but the test at the academy was basically, 'if you perfume you get removed'. But I only perfume when I'm turned on, and by the time I figured that out, all the other omegas had been removed. I did my best to stay under the notice of others. And on the off chance I came to school smelling like a sexually active omega, everyone assumed I was just sleeping with the one."

"When you figured out you could perfume, why didn't you tell anyone?" Aidan asked. "It must have been scary going through omega changes by yourself."

"It was," I said in agreement. "But my parents didn't want any contact with me. And even if I didn't have a lot of friends, I knew almost everyone in my school. I had my own room, I knew the teachers, I liked the classwork. It was familiar. Safe. And I also knew I hadn't seen a single omega since they disappeared to the center. For all I knew, omegas were dying there."

The males laughed at my imagination, but it had been a real fear of mine when I was younger—that hadn't really gone away. Omegas simply disappeared, and everyone said they went to a center, but where was the center? I didn't have any parents or siblings to get in contact with, and my friends were nice in the sense we work on school projects together, but we never hung out outside of the classroom setting. "I chose to keep going as I was. Everyone assumed I was a beta, and I didn't see a reason to contradict them."

"What about a pack?" Enzo asked.

"When it came time to decide between outing myself to the Compound or going to college…" I shrugged. "You can all see which path I took. I figured I could always go the Compound after I got my degree, but there was no guarantee whatever pack I found myself in would let me continue my education."

"Your education is that important to you?" Jen asked.

I made sure to stare directly into Jen's eyes when I said, "Yes."

My alpha nodded, but no one said anything about

the fact that I was still a student. Still attending an academy that would've happily kicked me out and sent me to the Compound if they learned the truth. Or maybe they would've sent me to my alpha now that I was bonded. Unless they fired him too because they thought he helped hide my designation.

"Woah, Koda, your emotions are—"

"Are what?" Enzo demanded, his voice either panicked or angry, when Jen cuts his words off.

"They started changing rapidly. It was too hard to catch on to a single one. What are you thinking about, little bear? Tell us, let's figure it out together."

"As a pack," Aidan added, making his way closer to me.

Enzo nodded his agreement, joining Aidan in closing in our proximity. Being able to scent all three of them calmed me—even if they all scented slightly of panic. Aidan and Enzo accepted me as their packmate, and Jen tolerated their closeness. It steeled my spine, making the words come out easier.

"Will you get in trouble, Jen, if they find out we're bonded?"

He seemed to consider his words carefully, which I simultaneously appreciated and hated. I wished the answer was easy enough for a simple yes or no. He looked at Aidan, as if checking to see if the other alpha had an opinion as he said, "If we're bonded, no. Alphas can bond betas, even if it isn't considered the norm. But if you go back to the academy and then get caught as an omega? Maybe. Probably."

I almost missed it. But I managed to catch the single most important thing Jen said. "There's no 'if', Jen. I spent two years at the community college, which I negotiated by the way, all to help prepare my future, and now I'm finally at Braker Academy. I have three more semesters. I'm not dropping out now."

"The academy has a lot of alphas that are separatists. They already argued against letting betas into the system, and they aren't going to be happy we're bonded if they don't know about your omega side."

"If they found out I had an omega side, they'd kick me out anyway. I'd rather have their hate but still get an education."

"So we keep your designation a secret."

The anxiety from the conversation had me biting my nails until Aidan grabbed my free hand, holding it away from my mouth and down in my lap. My forearm strained to complete tearing my nail off but eventually, I gave up.

"Will you get fired for being with a student?" I asked.

"I'm not worried about me losing my job. Aidan and Enzo by themselves both make enough so that I could stay home. So you could stay home too." I rolled my eyes at the comment but thankfully, Jen didn't linger on the idea. "But I'm not hiding my relationship with you. Neither will the others. Which means we come forward to Chancellor Kelly. We make everyone aware they need to adhere to the same social rules with you at the academy as they would if they passed our pack on the streets. We're claiming you as a pack beta."

That could work. I wasn't sure what the rules were for alpha professors in relationships with students since most were either in a pack or already had an omega—and I had noticed that Jen effectively evaded that question. I didn't want Jen to get in trouble, and there were so many little things that could've gone wrong and ruined our lives. Okay, maybe that was a little extreme, but my fly-under-the-radar-life had become increasingly above-the-radar. My little undetected blip of a life was now catching attention. Bright red and white alarm lights were flashing their warning. The last thing I needed was to end up on the news as some feign for taking a 'true beta's' place at the academy.

"Do we have to tell Chancellor Kelly? Can't we just ... not tell anyone?" I looked at all three alphas, wondering if anyone was in agreement with my plan but found no supporters.

"You ashamed of us?" Jen joked, but I scented the slight worry growing in his scent. That was one fear I easily dissuaded.

"Of course not. I'm nervous and slightly scared, but I've also never been happier. I kept telling myself I would be happy once I finished school, but I never considered I could have both. A pack and an education."

I had been so scared to take my chances with them. I had pushed them away, convincing myself it wouldn't work. Fuck, was I wrong. Thanks to a few drinks, and a lot of omega instincts, I now had a support system. A pack to help carry the burden of being me. A pack to help carry the burden of my lies.

"You know," Aidan said, "I have a copy of the academy's guidelines. I don't think it's ever stated that relations between a teacher and student is forbidden. It's only been updated once, recently, and that was when it changed the rules to allow betas to attend. But I'm sure Chancellor Kelly will let us know when we meet with him."

"I guess the main question is whether you'll be allowed to continue taking my quantum mechanics class," Jen said.

I nodded, absorbing all the information being thrown my way. It would suck to have to take the same class over again, but I could probably still fit it into my schedule next semester to make sure I graduated on time.

And really, if that was the worst-case scenario for our bond, I'd take it.

"Do I still smell like a beta?" I asked.

"Yes," Enzo said, immediately.

"Definitely," Aidan added.

Jen growled, frustrated because the males admitted to scenting me, but still comforted me. "Completely beta."

"Then no one will know I'm an omega. But if you want to claim me publicly, as a pack beta, we do that. Everyone will know I'm yours." I waited for the look of approval from Jen before I turned my attention to Aidan and Enzo. "I'm all of yours."

Instead of meeting my eyes, Aidan's gaze was locked on the space below the collar of my shirt. Even with the claiming mark hidden, I knew Aidan was staring directly at it. The portion of my heart dedicated to loving Aidan broke when I scented tendrils of jealousy clinging to him.

"Why didn't all three of you claim me?" I asked.

Jen tensed next to me, but I was starting at Aidan, watching as his lips parted in shock. When I glanced over at Enzo, his eyebrows were pulled together, a confused look on his face. Did the other males not know I would've wanted their claiming marks as well? Not only did I want to bond with them, but if Aidan and Enzo both claimed me, then the jealousy would be over. We'd be a proper pack—like Hannah was with hers.

Why hadn't I thought of this sooner? Better yet, why hadn't the males? I needed to invest in an espresso machine for this place if it was going to take me this long to come up with common sense ideas.

"How much do you know about alpha and omega relationships? Or about packs?" Enzo asked.

"I've watched movies, read magazine articles. I

have social media so it's not like I'm completely in the dark. Every year I take a mandatory beta relations class about what to avoid with packs and omegas. But I didn't get the formal education like at the Omega Compound."

"Well, typically, there's a waiting period between alpha claims, Orsetta."

"Why? Wouldn't that cause more ... tension in the pack?"

"Alphas tend to become very possessive in the beginning of a bond—even with their own packmates. It's safer for everyone if a newly bonded alpha has alone time with their omega. Typically, another bite too soon is seen as a threat instead of an addition."

"Oh." That was all I had. I hated the idea that there was information I was missing. But I couldn't risk going to the Compound for answers and being pulled out of school. I was lucky enough to find alphas that supported my education prowess. I did not want to risk being dropped out for information I could easily obtain elsewhere. Like online. Or from a friend.

That was when I remembered. "Where's my phone?"

Three alphas' undivided attention was a lot to handle so early in the morning, but that was the result of my question.

"I think it's charging in the living room," Jen said, reluctantly. "We plugged it in for you last night before we went to your nest."

"I'll grab it." Aidan was already heading down the hallway toward the bedrooms before he'd finished talking. When he returned, he handed me my phone but refused to let it go just yet. "You're not planning on leaving, are you?"

Jen growled. "Of course she's not."

"I'm just making sure."

Despite the aggression pouring off Jenson, Aidan looked to me. I didn't know the proper response to give him. Did I shake my head no, I wasn't going to leave? Or did I nod my head yes, his statement about me staying was correct? Ug, maybe I needed a third cup of coffee. They were smaller than I was used to, and they didn't have any espresso shots. I blamed my confusion on that.

"I need to see if Hannah texted. You gave her my number, right, Addie?"

"Yes, I did, Koda bear." Aidan preened at my use of his nickname and finally released the phone to me. With the other males so close, Jen pressed between my legs, one hand on his coffee mug, the other high on my thigh, definitely saying that I was his. Aidan stood to my left, his stomach occasionally touching my knee when he exaggerated his deep breathes. Enzo was on my other side, not touching me, but watching every point of contact with the other males like he was making sure nothing untoward happened.

My phone was already on with a text from an unknown number stating it was Hannah. The time stamp said it was sent about fifteen minutes ago. I saved the number before hitting call, my leg shaking with nerves.

It only rang twice before a female voice screamed my name on the other end. "Koda, I'm so glad you called. I was worried when we got separated last night. Aidan assured my alphas he and his packmates would take care of you, but I wasn't sure, you know? And then I kept thinking, what if you didn't want to go home with them but you had to because you were drunk? But Han said if I didn't hear from you today, he would help me find you. Are you okay? Are you safe?"

I laughed at Hannah's ramblings, feeling more confident about my decision to call and ask for her help. "Good morning to you too, Hannah. And I'm all good. I wanted to go home with Aidan." Jenson growled, obviously displeased in being left out, so I added, "And Jen and Enzo."

"Good. How terrible would it be if I let my new friend get kidnapped?"

"I can assure you I am definitely not kidnapped. But I was calling to see if you have plans for today?"

The silence from Hannah's end of the phone made me nervous, but Jen purred softly, comforting me.

"Hey, so, change of plans today," Hannah's muffled voice said, indicating she wasn't talking to me but holding her phone away from her ear, as if because she couldn't hear me then I couldn't hear her.

I couldn't hear what her alphas said, but I just barely made out her end of the conversation. "Because Koda wants to hang out. Yes, I get that. No, I'm not worried she's trying to lure me to a trap, Jackson. For fuck's sake, Seb knows her alphas. Because I don't know if she's an omega. Well, I'm going, so one of you can come with me or I can—I'm not against her coming here, but don't you think it'll be a little much with all four of you? Hey, Koda?"

"Yep, still here."

"Perfect. I'm free today so long as one of my alphas can come with. You know, for safety and whatnot."

"Yeah, I get it. I think I might have a tagalong too." I glanced at Jen, who nodded. "Want to do brunch?"

Hannah recommended some bougie place whose name I recognized but couldn't pronounce, and we planned to meet in an hour before hanging up.

"I thought you said you weren't leaving," Aidan said before the screen on my phone had even dismissed my call with Hannah.

"I'm not leaving. But I've been so busy focusing

on school and keeping my secret, I haven't had a chance, or the guts, to make a friend. Hannah is the first person I've felt comfortable getting to know. Not to mention she has a pack with four alphas who have all claimed her. She might have some tips on how to manage…" I gestured to the four of us. "…during the waiting period." Plus, I had lots of questions I needed to ask about knotting, my new bond, and loads of other shit only Hannah would know as a proper omega.

For the first time in my life, my heart hadn't ached at that thought.

I chose to ignore the all-too knowing look from Jen. Instead, I told him to hurry his ass up and get ready, because I was not wearing boxers to breakfast, which meant we had to stop at my dorm room.

Chapter Twenty

Hannah had started talking before I'd even stepped out of Jen's car. "I already got us seats."

We'd arrived slightly later than planned, but there had been some unexpected tension Jen had to work through when we stepped into my dorm building and he inhaled all the scents around me. And then there was the big question of what I should've worn? Did I dress up for my friend-date or were we going in basically pajamas? I'd wanted to slightly dress up for Jen—and to match his attire. I was glad I did now that I saw Hannah's outfit.

She wore sparkling fishnet tights and a red and black plaid dress with a fluffy coat draped over her arm. Despite nearing winter, it still wasn't too cold while standing in the sun. Her outfit was cute and matched the winter aesthetic like she was plucked from a punk magazine photo shoot, rocking out on a guitar in front of a decked-out Christmas tree.

My own outfit was made of dark blue flare pants with white dots that looked like snowflakes and a white long sleeve shirt. The fabric tightened on my wrists and around the collar, letting the sleeves flow. Originally, I'd wanted to wear a shirt with a deep V, showing off my new claiming mark—or the bandage over the mark, technically—but Jen heavily suggested he preferred for my mark to be exposed when the bandage was off. My key necklace was tucked under my shirt, hidden and occasionally making me wince when it bumped against my bandage.

My alpha's own outfit was made up of a dark blue shirt with a cream cashmere sweater over it. The buttons were only done up to his stomach to reveal the shirt underneath. His dark tan pants were perfectly form fitting, almost like skinny jeans if the fabric was different, but alas, the thick pants were the perfect mix of flair and hugging. He looked amazing, but that was to be expected for Jen.

"They have heaters set up for the outside seating, and I figured that would be best," Hannah continued. "You remember Jackson, right?" She motioned to the big alpha behind her, acting like a shadow but very much real.

Wearing a leather jacket and jeans, Jackson looked like he belonged in a motorcycle club, or even on the front of a rebel magazine, smoking a cigarette, with some female between his legs. He and Hannah complemented each other's styles well.

"Yes, I do. Hi, Jackson." I tried making eye contact with the other alpha but only made it to his chin before instinctively seeking out my own. It must've been my new bond and crazy omega instincts—or maybe it was because Jackson had an air of intimidation around him that frightened me—but I had the sudden feeling of free falling without anyone to catch me. Down and down I tumbled, wanting to back away from the looming alpha in front of me but too scared to move my feet.

"I'm right here, Koda," my alpha coaxed. He stepped up to my back, pulling me against him so I could inhale his scent. I clung to his forearms, scared he was going to toss me over to the other alpha that didn't want me. The thoughts weren't logical, but I couldn't fight them off or stop my brain from feeding panic into my nervous system. I was seconds away from asking Jen if we could just go home, or maybe if he still wanted me.

A growl I didn't recognize hit my flight or fight instinct so suddenly my body froze, unsure of what to do. If I had control of all my faculties, I would've acknowledged freezing was a terrible response to a not-my-alpha-growl.

Another, more familiar and more violent growl, filled my senses. Despite the blatant hostility coming off Jen, my body relaxed at the sound. A feeling of calmness, of being loved, being protected, washed through me. My senses came back, my nose slammed with a flurry of scents coming from my alpha: aggression, jealousy, frustration.

Looking up at her, I saw my new friend was smiling wide as her alpha kept her pressed tightly into his side. She playfully rolled her eyes, as if the whole scenario had been ridiculous male posturing, and not me on the verge of a panic attack.

"You have to let your jealousy show." To my surprise, it was Jackson who spoke up, not sounding angry or put out—at least not more than his normal voice sounded perpetually annoyed.

"I know," Jen half growled. His hand was fisting my ponytail in a move clearly stating he owned me and demanded all my attention. And I fucking loved it. Maybe even too much. I should've been embarrassed about the way I was acting in front of Jenson, and my new friend, but I had too many other emotions running rampant to really give in to embarrassment.

My omega side was pleased at the display of dominance. I was concerned about how my omega instincts were affecting my beta side so strongly.

"I don't know how it works for betas, but bonded omegas need the show of ownership. Need to feel claimed and wanted and shit in the presence of an unfamiliar alpha," Jackson said, looking at me and ignoring the threatening sound my supposedly poised alpha made. The grip in my hair started loosening, my neck finally able to relax and most surprisingly, my pussy already craving more from Jen.

"I'm sorry, little bear. I've seemed to have forgotten my classes on dealing with bonds." Jen lowered his voice so only I heard him when he added, "Maybe a refresher for all your alphas is in order after..." I knew what Jen was going to say and chose to ignore the comment about how my alphas had only dated betas recently. It made sense Jen would be used to holding himself back in order to make past betas comfortable with their different designations—hopefully nobody would put together the different way Jen acted with me and chalk it up to my preferences or the bond.

Turning my head into his chest, I inhaled his scent, content to find traces of my own scent, even if it was the beta version of me, on his clothes now.

And forever.

Yes, that was calming indeed.

Hannah winked conspiratorially, making me laugh.

With this new information, Jen didn't let me go. Even though I'd just freaked out, I felt better. Calmer. And that must've shown down the bond, because Jen nodded and gestured for me to lead the way.

I followed Hannah, who was smart enough to take us around the side of the building and enter through a little gate to the patio sitting area. There wasn't anyone else outside, despite the heaters. That realization helped me relax even more.

The moment I sat down, before I'd even scooted my chair in, Hannah said, "So you've been claimed. As a beta or an omega?"

Her bluntness shocked me into silence. Looking around, I confirmed no one else was around to hear it. I was sure a passing stranger wouldn't have cared, but anyone from the academy might've. Hell, anyone from a gossip column might just spread the information too, although that was a little generous speaking on my behalf. I doubted I was special enough for anyone to run to social media about. Just because broken omegas weren't on the daily news didn't mean there weren't more out there like me. We just had no way of contacting each other since I wasn't taking the risk of being outed as an omega.

Leaning closer to Hannah, I whispered, "Beta."

"I see." She leaned back, sitting normally, before asking, "Where did he claim you?"

I pulled down the collar of my shirt, just enough to barely show off the bandage covering the mark before the back threatened to decapitate me. The bite mark had been red and tender, before being covered in numbing ointment and a second skin bandage. There was some weird voodoo that allowed the bite to bond mates, but there was no way to heal it before it was ready. When it came to the bonds, I had no idea how it worked. That kind of information wasn't given in the mandatory beta relations classes.

"On your collarbone? That's actually really sexy. You'll look hot when you're all healed up."

"Where are yours?"

"I've got two on my ass cheeks, compliments of Han and Zeke. Sebastian claimed me on my right side, in a hell of a sensitive spot between my boob and armpit, and Jackson got here." She turned around, holding her hair up to show a bite mark on the back of her neck, just below the hairline.

I winced. "That must have hurt."

She nodded. "Like a bitch. But it serves its purpose and all that. Just like the mark from your first alpha does."

"What kind of purpose?"

Unfortunately, we got interrupted by the waitress

before I got my answer.

A growl started to rise at the new female's presence, but it was quickly cut off when Jen stood from the little table he and Jackson were occupying— pretending to give us space—and lifted me up so I was sitting sideways on his lap in my chair. Jackson came and stood behind Hannah, the other omega preening at her alpha's attention.

I scented the waitress—a beta. The majority of her scent was calm and unsuspecting, but I exchanged knowing glances with Hannah, who would've also been able to scent the underlining irritation from the male's displays of ownership.

Hannah didn't show any sort of discomfort, but she did catch my eye. If she'd doubted that I was an omega, my excellent ability to scent designations and the emotions that came with it would clue her in. Betas weren't great at scenting emotions like omegas were— even worse than alphas—but they were good at distinguishing between the designations. A survival technique to stay clear of others not in their designation.

"Good morning, everyone, I'm Renee. Thank you for waiting so kindly while I made my way out here. I can get you all started with some drinks and let you know what's on the menu for today." Yep, this restaurant didn't have menus. Something about helping the planet—which I was totally behind—but it didn't help with the decision-making aspect of ordering. "We have some healthy smoothies, a café if you're familiar with those types of drinks, freshly pumped juices, and of course, water with your choice of toppings."

Hannah ordered a smoothie, Jackson water—no toppings, Jen juice, and I got a macchiato with caramel drizzle. Because espresso. I'd stoutly ignored my mate's grunt when I'd asked for an extra shot.

Our drinks arrived quickly, then our waitress sprouted out the menu from memory. By the time it was my turn to order, I just managed to blurt out the first thing I remembered. When Renee walked away, Jackson pulled the two-seater table and chairs next to ours so we could all sit together. Reluctantly, Jen moved back to his own seat, keeping one hand on the back of my neck.

"So I have to ask…" I lowered my voice, ignoring the alphas' conversation about Jackson's work in security. "I don't know anything that is taught at the Omega Compound, and I was hoping you could tell me if there's anything I should know. I mean, I've been given courses on bonds but as a … a beta, the lessons are usually quick and along the lines of how not to piss off an omega."

"Like what?"

I shrugged, listing off the main points from every beta relations session, "Date within your own designation. If you're going to spend time with an omega, make sure his or her alpha is around. Make sure you don't touch a bonded alpha or omega because you might enrage their bondmate."

"That's terrible. No wonder betas hate omegas." She shook her head. "Betas can have packs just like omegas can. Hell, there are no rules as to what constitutes a pack so long as everyone is willing and happy, but people take what's common and force it like it's the expected."

I nodded my head along with her words, because she was right. That standard hadn't stopped my alphas from pursuing me, however. Meeting my pack, the flirting, even when I first kissed Enzo before my scent perfumed, they'd thought I was a beta. And while I was going to school, they were going to have to keep up the façade. They hadn't said anything to make me feel like my designation mattered except that I shouldn't get caught at the school. But I couldn't blame Jen for not wanting to get fired from his job. No one wanted to get fired.

"But shoot, what sort of questions do you have?"

I peeked over at Jen, finding that I needed to assure myself of my alpha's presence. Sure, I felt him and was surrounded by his clean laundry scent, but...

"That's normal," Hannah said.

"What is?"

"The need for reassurance. OC—the Omega Compound—says you'll never like being away from your bondmate, but in the first month it's the worst. Side by side contact is almost a necessity or else the alpha gets jealous, and the omega feels rejected. I've been bonded for a year now, and I still can't handle any of my alphas traveling without me."

"How quickly did you bond with all of yours? I tried to get Aidan and Enzo to bite me this morning. but apparently that's not recommended."

Hannah giggled before trying to school her features. "It really depends. For example, with me, I took all four bites in two months. Jackson was first, then Sebastian a week later. Zeke and Han were together the following month." She blushed slightly, obviously remembering her bonding with her alphas. I forced myself not to pressure her to spill all the information right now and instead put my energy into enjoying my macchiato until she was ready.

"But the reason I spread them apart in two groupings is because of the relationships within the pack. Jackson is first alpha which means he's the most dominate and needed to be bonded to me first. That's what you have with Jen. Sebastian was next because he's closer to Jackson. My first alpha didn't feel as threatened with Seb as he might have trying to take on Zeke or Han. Plus, Zeke and Han do everything together, so it made sense for them to bond me together."

Hannah blushed again, but this time it caught the attention of her alpha who pulled her face against his neck and let her breathe him in. As the two shared an intimate moment, I turned to my own alpha.

The stubble along his jaw was spikey and definitely gave me beard burn even with a chaste kiss, but the pain was worth it for my alpha. With a thinner beard, his lips appeared fuller and even his cheeks looked more rounded.

Hannah cleared her throat, a little more pip in her tone as she continued. "That means a lot of sex and a lot of claiming. But like, I stayed home. My alphas did too in their first month of claiming me, and even after that they did their best to take time off or work from home. But I still always have an alpha around. Like, now, with Jackson. And if I was home? Han would be there even if he was working. So, around."

That wasn't the news I'd wanted to hear, but I tried to hide how upsetting Hannah's words were. "How did you deal with the ... pack aggression after the first alpha's bite?"

"Obviously there are things you can do to help, but it's not your job to deal with the alpha possessiveness, Koda." My disbelief must've showed, because Hannah reached out to touch my hand. "I don't know what you've been taught at Braker Academy, or anywhere else really, but alphas are responsible for their own actions and tempers. And if anyone tells you different, you should take a look at that relationship. Seriously."

"She's right, little bear," Jen said, joining our conversation. "Although I think she was not so subtly hinting at our pack, but you never have to worry about my relationship with Aidan and Enzo. We've been friends our whole lives and packmates since we graduated high school. This is a challenge, but we'll get through it."

"I get that. I do. But if I want to keep going to the Academy, I need to do my part. Plus, it isn't just you that's possessive. I'm going to have to figure out how to deal with those girls flirting with you after class."

Surprise crossed over Jen's face. And then his scent changed, adding the heat that told me he liked the idea of me being jealous. His hand tightened around my nape, and he brought his face to my neck, inhaling deeply, and letting me feel his smile against my skin.

"Okay, everyone, I think we have everything." Renee appeared, not hesitating as she moved around the table, dropping off plates, sides, and toppings.

When she leaned down to place my blackberry cream crepes in front of me, I didn't know where to look. Her face was inches from my own, and then I saw it. The movement was so quick I almost hadn't noticed. Her nostrils flared, scenting my plain beta perfume.

I felt my panic growing. How would the beta feel about an alpha and beta together? I knew that I was going to have to deal with people disliking our relationship—that was a given at Braker. Despite the modern teachings, the proper ideals of the staff, and some students, was lacking. But I worried about Jenson's reaction so soon after the claiming. What if Renee resented inter-designation relationships and reacted poorly? Then Jen might've tried to keep me from going back to school.

Jenson pulled at my hand, obviously sensing my distress and trying to get me to be closer to him.

Renee made a few trips to fill up everyone's cup but my own, saying she'd come back with a whole new mug. I almost wanted the beta to freak out. Maybe shriek how happy she was about the designation mingling or refuse to serve us any longer. I just wanted to get a gauge of how someone would react when they found out. I was sorely let down when that didn't happen.

"So," Hannah said, "you're going back to the academy?"

"Yep. Next class is on Monday."

"You don't worry about how people are going to react?" The hesitation in Hannah's voice pulled my attention away from my delicious breakfast. I glanced up at the omega, who discreetly nodded in the direction the waitress went, obviously hinting at what I had just been thinking about.

"I know it's odd for a beta to be claimed in a pack, but it isn't unrealistic. When we met, those bouncers were assholes and didn't like the idea of a beta in a pack, but even they believed it was possible."

"The bouncers?" Jenson asked, clearly not caring about the social boundaries of conversations. "At Aidan's club?"

I nodded.

"What did they do? Did you tell Aidan?"

I was about to say 'yes', but I found myself hesitating. "I think I did?"

"I talked to Aidan about it when he was at our table last night," Jackson said.

Jen accepted this answer, but he gave me a look that said the conversation wasn't over. It wasn't that I'd wanted to protect those alphas, or that I didn't feel comfortable talking to my alphas, but I'd literally forgotten. A lot had happened since.

Hannah easily brought me back to our conversation. "I'm just worried. Sure, betas in packs have started to appear in progressive TV shows. Maybe even a song or two is written about alpha-beta or beta-omega love. But you're going into the heart of alpha culture. Weren't betas just recently added to the school? And I think they only allowed the two designations to mix because they assumed alpha packs wouldn't claim betas."

"Or that any alpha pack would allow a bondmate—even a beta—to go to the academy," Jackson added.

"And you have to consider even those that would give you the benefit of the doubt that you might have an omega in your pack," she said, and I knew she was thinking about the waitress, "would know that's not true with Jenson. The academy is about to be all up in your private business."

I stared at the other couple, shocked by their statements and feeling slightly overwhelmed. This wasn't new information, but I must have compartmentalized my fear, focusing on the nerves with the pack. My body suddenly felt as if I'd been trying to wade in the ocean. The waves kept getting bigger and bigger, and my legs were on the verge of giving up.

Jen threw me a lifejacket. "We'll make it work, little bear. We're just in uncharted territory."

"Your alpha is right, Koda," Hannah said, already jumping off the ship of doubts. I guess it was easy to point out worries when you didn't have to be on the receiving effects of the actions. Or maybe that was what having an overactive friend was like. "Seb says he's never heard of someone like you. Really, he's quite fascinated with studying you. I had to tell him that most friends don't want their friends' alpha studying them. But I did tell him I would put that knowledge out there for you to pick up on if you wanted."

I did my best to hide my wince. I knew Hannah didn't mean it like it sounded, and I knew I didn't fit in as either an omega or a beta. Was I half-beta-half-omega, or simply a broken version of one? Now that Jen and the others knew I had an omega side, were they happier? Were they settling for me as a beta, or did they not want an omega and were settling for that side?

"I don't know what you're thinking about," Jen whispered, "but you need to knock it off." It wasn't the words, but the aggressive way Jen said it, like he was ready to go to battle against my negative thoughts, that snapped me out of my pity party. "We chose you, little bear. Don't insult me by doubting that."

I nipped playfully at Jen's chin, unable to speak with my throat clogged with emotion but wanting to let him know I'd heard him. He didn't accept the little nip, however, pulling me in for a long kiss, one that heated my whole body as his tongue searched out my own. I started to turn, wanting to feel my alpha pressed against my chest right at the ache he'd creating in my heart, but he pulled away, biting my lower lip almost to the point of breaking the skin, like he was punishing me for having to stop.

"If she's determined to go back to the academy, she should wear your scent," Jackson said, dragging Jen and I out of our private moment. He only looked at Jen as he spoke, and I was starting to think that was intentional. "When you're home, that's when she should wear your packmates' scents with you holding her. That'll help the jealousy. Get you used to her being safe and smelling like who you trust."

"Thanks," Jen said in a clipped tone, not sounding thankful at all.

"What else do you need to know?" Hannah asked.

I bit my lip, debating on whether or not this was the appropriate place to ask questions. But I wanted answers. And media platforms had a tendency to either glorify or horrify alpha-omega relationships.

"Does it hurt?"

"What?"

"Knotting?"

Hannah's eyes went comically wide. She looked toward her alpha before falling into a fit of laughter. "Absolutely not. It's only pleasure. At least, it was for me." I knew what she was hinting at—that there was a possibility I was more beta than omega—but I could feel it. I could take a knot. Not that I was going to share that with Hannah. "Taking a knot is a natural omega instinct, but it isn't impossible for a beta to learn to take one either. You just learn through experience what makes it better or worse for you. But the most important part is picking the right partners."

My hand reached to trace the bite mark over my shirt. Choosing Jen, and his pack, hadn't even been a conscious choice. I could've blamed the alcohol, but liquor didn't make my omega more trusting. It usually had me inside my nest, hating all the sights and sounds of strangers. No, choosing my pack had been all instinct. They were always meant to be mine.

"Anything else?" Hannah asked.

"Honestly? I don't even know what I don't know. Betas are simply taught to stay away from omegas—not that we are ever around them. We're also told beta on beta relationships are best for long term since only the rare beta gets accepted into an alpha-omega pack. And if you are a lucky beta, your job is to take care of the alphas that aren't being pleased by the omega. And then you are to take care of the omega with cooking and cleaning. It is also your job to remind alphas to buy their omegas gifts."

The look of horror on Hannah's face was exactly how I felt learning the information. I remembered how excited she was last night to meet a beta that liked her, and I didn't doubt other betas had been rude to her. Everything we were taught was a direct competition with omegas that we always lost. Like dangling water in front of someone dying of dehydration but telling them that someone else needed it more and they had to wait to see if there was any left over. And most of the time, there wasn't.

"Okay, well, you have my number now, so just text me if any questions come to mind. And I'll text you the number of my hairdresser." Her own alpha growled in response to her words, but Hannah merely waved him off. "And if you decide you want to be studied, just let me know. Seb would die. Of happiness that is."

"Thank you, Hannah."

We finished our breakfast, getting to know one another better on a less serious note, asking random questions while the alphas sat back.

Jen had dragged me back onto his lap when he finished eating, pulling me backward so I leaned against him.

The biggest surprise came with the bill when the waitress handed a receipt to Jackson but told Jen our breakfast was on the house. She winked when I simply stared at her but didn't say anything else. That slight amount of hope made me hold my head a little higher when we left and said goodbye.

I had been so worried about all the bad reactions that I'd forgotten not everyone was cruel. Just like Jenson and his pack were willing to date betas, there were others who didn't follow the strict social rules defining their designations. And I didn't have to put myself out into the world as a beta representative. I just needed to place myself back under the radar and take my pack with me.

Yes, I could do that.

JOSEPHINE LIGHT

Chapter Twenty-One

I asked Jen to stop at the dorm room so I could grab my things. Most of the stuff in the room was from the academy, but the pillows, clothes, and all my bathroom essentials were coming with me.

Jen had been in my room earlier when I'd gotten ready to meet Hannah, but we'd been in such a rush to make it on time—okay, I was stressed about being late and Jen was accommodating my panic—and now I was nervous about Jen taking in my dorm room. It wasn't dirty. There weren't bugs or dirt. It was just cluttered. I'd turned the closet into my nest and didn't have a better place than the bed for all my clothes.

My alpha was so put together at all times. I was worried what he was thinking of having a messy mate. I was holding out hope I could somehow get him to ignore the state of my room if I didn't bring it up.

"Do you have a suitcase?" Jen asked, pretending like my room wasn't bothering him. I winced when his eyes lingered on my bed. My foot tapped mercilessly on the carpet flooring. "Or should we just carry everything down to the car in multiple trips?"

"I have a suitcase. I had to put it away to make room. Its current location is slipping my mind, but I would guess it's under the bed. At least, if I had a suitcase in my hands now, that's where I'd store it."

I moved random articles of clothing that were half-falling off the bed, trying to search under the bed frame. I hadn't noticed Jen opening my closet until he choked out, "This explains the clothes on the bed."

Every hair on my body, every nerve ending, told me I was in the presence of a predator. Even my heart slowed, beating softly, as if it was scared to beat fast and draw attention. Still on the ground, my body refused to move, the line between my beta and omega sides blurring.

Jen growled, his dominance in the very sound he made.

My thighs pressed together, as if that would've stopped my pussy from leaking. The old scents of my arousal-soaked pillows left my closet, forcing me to inhale them, making me wetter and feeding into Jen's aggression-filled arousal.

His fresh-laundry scent, mixing with his arousal, was becoming heavy, trying to permeate the air but struggling in the wake of the older scents leaking from my closet. I bit back the demand for him to close my closet door before the scents left and new ones entered. Jen was in charge.

"Come here, Omega," Jen growled.

My heart stopped for one beat. Two. Then it stuttered to life, pounding away and trying to draw attention to itself. I realized I hadn't moved when Jen snapped, "Now, Omega. I won't ask again."

Body moving into action, I threw myself at my alpha, seeing his surprise before delight filled its place, making his brown eyes appear lighter.

My alpha took what he wanted from my body, forcing my legs to wrap around him until my ankles barely touched. He was holding me up by my ass cheeks. His grip tightened as he rubbed my pussy up and down the bulge in his pants.

My lips parted on a silent gasp. I tried focusing on why we shouldn't be doing this here, but I couldn't. I breathed in Jen's delicious scent, felt his warm body pressed against mine, his strength holding me up, his arousal through his jeans. He'd barely touched me last night when he bonded with me, and I was somehow even more desperate for him.

He kissed and nipped down my neck, his claiming mark tingling with wanted attention. I yanked my shirt up and over my head, throwing it into my nest behind Jen before lifting my chest and trying to angle my claiming mark near his lips. I knew he felt my desperation through the bond, but he took his time, kissing along the bandage, outlining my exposed skin with the tip of his tongue.

"Bite. Bite, please, Alpha." I clung to him, my body tightening as I waited for the pain of a bite that didn't come.

Jen growled. "No bite, Koda. You're still healing from the first one."

I whimpered, the sound instinctive from being turned down, but it was quickly cut off when my back slammed against a wall, my breath leaving me on a hard exhale.

Jen's lips pressed against my own like he was trying to give me his own air, and I took it willingly. His hands roamed my body, and I had to squeeze my legs even tighter to hold myself up.

My hands found their way to his hair, but there was barely enough to hold onto. "Please, Alpha, I need to come. Please make me—help me. I need it." I pleaded over and over again until Jen broke, and I found myself thrown to the ground, grateful for the pillows and blankets to gentle the slam.

Jen didn't waste any time, pulling and yanking my pants open and down my legs unceremoniously.

"Clothes off," I begged.

Jen growled at my demand for him to get naked, purposefully ignoring me.

I narrowed my eyes, trying to reach for his clothes.

He grabbed my wrists and planted them above my

head, holding them there like handcuffs.

"I need to see you. To feel you."

"When I say so, Omega. No sooner. Now be a good girl for me and keep your hands right where I put them."

If I wasn't high with arousal, I would've preened at being a good girl. Instead, I struggled against his hold, testing his restraint, his strength, his dominance.

With my feet planted on the ground, I tried to buck and grind my hips against Jen. I was successful for only a sweet moment of bliss before pressure on my throat had my eyes snapping open.

The alpha in front of me was gone to his lust, and I'd pissed him off. He didn't cut off my air, but his fingers pressed into the sides of my neck, letting me know he could. My life quite literally bent to his demands. Instead of panicking, my pussy got impossibly wetter, officially ruining my underwear, and my body stopped struggling, submitting of its own accord.

"Hips up, Koda." Jen's voice was more growl than his normal educator voice. Usually, his words were clear and precise, with a level of superiority that would be annoying if he hadn't earned the right to be cocky. Now, I barely understood him. No, that wasn't true, I knew exactly what he wanted when he put his hands under my butt cheeks, lifted, and yanked down my underwear. It was his words, muffled with lust and aggression, that were hard to understand even if every growl from him had slick running down my thighs, staining the blankets under me.

With all his patience run out, Jen shoved a finger past my pussy lips, sliding in embarrassingly easy. One finger wasn't enough, but there was something different about it—about someone else touching me that had my arousal scenting stronger. My core muscles were trying to clamp down on a knot that wasn't inside me, the emptiness becoming more painful as my body begged the only way it knew how: with slick. Lots of lots of slick.

He shoved his finger in and out a few times, then pulled out, circling my engorged clit. Just the light touch had my hips bucking, but Jen didn't stand for it. He slapped one thigh, the pain sharp and forcing a gasp from my lips

"Hold still," he growled, shoving in another finger. Instead of just thrusting, he swirled his fingers around inside me, spreading and pressing against my inner walls, making me feel fuller.

My eyes shut, but I tried to flutter them open, wanting to watch the glances Jen shot my face to make sure I was enjoying his given pleasure. I let my hips move however they wanted, but another sting along my thighs had my body straining to hold still.

"Do not move, little bear."

"Why," I whined.

"I'm giving you pleasure. Your job is to take it. Can you do that and be a good omega for me? Can you take the pleasure I'm giving you?"

It was a rhetorical question, I knew that, but I nodded anyway. Holding myself still felt like an impossible task, but Jen understood exactly what he was doing with his words. He'd offered me a chance to please him—I would've done anything to please my alpha. And, he'd offered me a chance to be his good girl, enticing my beta side.

Jen continued playing with my pussy, moving his fingers around, using the outside fingers to rub near my clit, teasing me. His body leaned over me, one hand still between us, the other arm on his elbow near my head as he held himself up. He kissed me hard, forcing his tongue between my lips.

I moaned, fisting my hands in the blankets to keep from forcing his head to remain where I wanted. I couldn't seem to focus on more than one thing.

His tongue played with mine. When he finally pulled away to let me breathe, his lips found purchase on my neck, sucking and biting, leaving fake claiming marks. Every nip and lick were directed to my core. It tightened around his fingers, leaking wetness. And when he moved his lips over the claiming mark, gently brushing the bandage with delicacy, my pussy clenched so tightly it had Jen groaning. He muffled the sound in a harsh bite on the side of my breast.

Licking over the rough bite, he moved closer to my nipple but didn't quite touch it. Pulling his fingers out of my pussy, he drew a wet line from my pubic bone up to my stomach, his fingers circling my belly button, before he continued up to my breasts. He pinched one nipple at the same time as he took the other in his mouth, the warmth contrasting with the cool, wet fingers.

The tension of holding my body still as my arousal was forced higher and higher was becoming borderline painful. Beads of sweat had formed and fallen down the side of my head, down from the crease behind my knees, and I didn't even know how I felt the droplets, but it was like my body was over-sensitized to a frenzy of feelings. I focused on holding my body still as he stroked me with touch, kisses, and licks all over my body. He didn't need to hold me down for me to feel his dominance—not that I would've been against it—but the fact that he was controlling me with just his words was proof he was a good alpha. A strong one.

And mine.

"Have you ever taken a knot, Koda?"

The question startled me, and I immediately started shaking my head no. But I didn't want him to think I didn't want the knot, because I really fucking did, so I started nodding my head yes. Wait, what was the right answer? I went back and forth between nodding and shaking before Jen grabbed my cheeks, stopping my movements. He shoved two fingers, tasting like my own arousal, into my mouth.

"Suck." I did without hesitation. "Now I asked you a question. No words. Just a nod yes or a shake no. Have you ever taken a knot?"

I shook my head.

"Do you want to?"

I nodded.

"Is this nest good enough?"

That question had me hesitating. I looked around the space—well, the closet—and noticed the dim yellow light was on and the door was open. The former was not ideal but tolerable since it didn't hurt my sensitive eyes. But the later set my nerves on edge. I did my best to hide that from the bond. No, this nest wasn't optimal. It wasn't safe, and I didn't even consider this my nest anymore, but I wanted Jen more than I wanted the perfect nest at the pack house. But even as I came to that conclusion, I could feel Jen pulling away. He'd read my emotions, but without the commentary of my thoughts, he didn't know I craved his knot more than the nest.

Logically, I knew the rejection was for my own good, but it didn't make the sting hurt any less. Emotions beat logic in a fight every time. Even against a stubborn alpha like Jen.

"Knot me, Alpha." I reached for his pants, yanking at the fancy belt, tearing open his zipper, and pushing down his underwear so his dick popped out.

He was still completely dressed except for this little leeway I'd taken. The look Jen wore was pained, like the possibility of denying me was actually hurting him. And maybe it was. Maybe that was the curse of the alphas, to hurt when denying their omega pleasure.

But if that was true, the curse of an omega was their need for pleasure. And a beta's was the need to be wanted. All of my thoughts were surrounded by the need for a knot. His knot.

"Please, Jen. I don't care about the nest. I want to be filled by you. Knotted. It hurts to be this empty, and only you can fill me up the way I need. I'm already wet for you, see?" I moved my hips so I rubbed my wetness along his cock like I could convince him to fuck me if he felt how wet I was for him. My swollen clit bumped against the fabric of his slacks, making noises come from my throat I was sure I'd be embarrassed about later.

When I felt his hands grip my hips, steadying me, I was sure I'd lost, that he was going to pull away from me, but then he was crushing me with his weight, shoving his lips on mine in a harsh kiss before pushing inside me. The tip of his cock moved in and out, each inward thrust going deeper and deeper until he was finally seated all the way inside me, forcing my back to bow in order to take his full length. I felt so full, like I couldn't move but in the best possible way.

And then Jen pulled out, slowly, letting me feel every inch of him before slamming back in. He pushed my knees toward the sides of his ribs, gripping my hair, forcing my neck and back to bow again.

"Is this what you wanted?" Jens asked, pulling out and slamming into me harder. I felt his hips smack the back of my thighs, his balls beating against my ass as he grinded against me before pulling back and thrusting again. "Answer me, Omega. Is this what you want? For me to claim you all over again? To feel my cock ride that wet pussy?" He made a circle with his hips after each question, teasing me with the penetration I desperately wanted.

"Yes. Yes, that's what I want. Please, Alpha, fuck me. Knot me. Please."

I couldn't tell if I was screaming the words or just repeating them until my voice went hoarse, but the result was the same. My throat hurt and my words were on repeat until finally—finally—Jen swore and started thrusting into me like I wanted.

Over and over again, he slammed into me, holding me by my hair so I didn't move far away. And then he sat back, straightening my legs so they rested against his chest with my ankles on his shoulder. When he pushed in again, it somehow changed the angle and I screamed. Every muscle in my body tightened, and I was so close to coming, but I didn't know how to get there.

Jen pushed against me, my legs still in the same position, but folding me in half, going impossibly deeper. He took one of my hands and started sucking on my finger. Each pull was like a direct line toward my clit, making me more desperate for the finish but infinitely wishing it would never come.

He reached out with one hand and cupped my throat like he had earlier, but this time he didn't just pretend, he tightened his fingers, so my air was slightly cut off. I could still breathe, but it was limited, and that control he had over me was what finally helped push me over.

And over and over and over.

My muscles spasmed, pleasure running through my veins, taking all coherent thought with it and leaving me somehow broken but more put together. When I came out the other side, Jen was shoving into me without any grace. He was using me for his own pleasure and every muscle in my body was too weak to do anything other than take it. Even my lips were too tired to form any words—not that any came to mind right now expect needless begging.

The rhythm of his thrusts started to slow as the pressure inside me increased. More and more, Jen's movements became jerky as hit knot grew, refusing to let his cock pull out of me fully, until he hooked onto my cervix.

Unprepared for the pain, I screamed at the same time Jen roared with his release. Disconnected from my body, I felt his cock expand with each release of cum. I felt his heart beating rapidly as he half-collapsed on top of me. The pain started to ease, but my muscles were tight again, straining with holding myself impossibly still so I wouldn't feel the tug of his knot against my cervix again.

We were both breathing heavy, but when Jen tried sitting up, I gripped his shoulder hard, trying to hold him still. And that was when I become aware of our position. The open door, the fact that we were in a dorm room, all of it hit me like a wave and dragged me under with the current.

"Koda, are you okay?"

I wanted to answer, but I didn't move, didn't speak, afraid it would somehow move my cervix.

"Shit, did I hurt you? Don't be scared, little bear. My knot will go down soon."

I had to fight the instinct to crawl away from Jen, to hide myself in the makeshift nest, because I knew that path only led to pain. More than the pain from laying on several lumpy pillows. But I didn't like how out in the open we were.

Knox had the key to my dorm in case of an emergency, and the nest wasn't closed, which meant our scents were leaking out. Not to mention we weren't safe.

Those three words rolled around in my thoughts.

We aren't safe. We aren't safe. We aren't safe.

"Koda. Focus on me, little bear. Eyes on me."

I could hear Jen's voice, but it didn't pass the cloud of panic in my head. A sharp tug on my cervix caused me to yelp, pulling me out of my thoughts.

"That's it, little bear, I want you to look at me. You're safe. We're safe. But I'm going to pick you up and move us farther into your nest, okay?"

I nodded, unable to get the words out. My throat was already in pain as tears started forming, and I fought them back. Heat rose in my constricting throat like I was suffocating from the inside out.

Every movement of Jen's was painful, and I did my best to cling to his body. He was barely undressed, his pants acting as a cage for his legs, restricting his ability to stand up without attempting to dislodge me, making the whole scenario even harder.

I kept my head tucked into his neck, trying to breathe through the pain by inhaling his scent. His scent was tinged with worry, distracting from the usual calming smell of freshly cleaned laundry.

Eventually, after what felt like hours, we were covered in only the dim orange light from the closet, and Jen was on his knees, sitting back against his ankles, still holding me. Whatever instinct inside me that demanded a safe nest was more appeased by the shut door.

"Here, lean back slightly, Koda." Jen's tone held no room for argument, every word from him now like the professor he was in the classroom.

I moved slowly, not knowing until too late which positions would hurt.

Jen took his shirt off, not trying try for his pants, and I didn't offer. He motioned for me to lay back against his chest again. The skin-to-skin contact was like a soothing balm over my worries. I took deep breathes, resting my forehead at the base of his neck, calmly stroking the light smattering of hair on his chest as Jen's hands ran all over my body, continuing to soothe me.

When I finally fell asleep, Jen's knot was still firmly stuck inside me. He was massaging my scalp, his purr going strong.

Chapter Twenty-Two

I woke up to a beautiful voice that refused to stop talking despite me covering the sound with my hand. Chuckles vibrated my hand, and I finally managed to lift my head, opening one eye.

Jen was still laying down in my dorm room closet, his shirt off as I laid on top of him, but the happiness I thought I'd see after he finally claimed me— sexually— wasn't there.

Instinctively, I scented my surroundings, wanting to ensure we were still safe and alone. I was slammed with the scent of grief and anger coming from Jen, overshadowing the joy and possessiveness I could just barely detect. And probably only because we were so close.

"Jen? Are you ... mad that I fell asleep?" It was the only thing I could think of as to why he would be upset. Maybe he hadn't wanted to stay here, but he had to because he literally fucked me into exhaustion.

I sat up, noticing his knot had finally receded. Despite falling sleep, our mixed cum still spilled out of me. The realization had me blushing, wanting a blanket to wipe up the mess. Before I could reach for anything, Jen grabbed both my hands, holding them against his chest.

"No, little bear, I'm not mad at you. I'm frustrated with myself for not having more control."

The sadness coming from Jen had me looking away, not wanting him to see the tears forming and falling without my permission. "You regret having sex with me?" I didn't know why I asked. I didn't want the answer, but I also couldn't stop the words from coming out.

"What? No. Of course not." Jen sat up, trying to meet my eyes, but I kept them casted downward, as if I couldn't see him, he couldn't hurt my feelings more. "I'm really making a mess out of this, huh? Look at me, Koda. Please, little bear? Let me see your gorgeous eyes."

After a few breaths, I managed to get the tears to stop. I looked at Jen. I knew he could see the red eyes and dried tear stains on my cheeks, but he gracefully ignored them. "Koda, as your alpha, it's my job to keep you safe. Keep you happy. I felt how much you disliked this nest, but I still fucked you. And then when I knotted you, you didn't feel safe, and it was like I was being gutted. I did that to you. I made you vulnerable. You panicked and cried all because I couldn't tell you no."

"No, Jen, no." Now it was my turn to comfort my alpha. I was low-key excited about the prospect, even if I hated that he was upset. Apparently, all I needed was reassurance my alpha enjoyed himself and my emotions realigned properly. "Sure, I freaked out a little in the end but … well, I don't care. I'm all good now. Better than good actually."

"It was your first time and I ruined it."

"You didn't ruin it. I made the decision to ignore how I felt about the nest because I wanted you. And I'm really glad I did because … well, because I enjoyed it. A lot."

Don't blush. Don't blush. Don't blush.

"I did too, little bear."

I could feel the truth from his scent. Although, his lingering sadness reminded me of listening to a playlist meant to make you cry. I got it. Words weren't always enough—even if I wanted to force Jen into a happy mood to match mine I couldn't. It was a weird feeling of helplessness to know I couldn't help Jen's mood. He had to come out of it himself, and to do that, I needed to be happy. Which meant I couldn't be caught in a vicious cycle of worrying over Jen, making myself upset, and in return, making him upset.

There was even a small part of me—one I hated to acknowledge but couldn't deny—that liked Jen being upset. Not the emotion, but the fact he felt more real in this moment. My mind had a tendency to intertwine Jen my professor with Jen my alpha, but in this moment, he was truly only my alpha. Which was something I needed after he went all strict teacher on me earlier. I loved both sides of my alpha, but the key was balance.

"Let's get my stuff all packed up," I suggested. "Aidan and Enzo are probably wondering what's taking us so long at breakfast."

Jen nodded, his relief that I was dropping the topic a silent emotion between the two of us. It was slightly awkward for me as I made my way to the bathroom to clean up. Thank goodness we hadn't started packing up yet. It meant all my odor reducing washes were still in the shower. It was a quick in, wash, out, and get dressed before focusing on packing everything up.

My only personal belongings consisted of the blankets and pillows in my makeshift nest and my clothes. I knew from moving into the dorm that my wardrobe fit in two large suitcases, but the pillows didn't have a way to be carried except by hand. The only problem? My nest material smelled heavily of omega perfume, even from before today.

Even with the door closed and Jen still inside, the barest hint of toasted marshmallow and arousal crept through. It wasn't enough to draw the attention of anyone outside my room, but someone would surely notice if I took the fabric down the hallway. Betas might have the weakest sense of smell, but no one could ignore how drenched the fabrics were.

And even if they considered I simply broke the rules and snuck an omega onto campus, fucking them in my dorm, how would I explain away the additional alpha arousal when it was only Jen and I?

The door opened to my closet-nest and despite his put together appearance, I could still scent the wayward emotions coming from Jen. Plus, my alpha's muscles were tensed, making him appear like a stiff board instead of the loveable alpha concerned for my well-being. That meant it was my turn to take care of him.

"I have scent blocking washes in the shower. Why don't you take a quickie, and I'll start packing the clothes?"

Jen nodded, giving me a smile that was probably only seventy percent real happiness, and then headed to the bathroom. The door had just shut when a boring phone ringtone went off. Immediately, I knew it was Jen's phone since even my default ringtone was customized to a windchime-esq sound.

"Who is it?" Jen yelled from the bathroom.

I found the phone on the clothes on my bed, most likely from Jen simply throwing it. "Enzo. Do you want me to bring it to you?"

I was already walking toward the bathroom when Jen called back, "No, you get it, little bear. Tell him I'm taking a shower."

There was a rush of excitement at answering Jen's phone, followed by deep laughter coming from the bathroom, but I didn't even manage a single word before Enzo started talking. "What the hell's taking so long? What are you doing? Is my Koda okay?"

"Koda is fine. In fact, she's happy to hear from you."

"Orsetta," Enzo said on an exhale. "How are you? Why are you and Jen not back yet? This is my third time trying to get ahold of Jen."

"We stopped by my dorm to pick up my stuff to move. We sort of got distracted and fell asleep."

Enzo chuckled, the sound somehow affecting me even through the phone. "Is that right?"

"Yes," I squeaked.

He sighed. "I guess I couldn't have expected him to wait to pound your sweet pussy when he had you all alone. Tell me you're coming home soon."

"Um, we still have to pack everything up in the car."

"Is that what Jen's doing now?"

"No, he's, um, he's in the shower."

"I can imagine he's not very happy about that."

"He not ecstatic right now." I didn't want to lie, but I also didn't want to put myself in the relationship between packmates. I'd bonded in my own way to each male and each alpha had their own relationship with the others of the pack.

"I would not be either if I had to wash off the scent of your pleasure." I wasn't sure if it was his intention to turn me on or if he was simply being ruthlessly honest, but the result was the same. Was I supposed to be able to get this aroused by another alpha so soon after being knotted? My breathing became shallow, arousal heightening when I heard Jen chuckle from the shower. He'd obviously guessed what was going on. Or maybe he could hear with his protective alpha ears. But either way, it did nothing to help ease my body's increasing excitement.

"Please don't talk like that," I whispered to Enzo. "Not when you can't help me relieve the ache."

There was a long silence before I heard a shaky exhale on the other end of the line. "I will stop now, Orsetta, but soon you and I will not. Now put me on speaker and keep packing. I want you home as soon as possible."

I didn't tell him I hadn't started yet. In fact, I kept the phone close to my ear and turned to stare at the closet, wondering how I was going to get my pillows and blankets to my new nest.

"Orsetta? I don't hear you moving around."

"Um, I don't know how to pack up my pillows. They all smell like omega, and if I take them out to the hallway…"

"We can get you more pillows."

The whimper that escaped my throat was more instinctual than emotional. I wanted my pillows. The ones that already had my scent even if I wanted more later on. I'd always want more pillows, but it somehow felt disloyal to not take these ones with me. As if they had feelings and I'd hurt them by leaving them behind.

"Okay, okay, it was just a suggestion, Orsetta." I liked the way his accent made his words run together. "You have a duffle bag? Something to shove your favorite pillows in to mute the scent?"

"I only have the luggage carriers I was going to pack my clothes in. And even if I wanted to pack the pillows in them, there isn't enough space for all of them."

"Just grab your favorites. We can make a couple trips to pick up the rest of your pillows when we visit campus."

It wasn't my favorite idea, but realistically, it was the only option. I grabbed the suitcases from under the bed and started with the clothes. Most of them were already laid out so it was just a matter of carefully folding and placing them inside. I set the phone on speaker, setting it on the bed in a rare space absent of clothes, and listened to Enzo talk to me.

He told me about where he thought he'd find

more pillows for me. That maybe he could get me handmade ones that would smell of his home. He promised to get me more pillows than Aidan and Jen.

By the time Jen came out, I'd filled up the first suitcase with all my favorite clothes. I tentatively scented the air, but there was no more pungent odor of sadness or guilt. Actually, there was nothing except the chemical washes to remove scents. Since his hair was so short, there was no sign that he'd just taken a shower. Without a flush on his cheeks, I assumed he put himself through a cold one. But I didn't bring it up, not wanting to put Jen back in the poor mental state he had worked his way out of.

"How's it going, little bear?"

"She needs to pick out a couple of pillows from her old nest," Enzo said before I got a chance to answer my alpha. "We'll go back for the others later."

Jen could no doubt feel my stress over the little action when he asked, "Do you need help?"

I shook my head, exhaling the tension. Or trying to. It was hard to choose which pillows would get to come with me and which ones stayed behind. It might be weird to feel guilty over inanimate objects, but these pillows were steadfast fixtures in my life. They were around for happy cuddles, comforting me when I was sad, something to squeeze when I was scared. And they were mine. I didn't have any decorations, but I had these pillows and blankets, and every single one was one I'd picked out specifically because I knew it would bring me happiness.

Deciding to go with a random method, I closed my eyes, spun, and grabbed whatever my hand touched. It was like the trolley theory. I wasn't pulling the lever, just letting the trolley go on its path. It felt less like a backstabbing move this way.

"I think that might be enough for our first trip, little bear. We will come back for the rest, I promise." Jen took them from my grip and started folding up the single blanket my random picking managed to get. I helped him zip up the suitcases, and then we left the dorm. It felt like an unofficial goodbye, and I was surprised I was only a little bit sad.

"Professor Jenson, what are you doing with Koda's belongings?"

I should've noticed the pepper-like scent of my RA, but in my defense, Jen was very distracting, especially when he carried all of my shit like I'd break if I was forced to drag a suitcase full of pillows and clothes to the car. And even though I wasn't attracted to Knox, I appreciated the way her alpha posturing was in defense of me.

Resting my hand on Jen's shoulder to try to draw his attention my way, I said to Knox, "It's all good, Professor Jenson is my mate." I dragged down my shirt to show Knox the bond mark, but the female alpha didn't seem impressed. In fact, her scent became bitter with anger. My instincts told me to hide the mark, and I didn't hesitate to listen, confused on the why, but feeling the importance of the action.

"You bonded a beta?" She growled at my alpha. The air thickened with tension, as if making a single loud sound would send the alphas into a frenzy.

"I don't think that's any of your business," I said to Knox. I tried not to be aggressive with the RA who'd been nice to me, but I was feeling defensive. I was offended by her words, but I had to get used to this treatment. Even from supposed friends. Maybe that was what made it worse. Some stranger was kinder than Knox who I thought liked me—even if I'd thought she simply liked everyone.

The alpha looked over at me when I spoke to her, something like regret shining in her eyes.

Jen snapped, "Don't look at her."

Oh shit. This wasn't going well. Jen hadn't yelled, but he did have disapproving authority figure down pat. His scent, which had been hidden, was blooming with aggression.

"Jen, let's just go," I whined. "Knox doesn't mean anything by it."

I could see the struggle playing out through Jen's body and on his face. Part of him wanted to please me, and the other demanded he show his claim over me in front of another alpha. To demand respect for him and his bonded mate. Except it wasn't just another alpha now. The betas who were in their dorm rooms on a Saturday afternoon were starting to make an appearance in the hallway as the drama unfolded. Betas tended to stay away from aggressive alphas, but apparently their curiosity was getting the better of their instincts.

"Have you updated the Chancellor about this … relationship?" Knox asked.

"We will," Jen said, sounding like he didn't want to now that Knox had brought it up.

"You're in a relationship with an alpha?" a beta I'd never met asked. He looked between Jen and me like he didn't believe his own words. His tone sounded more curious than anything, and his attention was mostly on Jen, apparently waiting for the alpha to be the one to confirm our relationship.

"Koda is mine," Jen admitted.

I didn't mind the aggressive way he said it considering he was still in a staring contest with Knox. But the hostile scents coming from both alphas was doing more than attracting weary betas—it was making my omega scent perfume. I hadn't realized it at first, but the tension slowly leaked from Jen's shoulders, and the mixed scent of freshly warmed laundry and toasted marshmallows floated around me.

I was about to tell Jen we needed to get the hell out of here, when Knox decided to ignore the proper response of leaving well enough alone. "It won't last. At least not without an omega to ground you. All you've done is get the poor beta's hopes up while you think regular sex is possible for a long-term relationship. News flash, Professor, none of your other beta relationships have worked out. Maybe the common denominator is the alpha-beta portion, ever think of that?"

This conversation—hell, the whole hallway being blocked by an aggressive female alpha while several betas stared—was taking its toll on my nerves. I wanted to tell Jen to simply ignore Knox, but the words seemed stuck in my mind, refusing to be formed by my tongue. It wasn't shame, but something dangerously close to it that had me hiding behind Jen, not wanting to be the center of attention anymore. Or maybe ever again.

"You're going to ruin the beta with your carelessness, Professor."

"And you're speaking of things you don't understand, resident advisor."

Knox snorted. "Exactly. I'm the RA for the beta dorm which means it's my job to take care of each beta living in my building. Koda included. Because I don't care what you say, when you get tired of not being able to knot her, she will be forced to drag all her crap back to her dorm, a scar carved into her flesh, as you get you knot stuck in some random omega's cunt."

The growl that came from Jen was pure hatred. All the betas in the hallway dipped their heads in submission, and I was surprised to find Knox unwilling to bend to Jen's will. When the familiar boring ringtone of Jen's phone sounded from his pocket, I didn't hesitate to reach for it, incredibly grateful when I saw Enzo's name.

"Enzo? Jen and my RA are posturing right now, I need you to talk some sense into him." I didn't wait to make sure it was really Enzo and not Aidan calling from the wrong phone, or to be sure he heard me, before shoving the phone against Jen's ear.

The barely audible mumbling confirmed someone on the other end did hear me. I wasn't sure if the words of his packmate were getting through to him, but then Jen looked down at me tucked into his side, stared, his nostril flaring, making me realize the exact thought crossing his mind: I was perfuming. My body trying to calm my alpha.

Everyone seemed to be distracted by the aggression coming from the alphas, but the threat of exposure was there. And it seemed to have knocked some urgency into him.

"Let's go, Koda." Jen maneuvered all the bags to one hand—impressively—and managed to grab hold of me. He growled, the sound coming from his chest and vibrating with such potency it had me perfume stronger to calm him. That was new and definitely not good.

Surprisingly, Knox moved out of our way, but I could scent the frustration and guilt coming from her when we passed.

"Jen." My voice cracked on the single word.

"It's fine, Koda. But you need to try and not stress."

That advice was not helpful at all, but I didn't point that out. Jen told me to sit in the car while he loaded everything up and then handed me his phone—still on call with Enzo.

"Enzo?" I whispered.

"No, Koda bear, it's Aidan. Enzo handed me the phone so he could work off some steam before you get home—not that I'd ever say no to talking with my girl. I've been waiting patiently all morning for you to come home."

"I'm sorry I was gone for so long, Addie."

"Awe, sweet girl, don't worry about it. I'm going to get all my cuddles in when you come home—not that good sex needs any sort of advance notice."

I jumped slightly when Jen yanked the door open, but the smile on my alpha's face when he sat down was all confidence. His scent told a different story, his anger and possessiveness lingering around him. At least he no longer had the taint of the chemical de-scenter.

"Was that Jen?" Aidan asked.

"Yes. He just got it the car."

"We're on our way home now," Jen shouted much louder than necessary.

"Okay, tell Jen to drive safely, Koda bear. You're precious cargo, after all." And then Aidan hung up.

It took me a moment to realize he had indeed hung up the phone without saying goodbye. When the screen showed the phone call log, I didn't know whether to be angry or laugh.

"He just hung up," I said. "No goodbye."

"Aidan does that. But don't worry, we'll be home soon, and you can give him an ear full. He's never listened to either me or Enzo, and it bugs the hell out of us, but I know he'll listen to you."

I liked that.

Home. Having the same issues as Jen and Enzo. Nagging Aidan.

Even if Knox's voice still rung in the back of my mind like a nasty echo of an old bell, those thoughts made me happy. For now, I was going to ignore the dusty chime because there was nothing I could do about it. Or her.

****

The drive to the house went by in a flash. Jen and I sat in comfortable silence, his hand resting on my thigh as some radio station played in the background. Really, my mind was calm, and I had no doubts Jen was behind it, his angry scent quickly disappeared the farther we got from campus. He was now radiating calm.

That scent mixing with the slight purr gave me a calming space. The negative thoughts struggled to take root in my head, but I felt them looming over me, ready to strike at the first sign of a weak defense. Kind of like a shadow flying around in circles on the ground. The bird was obviously nearby, but all I got was the shadow.

"Little bear, are you listening to me?" Jen squeezed my thigh, the movement reminding me we were still in the car. Oh, and we'd arrived.

"Why are we sitting in the car?"

"Well, I thought I was talking to you, but I guess you were too deep in your thoughts, huh? Want to share with the class?"

I shook my head. "It was nothing."

"Little bear, you can tell me anything. Every thought that passes in your head I want to know." Jen's hands grabber mine, squeezing tightly—but not painfully. I squeezed back to let him know he had my attention. "I know we didn't get to talk about what happened, but I'm ready and waiting to break down all your fears and worries. What Knox said isn't true. We had decided to pursue you before we even knew you could take a knot. It doesn't matter if you're a beta or omega, we just want you."

"Really, Jen, I appreciate that, but I wasn't thinking anything. I know I'm worried about what happened, but I'm sort of in this numb place right now. And I really just want to stay here. There. In my mind. Once I open the flood gates, the stress will come rushing through without allowing me time to get on a life preserver. So for now, I just want to pretend everything is okay. We can talk about what happened at the dorms tomorrow, right?"

He stared at me for a long moment as if he was trying to decide if he should push me now but ultimately decided to cave to my wishes. "Okay, but I was having a whole conversation with you while you were not-so-purposefully ignoring me."

I blushed at the slight indignation. "Tell me everything again. I'm listening this time."

"Aidan and Enzo are worried about you." Almost immediately, I opened my mouth to tell him I spoke to Aidan, and he seemed fine, but Jen gave me a sharp look I knew well from class telling me not to interrupt him. "That means when we get into the house, they are going to want to touch you to make sure you're all in one piece. It's an alpha thing."

It might be an alpha instinct, but now that Jen mentioned it, I felt my own need for Aidan and Enzo. I wanted to be sure they still wanted me—drama and all. And then I wanted to be held and never let go.

"But we're still too newly mated, Koda. I won't be able to let you go and watch them with you without some display of authority."

"What kind of display?" I asked even though I thought I already knew. The temperature in the car had already increased, making the seat heaters no longer necessary. Slick appeared in the space between my legs. Luckily, I'd put on a new pair of underwear before I'd left the dorm, but at this rate I would soak the thin fabric before we got out of the car.

"The kind of display where we leave your bags in the car and I carry you into the house, all the way to your nest, and force Aidan and Enzo to simply watch as I fuck and knot you. I need them to know that before they can so much as make sure you're happy and healthy, I get my fill of you. But it won't be sweet, Koda. It will be hard and rough and dirty. Another version of claiming for my alpha instincts."

I felt like the oxygen slowly leaked from the car as Jen detailed what he needed to do to me. Every beat of my heart, every inhale and exhale from my lungs, every slight twitch of my fingers was surrounding me, engulfing me, until all there was in the world was Jen's words and the reaction they had on my body.

"Can you handle that, little bear? Because if you can't, you need to get out of the car and let me drive around for a few hours."

My muscles were coiled like they were ready to be attacked and be bent at extreme angles based on the images my mind kept throwing out of Jen and me together. My omega had no doubt that I was built to take anything an alpha could give. And my beta side was more than ready to experience an uncontrolled Jen. All the moisture in my throat was gone, but I manage a single nod. Yes. Yes, I could handle rough sex with Jen.

JOSEPHINE LIGHT

Chapter Twenty-Three

I sat in the car as Jen got out. I could only hear the mumbles of whatever he yelled to Aidan and Enzo, but I knew from the change in their stances, they weren't happy.

When Jen opened the door, he pulled me out of the seat and picked me up, needing to be in complete control. I didn't object. In fact, I rested my cheek on Jen's shoulder, inhaling his scent. Even though I wanted to look at Aidan and Enzo, verify they were still okay, scent them to ensure they didn't smell of anyone else, I managed to keep my instincts under control. For Jen. Not that it was a struggle to cling to Jen. My alpha somehow managed to get me riled up and keep me calm simultaneously.

The swaying motion of Jen's steps came to a sudden stop. With the breeze kissing my body, I knew we were still outside. The eerie silence had me lifting my head to see what was going on, but a firm grip had me putting my head back down on Jen's shoulder. I let out a huff of impatience and humor.

"I thought you wanted to fuck me, Alpha." I taunted him, ignore the warning voice in my head telling me not to push Jen when he radiated this much dominance. And maybe I was more omega than I realized, because I wanted to push and push and push until Jen snapped. Like it was a game to see if I could get him to fuck me before he got me to the nest.

Three sets of growls responded to my comment. An unexpected amount of slick filled my pussy, a frustrated moan leaving my throat when my pussy clenched down to find nothing filling me. The increasing sexual frustration quickly turned to anger when I realized we still hadn't entered the house—let alone made it any closer to my nest.

Without thinking, I let my instincts take control. I dug my teeth into the tender skin between Jen's collar bone and the top of his shoulder while rubbing myself against his body in the hope of creating the friction I desperately needed. I had been turned on since Jen told me his plans for my body and every second waiting on him was a tease.

Jen's arousal was evident in his scent, the hardness of his body, and the way his grip tightened on me. It didn't help that I knew Aidan and Enzo were watching me. Wanting me. And I wanted to be able to scent my other alphas, to be able to see them.

"Careful, Omega," Jen growled out, his words a whispered warning.

"Or what? You'll posture some more? Maybe one of my other alphas should tend to me so you can keep playing—"

I didn't finish whatever garbage I was spewing. Jen's hand gripped my hair, pulling my head up and forcing me to meet his eyes. My head didn't hurt, but I could feel the tension in my scalp. The inability to move my head without pulling my hairs out had me trapped, staring wide-eyed at an angry looking alpha.

"You need a good fuck that bad, little bear? The pounding I gave you earlier didn't sate your needs?"

Every word out of Jen's mouth heated my body. My stomach flipped with excitement, my pussy clenching with hope that Jen would give up talking and simply slam into me.

"Well, don't worry," Jen continued. "I'll take care of that naughty mouth."

Threat or not, it got Jen moving. He walked right past Aidan and Enzo, letting the other males trail behind us as he carried me to the nest. I could just barely make my other alphas out from the corner of my eyes.

Enzo was smiling, a look that told me he was going to enjoy my punishment for my words whereas Aidan looked like he was going to melt into a puddle from the heat consuming him.

"I'm not letting you out of my sight," Jen said. "So if you need to get the nest ready, I will have Aidan and Enzo wait out here. Decide."

It took restraint for Jen to allow me time to fix the nest, but I didn't have the same icky feeling I did about my old nest in the dorm room. Whether it was because I had all of my alphas present or this nest was more secure than the other, I wasn't sure, but there was no aching need to fix anything besides my current state of not being fucked.

"Shoes off," I reminded him.

"Be sure, Omega," Jenson warned. I admired his restraint, but it wasn't needed. Not in this. But I knew he was worried about what had happened last time.

"Shoes off," I repeated, making my voice stern.

I was adjusted against one hip and then the other, the soft clomping sounds of three pairs of shoes being taken off. Jen even remembered to do mine—which I'd forgotten about somehow—before throwing us into my nest, breaking through the invisible chains holding him back.

There was so much anticipation in my body, I could feel my heartbeat throbbing in my clit as my blood rushed to the bundle of nerves. Rubbing against the fabric of my underwear, the slight pain made me even hornier.

Jen didn't make me wait any longer. He slammed his lips to mine with enough pressure I absently wonder if lips could bruise.

His hands moved to take my shirt off and I let him

with ease, throwing my head back when he trailed kisses down my neck to my breasts. He traced around my nipples with his tongue, my eyes flying open when I heard a groan that didn't belong to either me or Jen.

How had I forgotten about my other alphas?

I wanted to reach for them, but I wasn't willing to risk upsetting the alpha sucking on my breasts. Especially when he bit down just beside my nipples, making me grab his shoulders, wanting to pull him closer and push him away at the same time. Everything Jen did made my pussy wetter and wetter, and knowing Aidan and Enzo were so close was like an endless tease. Their older scents were still soaked into the fabrics of this room, reducing me to begging.

"Please, Jen—Alpha, more. I need more."

"Like this?" Still standing, still holding me wrapped around his body, he shoves his hand down my pants, easily finding my wetness.

His hand had little mobility, trapped between our bodies, but it didn't stop his fingers from seeking out my hard clit. Just the little brushes made my hips jerk with nowhere to go.

I whined. "Don't tease me, Jen. Please. I need you."

"That's right. Only me. Say it."

I growled, not wanting to hurt my other alphas but needing more than the slow teasing circles.

Jen shoved a finger inside me, but it didn't alleviate any of the need in my body.

"Just tell him, Orsetta."

I looked for Enzo, wondering if I was so horny I'd imagined him giving me permission.

On the other side of my nest, he stood on the little walkway that went along the walls, his hand on his cock. He was darker than Jen, and not circumcised, which felt like a weird thing to notice, but I couldn't help it while watching his hand tighten, fisting himself up and down. "Tell him what he needs to hear so he'll fuck you."

I whimpered as the weight of worry only fell halfway off. Even in the fog of arousal, I understood that what Jen was asking me to do was a big deal, but knowing Enzo didn't hate me helped. But would Aidan?

I looked at the alpha in question. He stood in front of the door, like a silent guard, but there was nothing relaxed about his pose. His eyes were locked on my breasts where Jen was tormenting and teasing them with his mouth, tongue, and teeth. I may have arched my back more, making my breasts look more pronounced as he watched.

Aidan's eyes glanced up to mine. The smirk on his lips would be enough to soak my panties if they weren't already in that state. His hair was pulled up into a bun today that I desperately wanted to undo for no reason than because I could.

"Go ahead, Koda bear," Aidan said, winking at me like we were in on same inside joke together. "Tell him what he wants to hear so I can have a go with you."

I was pretty sure if Jen wasn't currently holding me, he would've attacked Aidan for such a claim on me. Either way, he settled for a growl before moving his lips back up to my neck and sucking on a new spot to temporarily mark me as his. It was his retaliation for Aidan's words while my actual claiming mark was still covered.

With both Aidan and Enzo on board, I managed to push the guilt aside. "Only you, Jen. Please fuck me now."

I was unceremoniously dropped on top of my nest, the pillows and blankets providing the cushioning for my landing—and destroying my nest—then Jen got to work quickly stripping down. I didn't wait for any directions, rushing to get my own clothes off. Jen ripped off my key necklace, throwing it off to the side as if he hated looking at it.

Already, I wanted to beg Jen not to tease me. I didn't know how much more wound up my body could become before I exploded from sexual frustration. But there wasn't time to plead my case as Jen slammed his cock inside me, not worried about my wetness considering I was literally dripping slick.

The pleasant pressure of finally getting filled had me teetering close to my orgasm. If I could just come, I would let Jen use me to his heart's content. Or his cock's content.

There was nothing gentle about the way Jen fucked me. His hips slammed against my widespread legs he held far apart like he was trying to keep me spread open, and hold on, at the same time. I grabbed ahold of whatever my fingers could grasp, trying to stop my body from moving away from Jen's with every thrust. When that didn't work, Jen let go of my legs to lean over me, chest to chest. One arm slid under my neck and gripped my hair, holding me in place, as the other ripped off the bandage covering my bite mark.

The pain of the adhesive ripping was dull and immediately cancelled out by Jen's tongue tracing the outline of his mark. All the while, he never stopped thrusting, the beautiful filling motion sending pleasure to my whole body.

Jen's lips made their way back up, licking the shell of my ear before whispering, "Look at your other alphas, little bear. Look how they wish it was them thrusting into this tight pussy."

Unable to do more than obey, I turned my head toward where I knew my other alphas were. Their lower bodies were covered from my vision because of the fluffy pillows surrounding me, but I could perfectly make out both alphas watching me—us—and using their fists to give themselves pleasure.

My entire body tightened, including my pussy, and Jen chuckled, knowing the reason. Despite the nearness of Jen, and the strong scent of arousal pouring from my bonded alpha, I could still make out my other alphas' arousals. Whether it was their scents soaked into the fabrics from last night, or they were aroused enough to permeate the air of perfume encircling me now, it raised my need to climax.

"Do you like the power you hold over them, Koda?" Jen asked louder than necessary and most likely for the benefit of our audience.

I couldn't speak, but I whimpered and added a nod.

My admission had Jen picking up speed, his grip turning around so he wasn't pulling my hair back but holding me down by my neck. The slight tension his fingers supplied had my eyes rolling to the back of my head.

When I glanced back at Aidan, I noticed two dots of silver near the bottom of his shaft, above his balls, that I wished I could get a better look at. Was his piercing for pleasure or simply decorative?

Why did I want to lick it?

I wanted to ask Aidan if I could lick his whole cock, maybe get a better look at the piercing. And there was Enzo. I wanted to run my fingers along his cock, feeling if the extra skin made the movement easier. But Jen's words before we started were a warning, I was not allowed to touch either alpha, so I bit my lip—hard—hoping to stop the words from spilling out unwillingly.

"Oh no you don't." Jen pulled my bottom lip

away from my teeth and shoved his thumb in my mouth. "If you need something to do with that naughty mouth, I'll help. Show me what that tongue can do."

I did my best to pretend Jen's thumb was something longer, something more desirable. Still, I did as I was told with immense joy.

Jen still maintained his grip on my neck while I sucked on him, but with every flick of my tongue, every hollowing of my cheeks, he groaned. His body was barely holding back from climaxing, but I knew what he was waiting for: me.

Not coming felt like some sort of cosmic punishment. Over and over Jen pounded into me, but all it did was raise my sexual tension higher and higher. I arched my back so my breasts were pressing against his chest, planted my feet so I could move my hips. Everything I did felt amazing, but nothing pushed me over.

Just as I was starting to worry that I'd never come again, Jen pulled his thumb out of my mouth, sliding that hand down our bodies until he found and expertly pinched my clit.

I screamed through my orgasm.

It was like fire running through my veins—in the best possible way. My muscles clenched, relieved the pinnacle they were searching for was found, before letting all the energy drain out as I finally came back down. And then my newly relaxed muscles had to work, had to stretch to accommodate the large knot forming. The pressure was intense, but not as scary as my first time. I did my best to focus on Jen, on the sound of his groan as he came and his knot expanded, on the look of pure bliss on his face, the soft, beautiful purr vibrating his whole chest and seeping into my body, and the way his head tilted down toward me like he no longer had the energy to hold himself up.

We were both breathing hard, but the multiple exhales and groans remind me we weren't the only ones that finished. I looked over at Enzo currently on his knees like his orgasm had brought him down. Then I looked at Aidan, leaning against the door, his head upturned toward the ceiling. Both alphas had made themselves come, the evidence on their hand and shirts, their breathing heavy with huge gulps as if trying to suck down oxygen.

Even worn out and tired, I wanted to lick their hands clean of their cum, but I couldn't get myself to voice my wants. I could blame it on being too exhausted to speak, which was partially true, but it felt like more than that. It was a deep-rooted worry that my request would turn them off. My body craved their cum, but I didn't have any experience with sex and what was or wasn't normal. I didn't even know why I wanted it so badly.

Jen, finally recovering from his orgasm, worked his arms around my body to make turning us over easy. There was only a little tug this time, but it was enough to make me wince slightly. A soft kiss on my lips was an apology from my alpha that was so sweet it made my heart flutter like hummingbird wings.

"You've just been thoroughly fucked," Jenson said. "Your emotions shouldn't be so turbulent. What's going on, little bear?"

I didn't get a chance to answer before Enzo made his way over to me, ignoring the growl from Jen, and offered me his hand. The scent of Enzo, and his cum, was enough to have me grab for his hand, sucking and licking at the available liquid like it was a fucking treat. And it was.

When I finally released Enzo's hand, another was offered out, but with much less confidence. I follow the arm up to Aidan's face, his pale face now sporting two pink dots on his cheeks, making him look much younger and even more vulnerable.

"I—" Aidan swallowed, looking so nervous I wanted to cuddle him up and protect him from whatever was making him act this way. "I didn't know you'd like a taste. There's only a little."

Realizing I was the reason for Aidan's tension, I made sure to say, "Thank you, Addie." I found every drop of cum on his hand and licked it off, humming my pleasure around his fingers.

With all three of my alphas around me, even if only Jen was physically touching me—letting me rest against him as if he was a pillow while allowing his knot to go down—I felt safe. And just like last time, I fell asleep from sexual exhaustion.

Chapter Twenty-Four

I woke up to the glorious scents of all three alphas nearby. My body was still using Jen as a bed but the rhythmic rise and fall told me he wasn't struggling to breathe, so that was good. Jen's chest didn't have as much hair as Enzo's, but it was enough that I was able to run my fingers through it while I let my body and mind continue its wake-up process.

When I was finally ready to make demands for coffee, I realized the alphas were in the middle of a conversation about what happened at the dorm building. Not exactly a pleasant topic to wake up to.

"She shouldn't go back there," Aidan complained. "She might have gone under the radar before, but everyone's going to be able to smell the difference with her."

That had me sitting up so quickly the room spun. I had to close my eyes, but I still managed to get the words out. "My scent's changed?"

"Relax, little bear." Jen sat up and pulled my head down to rest on his shoulder, letting me inhale his fresh laundry scent, no longer aroused, but now comforting and very pleased. His hands started rubbing up and down my bare back, making me acutely aware none of us had put any clothes on yet. If I wasn't seconds away from panicking, too much of my focus would be directed to all the exposed, naked males in my nest. "Aidan just meant you smell of us. It's expected when you spend so much time with mates. Totally normal, even for a beta."

"Well, normal for any betas that get bonded," Aidan added. Both Enzo and Jen glared at their packmate, but Aidan didn't wither from the looks. "There's no point in mincing words. She's going to hear worse at the academy no matter how closely we attach ourselves to her side like fucking fungus."

Jen's hands tightened around me before letting go when I shook my back, requesting he keep rubbing. He resumed the careful glide of his fingers, despite the huff of annoyance, which I thought he meant for Aidan.

Jen's scent didn't change in any negative way, which I would definitely take credit for keeping happy. Of course, if we kept talking about the potential people who would scoff at our relationship, I imagined all my alphas' scents would turn bitter.

Although thinking about telling others the truth … they'd still scoff with having an omega at the academy. There was no winning in this situation if I was determined to keep going to school. And I was.

Hannah was the exception to the rule. Her alphas were powerful enough, or maybe had enough money— although that was basically the same thing—or had the right friends to bypass the rules of higher education to allow an omega to take classes. Hell, maybe Hannah was posing as a beta in her online classes. But either way, she was a special case, and I didn't have the same options as her if I got kicked out of Braker.

I wasn't sure why I'd always been determined to see this through. At any point I could've turned myself in to the Omega Compound for an easy life of being pampered. I was always resigned to doing so when I was ready to start a family—

Oh shit.

A family. I was nowhere near ready to start forming one of those. With my alphas? Sure. Creating little ones, that was a hard pass. Even if the thought of a baby with the features of any of my alphas had my ovaries squeezing painfully with anticipation.

"You okay, Koda?" Jen asked.

"Perfect," I croaked out. The looks on my alphas' faces told me they weren't believing me, but there was no way I was going to admit I'd imagined our pack with children. So, instead, I said, "I know you all are worried about what everyone is going to say, but there's no way to come up with every response. Good or bad, we will have to deal with it. We need to focus on the things we can actually control."

I looked at all my alphas in turn, making sure each one nodded in agreement before I clapped my hands, ending the discussion. "Good. Now I need coffee."

Aidan and Jen seem shocked, but Enzo smiled. "Una ragazza secondo il mio cuore."

I wasn't sure what he said, but the words were enough to excite my body, sending goosebumps along my skin. Logically, I knew he was bilingual. His nickname for me and his accent was enough of a hint, but he'd never spoken in anything besides English before. I liked it, this other language. The cadence of the words flowed better. I liked the deeper tenor he used, even the mystery surrounding the words.

My thighs squeezed together, trying to hide the evidence of slick forming, only to be blocked by Jen's body. Without any clothes on—and my legs obscenely spread by Jen's hips—any hint of arousal was scented by my alphas. And while having another round with Jen was intriguing ... I needed more fuel in me.

"Coffee?" I asked.

"C'mon," Enzo said, standing and stretching, letting his cock bob at my eye level only an arm's length away.

More slick rushed to my pussy, but I ignored it, reaching for Enzo's outstretched hand. My legs were shaky and weak from being bent and spread for so long. Standing in the line of sight of three alphas, all looking up and down my body, did nothing to calm my heating skin.

But then my stomach growled, and it was like all the arousal disappeared from their scents.

"Maybe more than just coffee, huh, Orsetta? I'll make us lunch," Enzo said. The idea of a homecooked meal—or really just any food at all—was enough to have me nodding eagerly. I'd gone to restaurants on occasion, but my diet usually existed on cafeteria food and coffee.

Enzo and I headed to the kitchen, where he lifted me up and set me down on the cold island countertop. A shiver ran through my body, pebbling my nipples. That little fact wasn't missed by Enzo who smiled but surprisingly didn't touch me, despite the physical evidence he was turned on too.

He maneuvered around the kitchen, pulling out ingredients and pans. "I think I'll make a lasagna for dinner. It will take some time, but while it's cooking, I'll get you a snack."

It was strange to be on the receiving end of an alpha so different than my bonded one. When Jen took care of my needs, he did it as if pleasing me made him happy. Jenson liked to make himself useful, which explained why he would've wanted to be a teacher. That same need to help was the basis of our relationship.

But Enzo took care of me however he wanted. He was an alpha that would do what he needed to keep me happy regardless of what others might've thought or even whether he was happy. It was a heady feeling and one I had to be careful not to abuse.

And then there was Aidan. Sweet Aidan who needed to be needed and included. Aiden who used our relationship to fill himself up with love. Which was good because I had endless love to give.

Beta sex classes taught me that alphas were an

aggressive, sexually active designation. Honestly, I would've guessed the class was taught in a way to dissuade betas from wanting to be in a relationship with other designations. Did it matter that I should have never taken those classes? Nope. All that toxic bullshit was rooted deep in my being. Which was why I was using all three of my alphas to make me feel safe, treasured, and important.

"Did you learn to cook by yourself?" I asked, noticing he hadn't pulled out his phone or a cookbook when he measured ingredients.

"My mamma taught me."

"Is she still alive?"

"She is. She lives in Italy with the rest of my family. Once we bond, I'm sure she'll be begging for us to make a trip out there for you to meet her."

"How come you're here?"

"You don't want me here, Orsetta?"

Embarrassment turned my entire face red if the heat in my cheeks was any indication. "No, I didn't mean it like that, Enzo, really. I was just wondering what brought you here. Not that I'm not thrilled you're here, by the way. Because I am, if that's not clear. Like, really happy you're here."

Thankfully, Enzo put an end to my rambling apology with a large hand on my thigh. The amusement on his face enough to get me to glare at the alpha.

"I came here when I was about thirteen," Enzo said. "My mother was born in America, and my father surprised the whole family with a trip here over summer so my mother could see her parents. We were supposed to go back for Ferragosto, but I did not wish to return to Turin."

The realization he hadn't said, 'return home', had me smiling. Just because he was born in Italy didn't make it his home. This was his home. Here. With me.

"I asked my mamma if I could stay with my nonni and she said yes." Enzo pulled his hand away to throw things into the pan over the stove. He kept glancing at me, a little towel on his shoulder, as he told his story. "It helped that my father has his heir, Alonzo Junior, and my mamma has her little girl, Viola. Being the middle child has its advantages."

I nodded in agreement even though—to my knowledge—I was an only child. "So you stayed with your…"

"Nonni," he said, supplying the word for me.

"Nonni. And then you met Aidan and Jenson?"

He nodded, but it was Jenson that said, "Yes, he did."

"Curriculum in Italy is different, and our teacher thought I could use the extra help. She asked Jen to help me out."

Jen handed me a large shirt that surprisingly smelled of Aidan and a pair of underwear. To my shock, I didn't blush at Jen touching my underwear—he must have gone out to get my luggage without me noticing.

My alpha helped me off the counter and said, "Little did she know, Enzo was way beyond what we were learning in class. He just needed a little review since he'd done our lessons years ago. And then he was good to go."

After getting dressed, I looked down at my bare legs, the dark stubble telling me I needed to shave. Soon. As if to hit on that point, Jen lifted me back up to sit on the island counter and rubbed his hand up and down my calf. Even when I crossed my legs over one another to try and sneak my legs away, he still managed to rub the stubble. When I glanced up to see if he was disgusted, he simply winked. Whatever the hell that meant.

"Where's Aidan?" I asked.

"On the phone," Jen said.

"With who?"

Instead of answering, Jen looked past me to Enzo, the two having a silent conversation that would annoy me if worst case scenarios hadn't started running through my thoughts of Aidan on the phone with someone he was attracted to. He'd gotten himself off earlier, but I doubted he was too pleased about having to use his hand. The guilt of not pleasing Aidan sexually overpowered any claim I might've thought I had on him—because at that point, all we had were words. That we might one day bond. But maybe he needed something before then. Someone before then.

"Shit. Jen." Enzo stopped whatever he was working on, maybe putting sauce in some tin, and grabbed my face with both of his large hands. His pine tree scent was mingling with the spices he was working with, but it didn't take away from how comforting his scent was. "Orsetta, don't cry. Tell us what's wrong, and we'll fix it. Are you hurt? Should we take you to the hospital? Jen, tell me if she's hurt."

"She's not hurt. Just feeling … rejected."

Enzo continued wiping the tears as soon as they fell, like he couldn't handle the sight of them.

"Koda bear? Are you crying?" Aidan's voice added to the fray, the sharp inhale his first response when I looked over at him through blurry eyes. "Why the hell is our beta crying?"

"We don't know," Enzo growled out, his hands rapidly, but gently, touching every part of my body. "Are you sure she isn't injured?"

"I think she's upset Aidan was on the phone," Jen said slowly, like he was waiting for confirmation.

"Is that true, Koda bear?" The pain in Aidan's

voice was enough to make me want to deny the words except they were true. Aidan took Enzo's place right in front of me, the despair in his scent breaking my heart for a whole new reason. "I was thinking you might be on the phone with someone who could please you better."

I barely got the words out. I was an equal mix of worried he might confirm my fears and guilt for blaming Aidan for something he might not have done.

"Please me?"

"You know. Sexually."

I didn't know what I expected. Laughter that the idea was ridiculous, maybe? Nope. I got anger. Pure unfiltered alpha anger pouring off Aidan forcing me to submit so quickly I was surprised he wasn't the lead alpha in this pack. If Jen had more dominance than Aidan, I was going to be so screwed—and not in the good way. Aidan picked me up, setting me back down on top of the kitchen island, momentarily separating us from the other males. It was obvious I'd overreacted to a fake scenario I'd created, but my hormones were crazy right now.

Really, it was their fault for affecting my hormones so aggressively.

"Let's iron out these creases and then donate the shirt, Koda bear." I looked down at the shirt Jen put me in, wondering what the hell Aidan was talking about, before realizing he was talking about a metaphorical shirt. "You are the only omega for me, Koda. You are the only beta for me. However you define yourself, you can add 'Aidan's mate' to your list. There's not a body I would go to for pleasure besides yours. Understand me?"

"Yes, alpha."

"We might not have a bond right now, but we will. And that doesn't mean there isn't some form of relationship between us, because there is. The four of us are in a relationship, a pack. Jenson is simply the first four-leafed clover—lucky. But we will get there, Koda bear, don't you worry."

"All of us will get there," Enzo said in agreement.

Jen came to my side, kissing his claiming mark. My bonded alpha's feelings on the matter were plain to see when he wasn't glaring at Aidan for having moved me away from him.

"Okay," I agreed, the tears stopping as quickly as turning off the faucet.

"Now get back to cooking, Enzo. Our mate is starving." Aidan pulled back his dominance and gave me a kiss on the cheek that had my heart beating louder than a woodpecker on a metal chimney. "Now, about the phone call. I spoke with my mother, and she intends to come visit us."

Enzo chuckled slightly, but with his back turned to Aidan, he missed the glare shot in his direction.

"That should be fun," Jen muttered.

"Koda bear, this means you have a decision to make," Aidan said. He and Jen took a seat on the bar stools, giving Enzo space, so I scooted farther back on the island toward the two alphas. The new space sent goose bumps down my arms and legs from the cold temperature, even with the new clothing. Of course, Jen's eyes didn't notice the raised hairs on my body but seemed to focus directly on the peaked nipples showing through the thin t-shirt.

"About what?" I asked.

Aidan rubbed a hand across the back of his neck before placing it over mine, playing with each individual finger. "Well, my mother has made her displeasure known about the fact the female I am going to bond is a beta."

Ah, the problem was starting to become clearer.

Whatever showed on my face had Aidan wincing, but he didn't let go of my fingers, either needing the connection, or realizing I did. "I don't know how she'll react around you, but I don't think it's going to be welcoming. And if you do decide you want to tell her about your … omega potential, then there's a chance the secret won't remain a secret."

"How does she know about me?"

Aidan finally looked away from me to glance at Jenson. "It seems that RA has already contacted Chancellor Kelly. I'd bet you have a few missed calls and emails from him already."

"Chancellor Kelly told your mom?" I asked.

"Aidan's family owns Braker Academy," Jenson said, putting the information out in the open like it wasn't the equivalent to a two-headed giraffe—you want it to be cool, but it was actually terrifying.

"Your family, what, has stock in the academy?" I asked Aidan.

"No. Stock-style ownership would only work with a university that's owned by a private corporation. It would have to pay dividends to stockholders and really be beholden to those stockholders. The Academy is private which means my family very much owns it."

"So your last name is…"

"Braker," Aidan said.

"His parents dictate Chancellor Kelly's actions," Jenson added.

"Like a puppet," Enzo said, not even turning around.

"He's right." Aidan nodded his head in agreement. "And in my parents' social circle, it doesn't look good that I intend to bond to a beta. Dating them was one thing, and my parents already stated their displeasure, but betas in the past have always been temporary."

"Especially since he refuses to be Chancellor." Jen threw that little bit of information out like it was a joke, but I couldn't help but gape at Aidan.

"You're supposed to Chancellor?"

"No," Aidan said firmly. "That job shouldn't be one handed down but given to the best candidate. Education shouldn't be a business. It's a learning institution, but my family has the ability to control the curriculum based on whims."

I stared at Aidan wide-eyed, shocked by the passion but mostly turned on. Even if that fervor wasn't directed toward me, the confidence from Aidan was sexy. Not that he was ever lacking in that department.

Although, I felt the need to point something out. "Jen works there."

"It's only temporary," Jen said.

"How come? Don't you want to be a professor? You're a natural at it."

Jen chuckled. "I had an in with Aidan. He was able to help me get the job so I could have some experience under my belt. We never planned to stay here for too long."

There was a lot I could've asked about that last bit of information alone. I decided it was best to stay on topic. "Okay. Aidan's mom is coming out even though she is displeased by the rumors she hears, and I have to decide about taking her ire or risking my secret getting out."

"Yes." All three alphas spoke together.

"I don't want your mom to hate me," I said to Aidan. "But I want to finish my degree. I won't risk that."

Aidan didn't seem shocked by my admission. "And if my mom found out you're an omega, she'd definitely make that common knowledge to help boost her own image. So, we keep your designation a secret, even from family."

Everyone agreed, and then Enzo pulled out a second tray from the oven I hadn't even seen him put in, let alone make, and I dug into my snack.

Chapter Twenty-Five

Dinner the next two nights was fucking delicious. Saturday night was homemade Tagliatelle Bolognese, and the snack beforehand was bread Enzo called Focaccia, which he hadn't let the others eat.

Then last night was stuffed artichokes. The other alphas had shoved food at me throughout the day whenever Jen sensed my hunger building. Enzo had to tell them to knock it off when dinner was approaching so I would be hungry enough to eat. I hadn't minded all the constant attention.

After we'd eaten last night, I'd gone into a food coma, wrapped up in Enzo's scent—and clothes—but settled on Jen's lap. Apparently, my bonded alpha had taken the suggestion seriously from Jackson. I felt like I'd gained ten pounds in the last few days, but I wasn't going to complain.

Leaving it to the last moment, Jenson had finally looked at the missed messages from the academy's Chancellor after Sunday dinner. Apparently, we had a mandatory meeting already scheduled for Monday. And not just for Jenson. My alpha was instructed to bring his pack and the 'beta' student. Needless to say, I was nervous about the meeting. What was the point of being kicked out of the academy still hiding my designation?

Which meant Sunday had been a day of relaxing—for me—and working out logistics for returning to school since my alphas were determined to figure out how to deal with every possible scenario imaginable. Since Jen had classes, and he couldn't be by my side the whole time, he finally agreed he could handle the separation as long as I had Aidan or Enzo with me.

I hated to think of my mates' romantic pasts, but

since they were familiar with dating betas and keeping their instincts in check, it wasn't such a strain on them. Although I'd been warned about receiving an overload of affection when we were all together—which I totally supported.

Of course, the plan only worked for the short term. Aidan and Enzo had lives outside of escorting me to classes and sitting in lectures they didn't understand. Luckily, there were two of them which meant the males could take turns escorting me to classes. Aidan had said he was able to work on some stuff from his laptop while I was in class, and Enzo just told me not to worry about him—which wasn't helpful at all. But alas, it was the best I got from the burly alpha before the food coma demanded to be obeyed.

There wasn't much we could plan for considering we had no idea of the reaction we were going to receive. Well, except for the one too damn early in the morning.

We left for our meeting with Chancellor Kelly at the butt crack of dawn, and not even my strong coffee put me in a good mood. I might've been awake, but I felt ornery as fuck, which was not going to be helpful in a meeting where tensions were going to run high.

I had made sure to tell all my alphas to remain calm the best they could. Getting kicked out of the school because I snapped at the Chancellor I could've handled. Getting kicked out because my alphas got upset and my body perfumed to calm them down was less than ideal. Was I putting the potential blame wrongly? Yes. Was it too early to give a shit? Also, yes.

"Come on, coffee. Do your fucking job," I mumbled.

Enzo laughed, his arms rubbing against mine. I glared at the alpha who was sitting in the back seat with me. We were all carpooling together since the males wanted to be with me for as long as possible. Jen drove and Aidan was stuck in the front seat, apparently having lost the game of dibs to sit in the back with me. The sun wasn't even up, so I couldn't fathom playing any sort of game.

"Tell me about what classes we're sitting through today," Aidan said from the front seat. I wasn't sure how they decided the days, but Aidan was coming to class with me today and Wednesday. Enzo on Tuesday and Thursday.

I glared at the more awake alpha, taking another sip of my coffee, but obliged. "I have Jen's in the morning, which is quantum mechanics. Obviously."

"Obviously," Jen added. His eyes meet mine through the review mirror, and I stuck my tongue out.

"Then it's a little break before Intro to Solid-State Electron Physics."

Enzo whistled. "That's impressive."

"It's a lot," I admitted. "But I've made it this far." Even if I still had pretty far to go.

****

I wasn't sure what surprised me more. The early time for the meeting with the chancellor, or the fact his secretary was already in. Just the thought of how early she had to wake up had me gulping down my coffee.

"Welcome, welcome," the secretary said with a chirp. The little name plate on her desk said Anne Wallen, and a single inhale told me she was a beta. It was impressive that a beta was a secretary for the chancellor, especially since we weren't allowed to attend or work at this academy a few years ago. "You must be Miss Tucker. Mr. Kelly is looking forward to meeting with you. I'll go ahead and let him know you're here."

Instead of calling on the intercom or something more typical, Anne continued typing away on her computer. I watched her long nails rapidly moving along the pink mechanical keyboard, occasionally reaching for a bright pink thermos with the words, "World's Best Secretary" written in a pretty font. I was definitely seeing a theme. After a few moments, she told us to have a seat, motioning to the little waiting area to her right.

Honestly, I had no idea how the chancellor could be anything other than ready at this time of the morning, but I kept my lips busy working on my coffee. Each inhale brought me the scents of my alphas, delicious coffee, Anne's beta scent, and a strong scent of cut wood which I assumed belonged to the chancellor.

Five minutes later, the door to the office finally opened. Chancellor Kelly smoothed down invisible wrinkles on his vest that already look pristinely ironed. I wasn't sure what I expected from the chancellor, but the intimidating alpha in front of me was not it. His whole body screamed that the alpha worked out, and not in the lithe way like Jen. Oh no, this alpha was jacked, his pants and shirt working overtime to stay intact around his bulging muscles. He didn't have any hair on his head, making his features seem more pronounced but without any ounce of kindness. Which was a harsh description, but he did make me wake up before the sun.

The stereotype for omegas was to want alphas like Chancellor Kelly. Muscles were supposed to intrigue and invite us. Something about virility and fertility— according to erotica—but the only emotion I got from the large alpha in front of me was fear.

Jen reached for my hand, squeezing my fingers and bringing my awareness back to my body. If I thought the scent of wood was strong in the waiting area, it was nothing compared to now.

"Hello, Miss Tucker," the chancellor said on a drawl, his eyes immediately narrowing in on the grip

Jenson had on my hand, the disgust evident in the tightening of his lips. He didn't smile or make any attempt to put me, or my alphas, at ease, at least until Jen growled at the Chancellor.

He quickly cut the sound off, squeezing my hand in a non-verbal apology. "There's no need to stare," Jen said through gritted teeth.

Anger flashes in the chancellor's eyes but, in this, my alpha didn't back down. His confidence was evident in his strong posture—almost challenging in its presence—and I had to fight back the urge to remind Jen not to piss off the male that controlled whether I continued getting my education here. And his employment status.

Instead, I cleared my throat and stood up. "Yes, um, that's me. It's nice to meet you, Chancellor Kelly." Everyone in the room knew it was a lie, but I maintained the formality. He couldn't kick me out for perceived lies, right?

"Come into my office. There's no need for us to have this discussion out here." Kelly didn't wait for us to answer, turning sharply on his heels and marching back into his office.

I followed Jen, Enzo behind me. Aidan was last to enter, closing the door behind him. The tension in the smaller, enclosed space was borderline choking. Like smoke but somehow even less pleasant. Maintaining my beta status meant pretending the scents didn't affect me as strongly as they truly did.

Just like Anne's desk, there was nothing on Chancellor Kelly's desk to make it personal. The only decorations on his walls were his diplomas and other certificates he was obviously proud of if the expensive looking framings were indicator.

"So," Chancellor Kelly started off, "this rumor is

true?"

I almost snorted at the phrasing—and would have if Kelly wasn't glaring at my bonded alpha—because I knew there was no rumor. Or there wasn't until Knox directly told the chancellor. For some reason, I liked to believe the betas in my dorm wouldn't spread rumors about me being in a pack for no other reason than some preconceived designation solidarity. Although, was it technically a rumor if it was true? Either way, I didn't think the betas were behind Chancellor King demanding this meeting.

"I've bonded with Koda, yes," Jen said.

"And the others?"

"No. Just me." Chancellor Kelly seemed to relax, slightly, before Jen added, "For now. As soon as Koda is ready, she'll take on Enzo and Aidan's mark."

Those dark brown eyes took in Enzo and Aidan, and both alphas nodded in agreement to Jenson's words.

"You marked a beta?" I couldn't tell if Kelly was disgusted or interested, but either way, this wasn't a good line of questioning to go down. His scent was skillfully under control, giving me no hints to the way this conversation was going to go.

Jenson seemed to agree with my inner thoughts, because he responded in a tone that said he refused to expand on the question. "Yes."

"Do you care to tell me what went through your mind when you bonded with a student?"

"Respectfully, Chancellor Kelly," Aidan said, pulling the Chancellor's attention. "We don't need to justify to you, or anyone, who we decide to bond. Our pack is our private matter."

"This alpha is a professor who marked not only a student at this academy but one of his own students. Respectfully," Chancellor Kelly said tauntingly, "how should I handle this situation?"

"There's nothing to handle," Aidan said, shrugging.

Kelly snorted, obviously displeased and amused by Aidan's answer. "And that's why you were not fit to be Chancellor. Tough decisions need to be made, and you're ill-equipped to make them. This whole situation is unprecedented."

Aidan didn't seem bothered by Kelly's words and actually ignored the attack on his character to defend our relationship. "It's not against any of the academy's bylaws."

"Because no one needed to state an alpha and beta at this academy shouldn't bond."

"If you're worried I will give special treatment to Koda's grades, then we can have another professor review and grade her work," Jenson suggested. "I have plenty of friends in the faculty that would be willing to grade a single additional assignment."

"And what? Your relationship with a beta should simply be allowed to stand?" Kelly demanded. "Do you not worry about the toxic environment you have created for a bonded beta? Think of how the other students will treat her."

"Are you incapable of protecting your students?" Enzo asked, his voice threatening.

"Of course, we will do our best," Kelly said. His eyes slid toward me for only a moment before he looked back at Enzo. "But the students on campus are plentiful and outnumber the staff considerably. We won't be able to protect her fully."

Jen's grip on my hand tightened.

I squeezed his hand back, reminding him I was okay, that I still wanted this. Potential threats were not going to stop me after years of hard work.

"Her other mates are willing to guard her during her other classes for the time being."

"And if she is threatened?" Kelly demanded. "Who is going to protect the other students from her mates?"

No one spoke, having nothing to add to Kelly's comment. I didn't think adding that if a bully targeted me, he or she would receive whatever they deserved as a punishment from my alphas because I didn't think that would've been helpful. Though it was true.

It was Enzo that finally broke the silence. "You are basing all the scenarios as worst case. The students might be more curious than aggressive about Koda's relationship. Do not let your own opinions cloud your judgement on an innocent student."

Chancellor Kelly growled, the sound dangerous before he quickly stopped himself. "And what about you?" Chancellor Kelly asked Jenson.

"What about me?"

"Are just going to allow your bonded mate to trapeze about campus? You have responsibilities here, and I will not be permitting you to take a leave of absence since your mate is not an omega."

I hadn't considered that alphas were technically allowed a month's leave after bonding with their omegas. It wasn't technically a law, but most work environments found it necessary since alphas separated from their newly bonded omegas were typically aggressive.

"If you aren't going to allow it, then there's nothing more on that topic to discuss." The words sounded pulled from Jen, like he hated to admit it.

There was another pause before Chancellor Kelly leaned forward on his desk. "Fine. If Professor Jenson can find a faculty member to grade Koda's work, without the additional pay that comes from another student, and the majority of the other students do not protest, she can remain at the academy."

All the air seemed to rush from my lungs, making my next breath full, clean and filled with happiness. I smiled at Jen first and then Aidan and Enzo, content with the outcome. I hadn't been aware my position at the academy was already kicked out, but I'd been reinstated so I tried not to think too much about it. Because this was actually going to work. I was going to get my alphas and my degree.

I missed the last part of whatever Chancellor Kelly said, but considering he hasn't spoken to me at all during this meeting, I didn't really care. Maybe I should've been more assertive, but I didn't want to draw any more attention to myself than was necessary. I simply wanted to fly under the radar, and if that meant letting my alphas fight on my behalf, I was all for sitting still and looking pretty.

My alphas moved to leave, and I stood with them, but when I stopped to toss my empty coffee cup away, I couldn't help but look back at the chancellor. I didn't see the disgust I'd expected when I met Chancellor Kelly's eyes. It was there when he looked at my alphas, but when his eyes meet mine, there was a softness to them. Maybe he felt bad for the action he took against me, or he thought the same as Knox—that as soon as my alphas tired of a beta I would be tossed out.

It was harder than I thought to push away the concern following that train of thought. I wasn't really a beta, but I wasn't really an omega either. Would my alphas tire of dealing with a broken omega? Or maybe become too frustrated with dealing with the students here? Was I even strong enough to deal with a broken heart from Jen—let alone all three alphas?

No. That was an easy answer. I wasn't that strong.

"Stop worrying," Jen said, wrapping me up in a tight hug when we got outside Kelly's office building. His scent calmed me more than his words, so I got up to my tip toes, wrapping my arms around his neck to pull him down, taking deep breathes. "Kelly tried to scare us with what he assumed were logical question we hadn't considered, so we should take the whole encounter as a win."

The negative voice in the back of my head that had been warning me my alphas would tire of me was quickly drowned out with each inhale of Jen's calming scent and his soothing words. Typically, Enzo's scent had a drug-like feeling to best combat my emotions, but being able to scent the confidence coming from Jen was calming in its own right.

When Jen pulled away, I was swept up in a hug from Aidan, who spun me around, causing a very high-pitched squeal from me.

"Congrats, Koda bear," Aidan said, right before he pressed his lips to mine in a hard kiss. It was an awkward kiss since my lips were pulled thin in a smile and I was trying my best to not laugh as I literally dangled from Aidan's grip, but neither of those facts seemed to deter Aidan.

"Thank you, Addie." I wiggled my feet and Aidan got the hint to set me back down. My body swayed slightly as I tried regaining my balance from the spinning, and a new pair of hands steadied me.

There were no words, but Enzo pulled my back against his front. A gentle purr coming from his chest had my body relaxing and my eyes falling closed. I wrapped my hands on his forearms and pulled them around me, keeping myself tucked into him. When I felt the tip of his nose draw a line down my neck, my body couldn't decide if it wanted to be languid or taunt.

"I like the look on your face, Orsetta," Enzo said, his voice thick, making his accent stronger. I turned my head to smile at the alpha, half amused he had to break his neck to be at my eye level and half simply happy to have his attention. "I have to go now. There's some stuff I have to get done before I take you to class tomorrow, so give me a proper goodbye."

It wasn't a question from Enzo—simply a demand—but I didn't mind the authority.

Jen let out a playful growl—at least I thought it was playful. I wouldn't admit it, since I knew I'd have Aidan with me all day, but I was going to miss this alpha. Like a stupid amount. That thought had me rushing to push onto my toes, pulling down Enzo's head to force his lips on mine like he might've disappeared if I didn't kiss him soon enough.

His mouth opened without hesitation, letting his tongue play with mine.

My core clenched, ready to make slick if Enzo was determined to continue mouth fucking me. I ran my hands down his neck, lightly scraping my nails, until I reached his shoulders and then I held on for dear life.

Enzo's arms tightened around me to the point my back was starting to ache from the arch, but the pain had me trying to reach a point on my toes so I could be higher, kiss him harder, leave bruises on his lips—

"Enzo," Jen growled, the single word warning enough to have him pull away.

My lips tried to chase him for a moment, but he returned to his full height and my goal of his lips was lost. Sparks of panic came with the thought of letting Enzo go. It seemed even more impossible to ignore them than reaching his lips without climbing him like a freaking tree.

"You're picking me up after my classes, right?" I

asked. The words were weak, but I didn't care if Enzo knew I was going to miss him. No. I wanted him to know I would miss him, so he was thinking of me all day like I'd be thinking of him. Counting down the time until I could be with him again.

Enzo inhaled deeply like I had done with Jen, his grip tightened around my body as if he was ready to pick me up and sprint away with me. "Yes, Orsetta. I've told my band about needing a flexible schedule for the next few months. Stay with Aidan and when you're done with classes, meet up with Jen."

What I wanted to say was he'd need a flexible schedule for a lot longer than a few months, but since I didn't trust my tongue not to pronounce those traitorous words, I only managed a nod. Every step Enzo took in the direction of the parking lot made me want to call him back. I knew he had duties besides being constantly by my side. The same way I did. We both needed to be able to be separated, even if my reasoning didn't feel worth it right now.

I took a fortifying breath, tucking away my longing for Enzo underneath my need to get my degree and my happiness with having Aidan and Jen in my first class.

"Okay." I reached out for both Jen's and Aidan's hands, needing contact with both of them. "If I'm going to get through class today, I need more caffeine. Maybe a Romano with a double shot. Yeah, that sounds good. But we have to hurry if we're going to get to class on time. And by on time, I mean for Jen. Technically, it will still be early for me."

"I think you're already caffeinated enough," Jenson said.

I shook my head before he'd even finished talking. "Coffee, even the strong kind you have, isn't enough to get me through the day. I need an espresso shot" —or ten— "or I'll get tired and cranky."

"Don't want a crabby Koda bear," Aidan added.

"We'll get an espresso machine for home," Jen said in his signature, stern teacher-esq voice, earning a glare from me. There was something about being on campus that made me feel braver in regards to my relationship with my posh alpha. It probably helped that we'd just come from a meeting where he defended our relationship to a male that had the ability to punish him for his involvement with me. "Then we can work on cutting your caffeine intake back. But for today, I guess we will have to indulge your bad habits."

I was about to argue with my alpha when Aidan squeezed my hand, pulling my attention. He gave me a secretive wink. "C'mon, let's go get our mate's grind on."

Both Jenson and I groaned at the terrible pun.

JOSEPHINE LIGHT

Chapter Twenty-Six

My first sip of my Romano hit the spot. My second was just as good. But then Jen started leading us back toward his classroom, and my nerves grew sip after sip, my Romano becoming less delicious. I wanted to blame the drink for somehow losing its delicious flavor, but the truth was more than just my drink was ruined. My nerves were turning my stomach to lead, tightening my throat until every sip felt like work.

When we finally made it to Jen's classroom, the sun had started rising, but the temperature was still so cold that the inside of the room felt like I'd walked into a meat locker. After putting his stuff down on his desk, my bonded alpha pulled my shivering body to his, letting me steal his body heat as the heater got to work.

"This is going to be fine, little bear," Jen said softly. "Luck is on our side that this is your first class. It'll help us ease into separating."

Just the thought of not being near Jen had me panicking. I wasn't worried about my safety. I just didn't trust others to not flirt with my mate. My bonded alpha didn't have a mark saying, 'fuck off' or another pack member to make sure no one came too close. And I knew plenty of females flirted with my sexy professor. I'd literally been in a 'pay attention to me' contest with them, and I was sure surrounding his desk with pretend questions after class wasn't a one-time thing. My natural defenses kicked in, turning my nerves into anger at the prospect of anyone flirting, touching, or begging for attention from my bonded alpha.

I tightened my grip on Jen, suddenly wanting to wrinkle his clothes like the fabric could be my temporary mark on him. My omega side felt pretty confident I could hold Jen's attention against any betas, but my beta side was telling me we were replaceable in the view of an alpha. Wrinkling his clothes it was.

Small shoulder shakes told me my intentions weren't hidden from a laughing Jen, but he didn't let me go, tightening his grip around me, so I assumed he agreed with my plan.

Wanting to thrive off my natural omega confidence, I let that side of me take control. When I took a deep breath, and the sweet scent of an alpha's possessive pheromones filled my nose. The ones telling anyone nearby he wanted to grab me and run us back to my nest so no one could look at me, scent me, talk to me, really, exist around me. A shudder ran down my whole body, and I exhaled a shaky breath, finding comfort in the mildly aggressive scent.

"How come I can scent your alpha instincts more now?" I asked Jen, though my voice came out muffled since my face was still plastered to his chest.

"It's getting harder to distract myself," he said. "Taking you out yesterday was easy since my alpha instincts wanted to show you off. To prove to everyone you're claimed and mine. Plus, you were by my side for the whole time."

"But you wanted me to cover up my claiming mark."

Jen shrugged, a half-smile on his face. "Instincts don't always make sense. I want everyone to see the mark and know you're claimed, but I don't want anyone looking at you. A claiming mark on a ... beta would definitely draw attention. My brain and instincts aren't really aligned with you, little bear."

My alpha's gaze dropped to where my claiming mark was currently hidden under my sweater. The look on his face was a mix between annoyance and pride, which must make the worst kind of headache. I could relate. My own instincts were a constant contradiction to which side of me was in charge. It must've been hard to feel the alpha instincts toward an omega but treat me like a beta.

"Are we going to be able to do this?" I hated asking the question, and the subsequent guilt that made my beautiful alpha wince, but it was necessary.

"We agreed we would claim you, publicly, as our bonded beta. I think that's our best shot. Omegas and their alphas go out in public all the time, and all the students here know how to deal with newly bonded mates. And I have some experience being with betas. That should help me keep my instincts in check."

"Just remember," Aidan said, drawing my attention to where he was sitting next to us. "Despite whatever your omega instincts tell you, you don't have to worry about Jen. He is going to teach and then come find you. I bet he'll even cut his last class short to come see you."

Jen looked annoyed with Aidan but also pleased that the blond alpha was on my side. Yes, he was in for a headache, indeed. And a perfect summarization of us right now—walking, talking, breathing, living contradictions.

Soon after our conversation died down, and Aidan started working on his laptop while Jen placed pieces of paper saying "keep vacant" on all the desks immediately around me, students started showing up. Jen, my mate, quickly turned into Professor Jenson.

Students slowly filled the available seats.

A growl threatened to release from me when a female student found a spot in the front row by my alpha's desk. I was immediately distracted by the feeling of falling. Or technically, sliding. Aidan had moved my chair closer to his, so our shoulders touched. My body relaxed at the simply touch.

"Anytime you need it, you can scent me," Aidan whispered. "It might not be as comforting as Jen's, but my scent should help you."

I leaned into his side, purposefully scenting him and even kissing his cheek. "I love your scent. It reminds me of a storm. I can smell the rain, blooming flowers, and even the calming quite like all the animals are patiently waiting for the storm to end."

Aidan's eyes went wide, his scent becoming sweeter, turning my cheeks a bright red. His eyes roamed my face, spotting the color on my cheeks, which had one side of his lips turning up into a sexy smirk.

"You have a way with words, Koda bear." There was a sense of awe in his words that didn't match the lust in his scent. His tongue peeked out, licking his bottom lip in a way that was surprisingly seductive.

Enzo had started the fire in me before he left, but the heated embers were gaining oxygen. I tightened my thighs together, slowly moving one up and down as if I could alleviate the sudden need.

The smirk fell from Aidan's lips when his nostrils flared, obviously scenting my arousal. Since I wasn't leaking slick yet, it was obvious spending time near me had sharpened his nose to the changes in scents.

And why was that such a turn on?

The thought of how well my alpha knew my needs excited my body. I felt the slick leak onto my underwear. My layers—soaked in Jen's scent before we left the house—hid the majority of my scent, but any omega would be able to scent it. If I couldn't get myself under control, I would attract alphas.

My bonded alpha suddenly appeared, bending over my desk, his face so close to mine I couldn't look at

Aidan anymore. I locked eyes with Jen's brown ones, but his nearness—even his temper— didn't do anything to dissuade my arousal.

Jen parted his lips like he'd wanted to say something, but with his dilated pupils, harsh breathing, and rough grip, I knew he was feeling the consequences of my arousal through the bond.

When Aidan pushed Jen's chest away from me, I wanted to growl at the retreating promise of pleasure, but neither alpha focused on me, their attention solely on each other.

I couldn't focus on what Aidan whispered to Jen, but my bonded alpha glanced over at me, still posturing with his packmate. I didn't want them posturing, though.

"C'mon, Koda bear," Aidan said. He grabbed my hand, pulling me out of my chair and away from my bonded alpha.

My feet struggled, wanting to stay with Jen, wanting my alpha and the pleasure I knew he could've given me.

"Go with him, little bear." Jen's voice sounded hostile, but even with my raging hormones, my instincts would do anything to please my alpha. Even walk away when needing sexual release.

Aidan dragged me out of the classroom and all the way through the courtyard for this group of buildings. Then he hurried us into a bathroom. When he locked the door behind us, he wasted no time pushing me against it, slamming his lips on top of mine in a desperate kiss.

I didn't even hesitate. I needed release from the tension in my body, and Aidan was promising it to me. My pussy was fluttering around nothing, my core adding oxygen to the heat inside me, and my nipples tightened to such sharp points so quickly they actually tingled.

He started taking off all my clothes, not just the

ones covering my lower half, but he never stopped kissing me. His lips trailed down my jaw, along my neck, biting the sensitive skin with silent promises to mark me soon.

My hands reached for his hair, reveling in something to hold on to. I gripped the blond locks so I was putting constant tension on his head. Another growl had more slick running down my thigh, the air cooling it and sending shivers up my body.

Aidan went down to his knees, his face at the perfect level to kiss my pubic area and for him to look up at me, sending a wave of euphoric power into my system.

"We have to be quick, beta, before your arousal clings to me." Aidan licked the slick from my thighs, his tongue continuing to travel up until he met my pussy. He moaned like my taste was a delicious treat. His hands trailed up my thighs, his thumbs grabbing my pussy lips and pulling them apart so I was completely exposed to him.

I couldn't decide between letting my head fall back, closing my eyes, or watching Aidan as he fucking devoured me, licking at the slick leaking from my core, occasionally biting my pussy lips and thighs like he was ensuring I was paying attention to him.

"More, alpha. Please. Please." The words came out as a plea, a demand, a frustration.

Aidan let go of my pussy lips, pressing a long finger inside me while his lips moved up to capture my clit.

My walls tightened around the intrusion, wanting more. When he pulled his finger out, I whimpered, but he didn't pay me any attention. He placed his wet finger on my clit at the same time he shoved a new finger inside me.

I threw my head back, but the dull pain wasn't

enough to distract me as he started thrusting his finger inside me while his opposite hand rubbed the nub of my sensitive clit.

My feet went up on tip toes, trying to get away even as I pulled Aidan's head to follow my rising body. My lungs were simultaneously breathing hard and barely working, as if sucking in oxygen was no longer a subconscious activity and I had to force my lungs to work.

"You're doing so good, Koda bear. Do you need more to come?"

I nodded rapidly, not having the words but mentally shouting pleas for more.

Luckily, Aidan understood. I watched him suck on his own finger before demanding I spread my thighs a little wider and bend at the waist so my breasts were by his face. My body responded without hesitation. Instead of tonguing my breasts, Aidan spread my ass cheeks and pressed his wet finger into my back hole. My ass clenched on instinct and Aidan pulled his fingers out of my core to slap my ass.

"Don't clench," he growled, forcing my body to obey on pure instinct.

With one finger in my ass, he shoved two into my sopping pussy. Even on his knees, Aidan radiated pure confidence, giving me a smirk, before moving both hands. When one went in, he pulled the other out, constantly stimulating me.

My body was near its breaking point, my climax so close the pleasure was moments from exploding, and then Aidan pressed his thumb against my clit as he took one nipple into his mouth, biting, and breaking me.

Every muscle in my body tightened as the peak of pleasure rolled through me. My breath caught in my lungs, my legs started shaking from holding me up, and my stomach felt like I'd just done an abdominal work out. The blood that was pooling in my clit, making me lightheaded, started returning to my head, returning my ability to function properly, and I realized Aidan was still on his knees.

He finally pulled his fingers out of me, and his lips left small kisses along my hips. I watched every kiss, giving him a huge smile.

Satisfied, my omega side retreated, letting my beta instincts and scent envelope me.

"Good?" Aidan asked.

"Amazing," I said on an exhale.

Aidan chuckled and slowly stood back up, his hands never leaving my body. Not like he was trying to stroke my arousal but more like he was making sure I wouldn't fall over—which was entirely possible after that orgasm.

"I've been wanting to do that since we talked in the coffee shop weeks ago. But as much as I'd like to let you relax and enjoy the effects of a good orgasm, we need to get back to class soon," Aidan said, reminding me he just went down on me in a public bathroom. The blush didn't just stain my cheeks but somehow heated my whole face and down my neck.

We quickly washed up, making sure to clean off any dried-up cum on my body, and I tossed out my underwear, sighing at another pair lost.

"I'm going to need more underwear," I said, mostly to myself.

The look of pride on Aidan's face had me rolling my eyes.

Once we were dressed, Aidan pulled me against him for one more kiss. It wasn't hot, but slow and sweet, as if he was thanking me for letting him go down on me. I pretended like I couldn't taste myself on his lips and tongue because if I got turned on again, I would demand another round. And maybe even his knot. Definitely his knot.

JOSEPHINE LIGHT

Chapter Twenty-Seven

The door to Jenson's class was closed, which meant I was officially late.

With my hand in his, Aidan dragged me down the steps to the front row, his grip tight.

I stared intently at the back of his head, ignoring the feeling of the stares in my direction. Usually, classes weren't overwhelming with scents for my nose since people were typically relaxed. During the weeks prior to midterms and finals, the scents of stress became stronger, but the consistency was usually what helped me handle the overwhelming aspect. And this semester, I'd learned to not sit near any of the students lusting after Professor Jenson.

Now, though? The mix of emotions was like walking into a perfume store right after someone sampled every available scent. There was beta frustration, alpha disgust, along with curiosity and even lust. A headache immediately formed above my eyes, and I tried to discreetly breathe through my mouth.

Even the space Jenson commandeered to separate me from the others wasn't enough of a barrier. As soon as I sat down, I tapped on Aidan's shoulder, forcing him to lean in like I was going to whisper to him. Instead, I took several deep breathes of his scent, trying to drown out all the other emotions with Aidan's satisfied one. He might not have gotten off, but apparently having me come all over his face was enough to put the alpha in a good mood. His face smelled like my release, but my omega perfume wasn't too noticeable on him as long as no one got too close.

I looked up to meet Jenson's eyes as he was writing a page number on the board. The tension in his back was obvious, and the need to soothe him had me trying to get up from my seat.

A large hand on my thigh stopped me. "Offer me your drink, Koda bear," Aidan whispered.

My hand moved to follow the command without thinking, and I watched Aidan's lips take a sip of my drink. His instant pinched face had me giggling, drawing the attention of Jen and some other students behind me, who growled.

"Do not growl at my beta," Jenson snapped. Dominance rolled off him, and I held back a whimper, before he quickly pulled it back.

The tension in the room skyrocketed, but a few students mumbled apologies even if they sounded forced.

Apparently, I'd missed the part where Jen admitted he had a bondmate. When I tried to discreetly look behind me, I found several pairs of eyes already staring in my direction.

"There's no way he actually bonded her," a female muttered.

"He's probably just fucking her and had to say they were going to bond so she doesn't freak out," another female answered.

"Yeah, but why her?" the first female asked, an annoying whining quality to her voice telling me she was one of the post-class question askers.

"His whole pack only dates betas. There's no way they can each go from having their own beta to sharing one. She'll be kicked to the curb soon enough."

I did my best to focus on Jen when he finally pulled away from writing on the board to lecture, but I felt more like a dictation service, writing down all his words and diagrams without really absorbing the information. My ears were picking up whispers and I was constantly needing to inhale Aidan's delicious scent to calm my nerves and drown out the more unpleasant smells.

Aidan did his best to stay in contact with me, whether it was our thighs touching, our arms, or him grabbing the back of my neck, massaging the muscles to help ground me. Truthfully, it helped calm my omega side. But it was my beta side unable to focus on the lecture.

How would I graduate if I couldn't pay attention in class?

Class quickly came to an end, but before we packed up, Jenson announced, "I will not be available to answer questions after class for the foreseeable future."

Groans and complaints immediately followed his declaration, but my own heart leapt, and I had to fight back a smile. I should've hated that Jen had to change up his routine to make accommodations for me, but I hadn't asked him to make this decision. He was doing it for me and honestly, it felt wrong to not appreciate it.

"The Academy states you need to be available to all your students," a female said, placing an emphasis on the word 'all', her voice raising above the others to demand attention. She sounded suspiciously like the first female I'd heard talking shit earlier. Now that she'd drawn attention to herself, I had no quarrels with turning around to check her out. To say I wasn't even surprised it was the brunette bitch that argued with me a couple days ago around Jen's desk would've been an understatement. I was pissed, and both sides of my instincts wanted to growl at her.

"I will always be available to all my students, Miss Crow. If you have any questions, you should have my email in the syllabus. I will make sure to respond in an orderly time, but if you need more immediate help, there are tutors in the library. Their schedules are posted on the library doors, and I'll even make sure to get a schedule to hang up in my class. Now, you're all excused. Have a nice day."

The sound of everyone packing up wasn't enough to drone out the criticisms of our relationship from the females. I wished they would've suddenly become sick enough to not attend the academy. Not like, deathly sick, but the kind where they couldn't come to class for the next month. Or two. Then be totally fine.

There were only a few minutes I could spend with Jen before my next class started. My nerves about separating from him were getting harder to push away. The moment he shut the door on his last student, my legs carried me to him.

Without hesitating, he pulled me against him, inhaling deeply like he wanted to memorize my scent.

Tears burned the back of my eyes, threatening to fall. They were definitely turning my eyes red and making me snort to stop from rubbing snot on Jen's nice clothes.

The logical part of my brain understood I was only going to be away from my bonded alpha for like, two hours, but the emotional part felt like it was going to be forever.

With my head on Jen's chest, I felt the beating of his heart, the deep inhales he was taking of my scent, and the tight grip on the back of my clothes keeping me pressed against him. Usually, inhaling my alpha's scent would be calming, but I could scent the anxiety on Jen, which made me nervous, flooding Jen with my worries down the bond and continuing this vicious cycle between us.

That was the catch with Jen. He was always taking care of me, making sure I was happy. Like cancelling after-class questions and agreeing to come get me as soon as possible, no matter how inconvenient it would be for his other students.

"It'll be okay?" I meant to reassure my alpha, but my comfort came out more as a request.

"Of course, little bear. This is all just instincts, not logic."

I nodded along to Jen's words, knowing their truth even if it felt more foreign than an eyelash on my eye.

"I want you to stay close to Aidan, okay?"

Alpha command laced his tone, sending goosebumps down my arms, and teasing me with the opportunity to please him by following his order. "Yes, alpha."

"I'll stick to her like a fly on shit," Aidan said.

I chuckled against Jen's chest, turning my head slightly so I could see Aidan. He was wearing a wide smile, an obviously pleased look on his face from making me laugh.

There was something lighthearted about Aidan, like the alpha was determined to always be in a good mood. He gave off a carefree vibe that was mostly his personality, but his long hair and clothes definitely helped cement who Aidan was. But I'd seen the parts of Aidan he tried to hide behind his confidence. He had a need to feel as important as he perceived his other members of his pack, as if he felt like he could be forgotten, left out.

"Are you ready to go, Addie?" I didn't really want to leave my bonded alpha, but I had incentive to. While being late was a concern, what I really wanted was more alone time with Aidan.

"Definitely, Koda bear."

I went up on my tip toes to kiss Jen goodbye, and my bonded alpha didn't hesitate in taking my lips. But just as quickly as the kiss started, Jenson pulled back, licking his lips like he was savoring the taste of me.

"Your next orgasm is mine, little bear," Jenson whispered against my lips.

For the thousandth time—just today—I blushed, nodding, accepting the rule my bonded alpha just laid out for me.

Aidan playful growled, and I dug my forehead into Jen's chest like I could burrow into his body to hide.

"C'mon, Koda bear. I'm sure the professor here has shit to do before his next class, and we still have a walk to get to your class so you can claim a seat away from people."

Aidan already had his stuff packed up and my own bag over his shoulder. I grabbed his offered hand and walked away from Jen, even as it felt like my heart was left behind in the body of my bonded alpha. I leaned into Aidan, trying to drown out this temporary heartache by inhaling gulps of his scent. Maybe because he could sense I was seconds away from calling it quits and turning back, he began purring, the sound and vibration enough to calm me.

"Where's your beginner's class?" Aidan asked.

I snorted. "It's intro to solid-state electron physics."

"Beginner. Intro. Same thing."

I gasped like I was offended. "'Beginner' is like a first year taking classes. 'Intro' is the equivalent of having an understanding on the topic and being introduced to an advanced concept."

"Are you sitting okay, Koda bear?"

"What the hell are you talking about, Addie?" I stared up at him like his face might reveal something, but he wore a concerned expression, as if I was the one that started asking random questions.

"Well, I figured with those made-up definitions, you must be pulling dictionaries out of your ass. Your little tush must hurt."

I rolled my eyes so hard I was pretty sure I caught a glimpse of my brain.

"That was funny, and you can't convince me otherwise," Aidan said.

"You should quit your day job and be a comedian."

The smile on Aidan's face made me slightly worried he hadn't realized I was being sarcastic. "I think that's a great idea, Koda bear. I tell the others that, and they always disagree. But if you think I'm good enough, then decision made."

"Um, Addie…" I bit my bottom lip, unable to get the words out. If Aidan wanted to be a comedian, who was I to argue he wasn't good enough? All this alpha had done was take my own dreams into consideration, and I needed to do the same. "I think that's a great idea. The coffee shop I like, a little way off campus, puts up flyers for all kinds of events. I bet we could find one for an open-mic night."

Aidan suddenly stopped walking, his purr ratcheting up so anyone walking by could hear it. I leaned farther into his chest, admiring the deep tenor of his purr that felt like a direct compliment.

"You're too good for me, Koda bear."

I shook my head, refusing the statement.

A high-pitched voice I instantly recognized as the professor to my next class was calling my name, interrupting our conversation. Professor Bert Stockfield was probably a year away from retirement—I could hope, at least—with long grayed hair always falling flat like he purposefully straightened it, and a wardrobe consisting of blue jeans and a white button up. You could take a picture of him once a day for a week, mix up the photos, and never be able to tell them apart. He always looked that similar.

He also didn't like me very much. Originally, I'd thought it was because he was sexist, but I quickly learned he had no problem with females—so long as they were alphas. Apparently, Professor Stockfield had been teaching at the Academy for years and was against the integration of betas. I couldn't even imagine how he would've reacted to learning about me being an omega. Probably worse than him learning a beta bonded with an alpha.

"It's true then?" Professor Stockfield demanded. Several classmates had stopped making their way inside to watch our interaction.

"Is what true, Professor?" I did my best to look innocent, but the scent of his hatred, matched with his glare, made me glad Jen wasn't here to see it. Usually Stockfield ignored the betas, graded us harder, but he mostly kept his opinions to himself. Having passed as a beta for my whole life, it wasn't really unique treatment, but more like the expectation.

"You took a perfectly good alpha for your selfish self?"

I opened my mouth to agree, but Aidan beat me to it. "She didn't take anything," he growled.

Aidan was quick to anger. I'd been exposed to Separatist alphas, and even some betas, as long as I could remember. Even if no one had directly spoken this harshly to me before, I'd witnessed it. Seen it in media. Watched it happen to other students. I'd been too afraid to help them. But in a world that treated alphas with respect, Aidan wasn't equipped to handle toxic elites. And I didn't know how to stand up for myself against someone who controlled if I graduated. With that thought, panic seeped in.

Professor Stockfield snorted, his disgusted gaze turning toward Aidan. The two alphas sized one another up, but the posturing between them was quick. Aidan was younger, stronger, and more dominant. When Professor Stockfield tore his gaze away, he sneered at me but didn't say anything else, which was a miracle itself. I didn't doubt Aidan was the reason he didn't give me a detailed description of how he felt regarding my life choices.

Aidan's phone vibrated in his pocket, and he got it out, handing it to me without even looking at the screen.

"Hello, Jen," I said, tentatively. I knew I hadn't done anything wrong, but worrying him was my fault.

"What happened, Koda bear." It wasn't a question but a demand for answers. Jenson's strict teacher-voice sent a shiver down my spine, letting me know if he wasn't pleased with my answer I wouldn't be going to my next class. The students that had stopped had already moved on, but we still had some passersby staring and whispering.

"Nothing. Aidan handled it." It wasn't really a lie even if it wasn't the truth. The silence on the other end of the phone stretched for so long I pulled it away from my ear to make sure he hadn't hung up on me. "Alpha?"

"I don't like not knowing, little bear. And I know if you're hiding what happened, you think I might take you home, so I'm trying to stay calm and not demand answers or just say, 'fuck it' and go find you."

Jen let out a frustrated exhale before asking to speak with Aidan. We said goodbye again and, surprisingly, tears threatened to fall when I handed the phone over. I pressed my forehead against Aidan's chest, almost like I was resting, as I tried to fight back the burn in my eyes and down my nose. I listened to the gentle purr and the reassuring tone of Aidan's voice, both helping to remind my instincts I was fine.

When Aidan finally hung up, he said, "I didn't except such overt anger." I didn't have anything to say about that, and there wasn't really anything to say. "Your class is about to start. Are you ready?" His eyes looked between mine, waiting for my verbal answer as much as he was watching and scenting my reaction.

"Ready as I'll ever be."

Aidan nodded and held the door open for me.

All the classrooms were set up the same, with a desk set up for the teacher in front of either a projection or a whiteboard or occasionally both. Chairs with a little platform, typically on the side which could be pulled up, filled the rest of the room. Whereas Jen's classroom you entered from the back and had to walk down the stairs to get to the teacher's desk, Professor Stockfield's door was right next to his desk, making the students walk up the steps to find a seat.

When Aidan and I walked in, Professor Stockfield was clearing his voice in his signal he was going to start class.

Instead of waiting for him to comment, I made a beeline to the stairs and started climbing. I took a seat against the wall so Aidan could have my other side. While my alpha started unpacking his laptop, I looked up, feeling eyes on me.

Professor Stockfield was glaring in our direction, and I could actually see him considering kicking Aidan out of the class.

Some of the students noticed him looking in my direction and turned around to figure out what was distracting our diligent professor from starting class. But they only saw me and Aidan. Just when the whisperings started, Professor Stockfield got his focus back and started class, managing to ignore me for the rest of the time.

JOSEPHINE LIGHT

Chapter Twenty-Eight

Now that classes for the day were done, we were finally all home, and I felt the weight of the day fall off. My back and shoulders felt sore, like the tension I had carried all day was too heavy for me to bear.

I was adding the finishing touches to an essay due later tonight, sitting at the kitchen bar despite the perfectly available studying somewhere in the house. Jen had showed me all the studies that I could've used, but I'd wanted to be near my alphas, not tucked away. Of course, I could've done that at the dining table, but it looked too fancy for me to be hunched over, reading the same sentence again and again. I couldn't figure out why it sounded like I'd had a stroke in the middle of explaining which quantities were worth paying attention to and which should be ignored.

I let out a frustrated exhale, making Enzo laugh. All of my alphas were in the kitchen with me—Enzo cooking, Jen setting up his lecture for tomorrow, and Aidan on a phone call with some new-name whiskey distributor who wanted to be sold in his clubs.

"Need a break, Orsetta?" Enzo didn't try lowering his voice at all, which had Aidan glaring at him.

Of course, Aidan didn't leave. He just returned to tapping his pencil against his mostly blank notepad.

I nodded to Enzo, shutting my laptop—property of Braker Academy—and placed my head on it.

"Here. I made them to go with dinner, but you can dig in now. Just don't tell my mamma."

I grabbed the thin breadstick, expecting it to be soft and fluffy but finding it more like the consistency of a hard pretzel. Little crumbs fell on my laptop when I broke off a piece, but it tasted really good.

"You made these? Like, from scratch?" I whispered.

Enzo shook his head, lifting the lid of a pot on the stove. He stirred, decided it was all going well, and then turned to face me, resting his elbows on the opposite side of the island counter. "My mamma would beat me if she ever found out I served anyone frozen food. Especially my mate."

Aidan interrupted our conversation, kissing me on the cheek. "I missed a call from my mom while I was talking to the distributor. I'm going to take it in the other room."

"Dinner's basically done. Just needs a few minutes to cool down," Enzo said in warning.

"I'll be quick."

I wanted to follow Aidan and eaves drop on his conversation with his mom, but I figured he was leaving for my sake. I just wasn't sure if that made me feel better or worse.

"Do you talk to your mom a lot?" I asked Enzo. My voice felt extra loud since I'd been whispering, but at least now I didn't feel bad for disrupting Aidan.

"She calls about once a week."

"Wow." I wasn't sure why, but that felt like a lot.

Enzo chuckled. "The rest of my family has dinner together every Sunday. And I wouldn't doubt my mamma still calls them once a week."

"Do you miss them?"

"Yes and no. They're my familia, but I've lived the majority of my life away from them. I guess I got used to it. At least I have a good relationship with my genitori."

Somehow, Enzo had figured out that I liked hearing his other language. He'd started slipping in Italian words where I'd recognize their English meaning.

I mouthed the word for grandparents to myself so I would remember.

"What about you?" I nudged Jenson, more interested in learning about my bonded alpha than worrying about interrupting him.

"My parents? They're dead," Jen said, never looking up from his papers.

The blunt words made me flinch, and I regretted bothering my alpha. I focused my attention on wiping up the crumbs from my laptop. I didn't want the males to think of me as messy. After I spent some time looking around for the trash and refusing to ask where one was, Enzo opened a cabinet near the sink.

My cheeks burned with humiliation, and I silently tossed the crumbs away. Who hid a trash can anyway? With full hands, I wouldn't be able to open the stupid drawer.

Enzo grabbed me around the waist before I could return to my seat, handing me another breadstick to munch on. "He didn't mean to upset you, Orsetta."

"Who upset you?" Jen demanded, interrupting Enzo's supportive words as he finally looked up from his paperwork to glare at the other alpha.

"You did, fratello. Koda wants to learn about you, and you blew her off."

"He doesn't have to talk about his parents if he doesn't want to," I whispered. I understood that he might still be hurting from the loss of his parents, no matter how long ago they'd passed away. Even though I hadn't known, talking about them probably made him defensive, wanting to keep their memory to himself.Jenson eyes filled with too much emotion to meet.

Instead, I poured all my attention to cupping my hand and catching the new crumbs from my breadstick. Sometimes I forgot I barely knew my alphas. The bond might help solidify my place here on an instinctual level, and we were all attracted to each other, but we were still in the bloom of a new relationship. It felt like longer, considering I'd been hiding my crush on Jenson since I'd bumped into him on the first day and low-key insulted him. I'd been so nervous, but I'd had nothing to lose, so I was confident. Now, I was fighting to keep my alphas.

"I'm sorry, little bear." Jen ran a hand over his hair, the short strands barely moving. "There isn't much to tell. They passed away a long time ago, and I don't think about them much."

"You weren't close with your parents?"

"No." Jen extended his hands out to me, wanting me to join him.

When I tried to move, Enzo's hands didn't budge, keeping me pressed against his chest as he growled possessively.

I couldn't help but laugh even as Jen growled at the alpha for keeping me from him.

Enzo leaned down so his lips pressed against the shell of my ear. His teeth gently bit down, but it was enough to set my body on alert. Alphas were predators by nature and my unwillingness to lose an ear kept me in place, but the fear from having Enzo's teeth on me didn't outweigh my desire for his bite—to be claimed by another one of my alphas.

My core clenched at the idea of a knot. I hadn't had one in days, and the empty feeling inside was a tease with no ending in sight. A whine clawed at my throat with an alpha so close to claiming me if he'd just bite down a little harder. My omega instincts took control, causing me to grind back on Enzo, encouraging him to do more.

Whatever we were talking about was forced out by my arousal. We had the rest of our lives to get to know each other.

All I could think about was Enzo. The heat coming from his chest, seeping into my back. The little puffs of air from his nose as his teeth tightened down on my earlobe, keeping me firmly from turning around and demanding more. Even the feel of his cock hardening against my ass. I'd never hated clothes as much as that moment.

Jen growled again, but the sound was much closer. My eyes flew open, although I didn't remember closing them, and I looked straight at Jen's chest. Trapped between two alphas did nothing to calm me down.

Jen's proximity was gasoline to the fire, blooming my arousal so the scent of burnt marshmallows was strong enough to cover even the arousal of my two alphas. My omega growled at the loss of their scents, my body redoubling my efforts to entice them.

I reached for my bonded alpha, wrapping my fingers around his clothes and tugging him so close I could feel the pressure of his body against mine. Untucking his shirt, I ran my fingers up his stomach, letting the material bunch.

Jenson had faint outlines of his abdominal muscles which became more defined as I continued touching him.

The need to kiss or lick the exposed skin had me whining, wanting Enzo to let go of my ear. When he did, I didn't make it an inch toward my goal when his teeth lowered, clamping down on my neck, on the opposite side of my body as Jen's bite. I felt his teeth leave an indent in my skin, forcing my body to go lax.

"Please," I begged. "Bite, alpha. Claim me."

My alpha wouldn't be able to bite me before he knotted me, but that plan was my goal. My need for a knot was controlling all of my actions, and a small part of me was aware of that, but my instincts were in control, and they demanded I get fucked, knotted, and bitten.

I inhaled, trying to figure out if my alphas were gone on my pheromones enough to listen to my demands. It was a vicious cycle of inhaling the scent of arousal, ratcheting up our need, only for the scents to bloom stronger as we inhaled again.

I removed one hand from Jen's stomach to reach behind me. Grabbing the back of Enzo's head, I pressed his face closer to my neck like I could force his claiming bite on me.

My touch seemed to entice Enzo, as the alpha biting down harder. It was still not enough to break the skin and claim me, but enough for my body to tense with anticipation.

Instead of completing the bond, the alpha picked me up and started walking.

Panic had me squirming against Enzo. Despite the need to have him bite and claim, I needed my bonded alpha nearby. I needed to be able to scent him to ensure he was happy. I needed him to make sure I was safe while I let my instincts take over.

"I'm here, omega." The smooth confidence of Jenson's voice set me at ease, letting me sink into Enzo, who'd stopped just on the outside of the door to my nest. "You have to invite us in."

I didn't hesitate. "Come in."

The wording was weird since Enzo never let me go, carrying me in as he entered, but the intention worked. When the door clicked close, it was like the sound set my body in motion. I shoved Enzo into my nest, forcing my lips down to his so I could explore the taste of his mouth with my tongue.

Hands roamed my body, pulling off layers of my

clothes, but I ignored them, needing to push the alpha below me to the level of frenzy I was at.

Somewhere in my nest, I heard my bonded alpha speaking, but the meaning of the words was warbled. But the longer he spoke, the longer he refused to touch me. I finally pulled my lips from the alpha beneath me, turning to release a frustrated growl at my bonded alpha, demanding his attention.

My growl was cut off when a more dominant growl demanded my submission.

Despite the aggressive sound, I preened at my bonded alpha's attention. I wasn't worried about whether he was angry or not, as long as he was focused on me. My beta side was pushed so far to the back of my mind, she didn't even fear the dominant alpha growl.

"You need to think this through, Koda. If you bond Enzo, it'll make attending the academy harder."

The next growl from me was more aggressive. My thighs tightened around the alpha's body beneath me. My fingers gripped the shirt covering his shoulder—even if I didn't want the alpha in clothes, I was glad for the hold. I wanted this alpha to be mine.

My bonded alpha responded with another growl, his frustration bleeding into the sound. The muscles in his cheeks tightened making his jaw more defined. "I'm not saying you can't fuck him. And I'm not even disagreeing you should bond with him. But you're not thinking clearly right now. Are you listening to me, omega?"

A purr pulled my attention away from my bonded alpha to the male pinned under me. The sound was deeper than even my bonded alpha's purr, and there was a tone to it like it was more musical than an instinctual sound.

I inhaled deeply, enjoying the scent of pine trees filling my nest, giving me the safety to feel like we were outside.

I wanted to bond this alpha. My body was already primed and ready for a knot, slick running from my pussy and pooling in my underwear, the last layer between me and the alpha. My muscles were tensed, ready for a bite no matter the location the alpha chose. And my heart already belonged to him.

"Bite, alpha," I whined.

Enzo's blue eyes flared, and he moved so quickly I didn't even have a chance to get dizzy as he put me under him. As he ripped off my panties, I knew I'd have red drag marks from the fabric. Not that I particularly cared.

I tried clawing off the alphas' clothes, needing to feel his skin against mine, but I got distracted with the matting of hair on his chest. The dark curls called to me. I didn't even try repressing the urge to run my fingers through them. When he tried to pull away, I tightened my fingers, but the alpha growled, demanding release. I could scent how aroused the male was, so I let him pull away slightly, trusting he wouldn't leave me hanging now that I was desperate for him.

When he finally leaned down closer to me, I felt the head of his cock at my entrance. With one of his hands, he dragged the tip through my wet folds, always going high enough to rub against my clit.

"You want my cock, Orsetta?" The alpha's voice was thick with lust, making his words almost indecipherable with his accent.

I nodded. The movement was desperate, but I didn't care.

"You want my knot? My bite?"

I moaned and my pussy leaked with excitement at his words. My body was way past being ready for an alpha's knot. Now it was releasing slick to entice him, to demand he finally fill me up. Anything to have the steady alpha be mine. "Yes, alpha."

"And you're going to let me do whatever I want to this body." This time it wasn't a question, but I nodded anyway.

He finally slammed into me, stretching my inner walls as he thrusted every inch of his cock inside. There was no pain, despite his size, only pleasure. The male didn't waste any time for me to adjust, thrusting into me over and over again. It felt like my entire existence revolved around the pleasure thrumming through my body.

I parted my knees, tightening them around his hips to meet each thrust. The feeling was almost too much, as if he was trying to shove his cock through my whole body. Each thrust had me moving from the force, so I reached over his shoulders, digging my nails into the flesh.

He groaned, clearly enjoying the sting of pain mixing with pleasure. Not one to be outdone, a large hand came down to my throat, the fingers careful not to crush my windpipe but pressing into the sides of my neck.

With the weight of him over me, his body spreading my legs and his grip over my throat, I was held captive by the alpha. The thought only pushed me closer to my orgasm, and when I felt his knot expanding, I couldn't hold the pleasure back any longer. My muscles tensed, back arching, as my orgasm beat at me like waves determined to make it to shore.

I was breathing heavy when I could finally focus past my climax. My eyes blinked a few times as they struggled to open, but they manage to be pried open by pure will and determination. Just as quickly as I had gained control over my breath, I lost it looking up at Enzo as he continued forcing his expanding knot into me.

The pleasure he got from using my body was written over his face. His eyes were closed even as his eyebrows came together. His lips were parted just slightly, and his grip tightened around my throat, sending a wave of dizziness to my head.

And then his knot was seated fully inside me. His cock pulsed, releasing his cum, and it all felt like too much. Too much pleasure with no way to release it again. I was on the verge of tears when he pulled his grip away from my neck, and his teeth sunk into my neck in the tender spot just below my ear.

A scream was pulled from my throat, and I wasn't sure if it was in response to the pain or the sudden orgasm forced from my body. I heard movement around the nest, but I didn't have the energy to open my eyes this time. My body felt limp, my throat sore, and my soul completely rung out with pleasure.

I wanted to smile, but the effort to move my cheek muscles was beyond my strength. My omega was purring—no wait, I was purring. I took a deep breath, ready to fall asleep for a few years, only for a familiar scent to snag my attention.

Eyes flying open, I tried searching for the owner, but all I could see was Enzo. My new bonded alpha was leaning against his elbows above my shoulders, his forehead less than an inch from mine as his head hung. His eyes were closed, and his chest touched my breasts with every deep breath.

Tilting my head up, I kissed his forehead.

Enzo's head swung up at the contact, his eyes immediately finding mine.

My lips curled up in smile so wide, it hurt my cheeks. "Alpha," I purred, somehow finding the energy to flirt.

"I like the sound of that, omega." Enzo chuckled,

laughing at his own thoughts. "Mi piace comunque mi chiami. How does your neck feel?"

Without thinking, I touched the spot Enzo just bit. I flinched at the tenderness even as happiness filled me.

My new bonded alpha growled at the feel of my pain, and the need to comfort him had words rushing out of my mouth.

"I'm fine, really. It's only a little tender, but I don't mind. Actually, the soreness is like another reminder it's there, so I like it."

He sighed. "I like it too, Orsetta."

I wanted to stay cocooned in this moment forever, but the scent of another alpha still demanded my attention. Aidan.

But Enzo's body was too large to see anything except his brown skin. Before I could even get the words out, Enzo flipped us so he was on his back, and I moaned at the feeling of his knot tugging inside of me. His chuckle turned into a moan, reminding me he felt my arousal, and it was no doubt going to turn into a vicious cycle of arousal. To ensure we weren't locked together for too long, I gave him a quick kiss, and finally examined my nest.

Jenson was the closest, his pants undone as his cock went back down.

My eyes searched his surroundings for his cum, needing it in me, needing a taste.

He lifted his hand, exposing his fingers covered in cum before offering it to me. I managed to hold myself back from taking his offering immediately, inhaling deeply to scent his emotions. The scent of arousal still lingered, along with pride, but also the slight tang of jealousy.

"Lick," Jenson said. The command mixed with the need to please my first alpha had me reaching for his wrist without any more hesitation. I licked at the cum, sucking his fingers into my mouth until there wasn't a drop left. "Good girl."

I couldn't help the blush staining my cheeks. I'd just licked one male's cum while another was inside me still. And I wanted more.

I looked for Aidan, finding him too far away.

Instead of being in the nest with us, Aidan stood just inside the door, a look of distress on his face even as he tried to fake a smile for me.

Worry gripped my heart, threatening to bring sad tears into what was supposed to be a time for celebration. But I couldn't blame Aidan for his emotions. Of course, he felt left out. My beautiful alpha was sensitive. It was why I'd given him a nickname just for me to use. But my instincts hadn't taken feelings into account, and I'd let them take control. The throbbing on my neck seemed more apparent than it did a second ago, like a neon sign blinking and reminding me of what was causing Aidan pain.

"Alpha." I reached for Aidan, not making it very far with my core still locked around Enzo's knot. The tug on my insides felt like a harsh slap of reality. I wanted to comfort Aidan, but how did I do that without upsetting Enzo? I should've been paying my new alpha attention. And then there was Jenson, my first alpha who might not have been ready to add another alpha to my pack. Sure, he loved his pack brothers, but to have them claim me without making sure he was comfortable with our relationship was selfish.

"Little bear?"

I looked over at Jen, unable to stop the first tears from dripping down my cheeks.

"No, Koda, no crying." He moved closer to me and Enzo, wrapping me up in a hug despite the awkward angle. Enzo's hands wrapped around my hips, and both my bonded alphas purred.

"I'm sorry," I sobbed. I couldn't stop the tears, my guilt needing a way out.

"Koda bear, why are you crying?" Aidan asked. His voice was still far away, and the realization that Aidan refused to come into my nest had the tears falling harder. Rejection was like a wall surrounding my lungs, not letting my lungs expand to get a deep inhale, making each breath constricted.

I reached for Aidan, needing him to touch me, to prove he didn't hate me.

Aidan hesitated, his body obviously racked with indecision to join me. A sob fell from my lips and a pained look crossed his face. If he didn't want me to cry, why wouldn't he come to me?

"You need to invite him into the nest," Jenson said. "Use your words, little bear. He wants to go to you. Can't you see how he holds himself back?"

I did see it, but I'd thought it was because his mind and heart were at war—not because he was following his alpha instincts. I wondered if this was just another thing the Compound would've taught me.

"Please, Addie." I reached for him with both hands like I wanted him to pick me up. Whether it was the words or the action, he finally entered my nest, falling to his knees and holding me tightly to him.

As the pressure released from around my lungs, I finally took in a deep breath, inhaling Aidan's scent, ravaged with negative emotions. I wanted to whine at the knowledge, but I didn't want my alpha to think he couldn't have emotions, so I kept the sound locked away.

Under me, Enzo adjusted himself, sitting up so I had all three of my alphas surrounding me, touching me. Jenson's scent helped calm me, his hands traveling around my collarbone and breasts, hardening my nipples into points that begged for attention. Enzo gently scrapped his nails along my spine, causing my back to arch and my pussy to squeeze. And then there was Aidan, his hand having found a place in my hair, holding me tightly and close to him as his pain turned into arousal around me.

There was no chance for me to fight my arousal blooming again. My hips moved, rocking against the cock already inside me. Instead of helping, the movement seemed to make my arousal worse. With Enzo's knot still inside me, I felt full, but I needed more stimulation. I needed to be taken, for a cock to pound into me and an alpha to hold me down.

I groaned in frustration, my hips becoming frantic without any success. Enzo's fingers continue down my back, spreading my cheeks as one of his fingers pressed against my back hole.

Yes. That was what I needed.

I pushed against his hand, but he moved his finger away. Glaring at the alpha, I tried to move my ass farther back, but I was fucking stuck on his cock.

"You need something, Orsetta?" Enzo's teasing tone had me growling again. "I think our little omega needs to be filled up."

I nodded frantically. I pushed against Enzo's chest until he laid back down, and flattened my own chest against him, ignoring Jen's annoyed growl at losing my breasts. Grabbing one ass cheek in each hand, I spread myself until my back hole was exposed.

"Please, alpha," I whined. I didn't care which alpha filled me up, I just knew I needed it.

Aidan growled, the sound sending goosebumps along my body. I heard shuffling as the males moved around in my nest, but all I could do was wait.

"Open your mouth, omega," Jenson said.

I lifted my head and parted my lips, excited for another taste of my alpha's cum. I was already moaning at the idea of his cum running down my throat as I licked the head of his cock so my mouth could fit over it smoothly. The veins on Jen's cock teased my tongue as I licked down his length before going back up and taking as much of his cock as I could.

Male voices were speaking around me, but I wasn't listening. I wanted Jen's cum and popping off him to ask what the hell they were talking about would only cause a delay. Taking more of Jen into my mouth, my throat gagged on him before I pulled back. My tongue swiped against the head, swirling it around and digging against the slit like I could lick the cum from him.

A hand near my ass pulled a portion of my attention from Jen's cock. Despite being plugged by Enzo's cock, my pussy continued leaking a mix of mine and his cum. Fingers trailed up from my sopping pussy and between my cheeks. Wet from collecting my release, Aidan's fingers pressed gently against the hole Enzo had teased. I tried pushing back and this time, it worked. Aidan's fingers weren't calloused like Enzo's, which felt better against the sensitive muscles as my hole learned to stretch.

He started working the finger in and out before adding a second and then eventually a third. When he pulled his hand out, it was quickly replaced with the head of his cock. The pressure of him pushing into me was unpleasant at first, and I gasped at the intrusion. But the deeper Aidan pushed, the more familiar I became with the movement.

Just like he did with his fingers, he gently pushed in and out, going deeper with each thrust until he was pushed into me as deep as he could go. Seated all the way inside me, his piercing pressed against my ass hole, like a marker he'd reached the end of his length.

I could hear his heavy beathing, feel his fingers tighten around my hips as he fought for control. My own climax was dangerously close as Aidan became more aggressive with his thrusts. I let my alphas take control, opening my mouth and allowing Jen to fuck my face as Aidan took my ass.

"Are you listening to me, Orsetta?" Enzo asked, his demand for an answer somehow penetrating the fog of my mind.

I couldn't answer with Jen using my mouth for his pleasure, but somehow, Enzo must've noticed I was finally listening to him.

"Do you like having Aidan in your ass?"

I moaned, the sound almost pained, as I tried to voice my love for having my ass fucked for the first time by Aidan.

"I was thinking now would be a good time for him to claim you."

The alpha in question definitely liked that idea, his thrusts becoming harsher. The bite of pain coming from my first time doing anal was barely enough to get my thoughts to focus on understanding the words.

"Would you like that, Orsetta?"

I whined at the thought of being claimed again. Our pack would be complete, and that alone was enough to convince me, but the fact it was Aidan? My most beautiful alpha with bolstering confidence that didn't match his own self-image? I would do anything to make sure he felt loved—included.

"Lorenzo," Jenson snapped, pulling his cock away from my mouth despite my protests.

I wasn't listening to the argument about whether this was a good idea or the right time. Fate had brought this pack into my life. I'd lacked so much happiness. I'd been content to hide in the shadows, until I couldn't anymore. These alphas noticed me when I was overlooked, choosing me to complete their pack. And now, for the first time in my life, I had control. I wasn't at the leisure of anyone or any timeline. I could choose to be claimed now or I could wait.

And who wouldn't want instant gratification after years of hoping I might one day get delayed gratification?

"Bite, please, alpha." I tried pressing my ass against Aidan, but the knot still stuck inside my pussy hadn't gone down at all. "I need you—"

The pain of a bite came before I even finished begging.

My shoulders stiffened, trying to protect my neck on instinct, but Aidan's teeth had no regard for the muscles there. Then the bite became sharper, finally breaking the skin, forcing my body into submission. I was thrown into another orgasm, this one so unexpected it squeezed my organs like being thrown into icy water, but instead of the sharp pain of cold along my skin it was the warmth of pleasure.

I fell onto Enzo's chest, gasping for breath as his fingers immediately press against his claiming mark on my left shoulder, offering me comfort along with his purr. Another set of hands played with my hair, pulling it back away from my sweaty face and my neck. If I had more energy, I would've been embarrassed about the amount of sweat on my body, but I couldn't find the energy to care. A soft blanket ran along my back, wiping up the cum there. And then I was rotated on my side with Aidan's purr along my back.

A sweet smell lingered around my nose, forcing one eye open. Jen offering his cum was like whipped cream on top of a sundae, and I licked every drop up before my eyes could no longer hold themselves open.

Chapter Twenty-Nine

Everything was beautiful. Everything was wonderful. Everything was … whatever adjective was on equal standing with the other two. My omega side was purring, content with the situation, allowing her to curl up into a little ball in the farthest crevice of my mind like she figured her services were no longer needed. Well, until she was ready for round two with her mates.

My beta side was enjoying the beautiful harmonious purrs of my mates. All three of them were purring for me—even if I could scent the slight worry coming from Jenson—it wasn't enough to pull me from the moment. I didn't think anything could, really.

I was starting to get hungry, but not enough that I could be convinced to get out of my nest, which I imagined all three of my alphas understood based on the fact no one demanded to feed me yet. They must've also known I didn't want to talk about the inevitable outcome that would be attending the academy with three possessive, bonded alphas, because no one broke the silence.

Had I made a mistake? Probably. But it was a *beautiful* one.

A soft, beautiful song started, breaking the silence. It came from outside of the nest and if we had been talking, I was sure we would've missed it. Just as soon as it started a few notes, it was gone.

"What was that?" I asked.

I stretched my body, surprised to find I was no longer connected to Enzo. Despite the disappointment left behind, my body was grateful for the ability to stretch and move without limitations. Or, I guess, within the limitations of three large bodies surrounding me.

"The doorbell," Jenson said.

"Are we expecting anyone?" It was more of a rhetorical question since I figured if we were, one of the males would've gotten up to answer it.

Instead of brushing off my comment, Aidan froze. His muscles locked behind me, and I could've sworn he stopped breathing for a moment before he exhaled a large breath.

"I have an idea who it might be," Aidan said, but still didn't move. "If the rumors of us have made it to my mother, that will be her."

I turned my head so I could see Aidan's face clearly, scrunching my nose up as I asked, "Like here, here. Now?"

We all turned to look at the door to the nest as if we expected her to open this door. My omega instincts were paying attention now, ready to defend my nest, my mates, if any female threatened to come in. Of course, that was fucking ridiculous, and I did my best to shove those instincts away.

"Should we answer the door?" I asked.

That seemed to get everyone moving, putting on clothes.

I stood awkwardly, not wanting to put on my clothes from school. They didn't smell of my mates and even if they were cute, they weren't as comfy as I wanted to be.

"What's wrong, Orsetta?" Enzo was the first one to finish getting dressed and the first one to notice I still had all my clothes in my hands—minus my torn underwear.

"I want to change into something comfier."

With your scent on it, preferably.

"Enzo, get our omega some clothes," Jenson said. "Aidan, you need to go shower so—"

The doorbell went off again and regardless of the fact it made the same sound, it somehow came off as impatient.

Aidan sighed. "On it."

He made it only two steps toward the door before I was running at him and forcing his head down for a kiss. His blond locks were long enough to grab, and I didn't hesitate to tighten my hold on him.

My new bonded alpha wasted no time in meeting my ferocity in the kiss, his tongue pushing past my lips in order to taste mine. Aidan's kiss didn't completely take control, but he met me in my eagerness, letting me know he didn't need me to submit to him.

Our tongues played with each other before I moved my lips away to nip at his chin. We were both breathing heavy, but I still rubbed my cheek against his, laying kisses down his jaw, his neck, until I got to the collar of his shirt.

Aidan's hands cupped my cheek, pulling me back so I could look into his eyes. His dark green eyes started into mine, frantically searching for something. I did my best to push my feelings of Aidan toward the male so he could feel their truth through our bond. I was rewarded with a huge smile, and another chaste kiss on the lips.

"Get her a pair of my underwear. It'll fit her best." And then Aidan left.

I growled at him leaving my nest, but a new body came up behind me. Enzo. He turned me around so I faced him—and so I could only barely make out Jenson leaving the room behind me.

"How are you feeling, Orsetta?"

I parted my lips, ready to say, 'fine' but stopped myself from the careless answer. Enzo wasn't giving into social pleasantries. He was legitimately asking how I was, and considering he could feel my emotions, I assumed he was trying to force me to reflect on the two humongous life choices I'd just taken on.

"I feel good." I reached up and ran my fingers along his jaw, enjoying the stubble that had grown out slightly so it was more smooth than prickly. "Calm. Like I no longer have a single worry in the world. Anything is possible."

My new alpha puffed his chest out, apparently very happy with himself, and it had me rolling my eyes. No matter what, I could never forget my males were alphas—not just in their designation but in their personalities. They were protectors and providers in a way every omega dreamed: helpful, supportive, and somehow both willing to stand by my side and behind me in my endeavors.

I leaned my head on his chest, placing a quick kiss on his chest. "How are you feeling? The bond's only one way, you know." Bonds allowed alphas to sense the emotions of whoever they claimed, but it didn't work the other way. Apparently, biology just assumed alphas only bit omegas and omegas, with their incredible sense of smell, would be able to scent the changes in their emotions. And despite being able to scent his happiness, I couldn't stop myself from needing to be sure he was as happy with me as I was with him.

Enzo purred, running one hand over my hair before gently tugging on the strands as a signal for me to lift my head. "Mi rendi il più felice del mondo."

I didn't know what he said, but the way he said it, with the tilt in his lips, had me blushing.

"Koda, I have clothes for you," Jenson said, his voice muffled through the door. "Come put them on so Enzo can take a quick shower."

Before I could follow Jenson's directions, Enzo gave me a chaste kiss, biting hard on my bottom lip so it would probably be red for a few minutes. Perfect, that was exactly how I wanted to meet one of my mate's mothers—with another male's claim on my lip.

Enzo left just as the doorbell rang a third time. I felt bad having Aidan's mother wait outside, especially since I was pretty sure it was already dark out. Although, no one seemed to be in a rush.

"Don't feel bad, Koda." Jenson handed me a pair of Aidan's boxers with little buttons on the front pretending to be shorts and a large dark blue shirt with a little pocket at the breast.

I quickly changed, keeping my omega scented clothes in my nest.

"She's been outside for a long time."

"She wasn't invited, so as far as I'm concerned, she can stay out there all night."

Jenson's words shocked me. They didn't sound aggressive, more disinterested, but of all my alphas, I assumed Jenson followed social niceties the closest. Either that didn't qualify for Aidan's mom or for anyone who showed up unwelcomed.

When I finished dressing, Jenson reached for my hand, heading for the front door. I took a deep breath to try and calm my nerves, but the de-scenting wash coming from Jen burnt my nostrils.

"You showered quickly," I said.

"Your scent was stronger on Aidan and Enzo. I just needed a quick rinse, just in case."

I listened carefully to Jenson's words, trying to catch how he felt about the fact I'd just bonded two other alphas. Unfortunately, all I could scent was the stupid wash he'd used. It was hiding his emotions from me.

We walked down the short front hallway in silence before we reached the front door. It was a grand piece of wood, coming to a soft point at the top in a sharp oval, and heavy enough it looked like any sort of knocking would be impossible to hear from the other side. The door didn't particularly match the aesthetic of the rest of the house, and I wondered if one of the alphas had picked it out.

When Jenson opened the door, he kept me hidden behind his back, but I could scent the anger coming from the omega female almost immediately. She smelled like a mix of sparkling water and cranberry juice, her anger taking away any sweetness from her perfume.

My own omega side took control and growled, the instinct to tell any female to back the hell up a demand I couldn't ignore, but especially a female that had the audacity for strong emotions toward my alphas.

Wrapped around the omega scent were several alpha ones. I couldn't pull them apart, but one in particular stood out, reminding me of sea salt chocolate.

My alpha wrapped an arm around my waist, either to comfort me or to make sure I didn't fling myself at the offending female, I wasn't sure.

"Hello, Catherine," Jenson said, his tone even more stand-offish than when he was in teacher mode. "Roger. I didn't know to expect your visit."

"Where is my son." It wasn't a question, but a demand, as if being greeted by Jenson was some sort of insult.

I growled again, unable to stop the sound.

"Tell the beta female," Aidan's mother said, disgust filling her voice at the word beta, "that if she cannot control her primitive instincts, it is only appropriate to excuse herself."

Jenson shut the door, cutting off the female's raid and then turned to look at me. Without the smell of her and her mate entering my home, I felt myself immediately relax. It also helped that she started ringing to the doorbell again, and I couldn't help but crack a smile.

"She seems…" I trailed off, trying to find the right word, but Aidan spoke up, startling me even as his presence made me smile.

"Old fashioned? Socialist? Like a grade-A bitch?"

"Did you hear her?" Jenson asked.

"No, but I assume she said something offensive," Aidan said.

Despite the light tone, I could tell Aidan was trying to fight his hurt. It didn't matter how much his beliefs differed from his parents—it would still hurt to not have their support. Even as an adult.

I sometimes imagined my parents finding me and apologizing for abandoning me. Sometimes I'd forgive them. Sometimes I told them to go to hell. But it was all in my head. I didn't really know how I would react to actually facing them.

I reached for Aidan, wanting to comfort him. Just like Jenson, he smelled of the washing agents blocking his perfume. It made me want to simultaneously snarl and rub myself against him. I wanted my scent on my alphas, just not my omega one.

"Who came with her this time?" Aidan asked.

"Roger."

My usually laid-back alpha swore.

"What do you want to do now?" Jenson asked. His hands came down to rest on my shoulders and being stuck between two of my bonded alphas had me biting down on my bottom lip to fight off the embers of arousal threatening to relight in my core. My whole body was aching from being used, but the sore muscles didn't do anything to hinder my arousal.

"She won't leave until she says her piece," Aidan said. "I can go outside so you don't have to hear it, Koda

315

bear."

"No. You shouldn't have to face her alone." I rested my chin against Aidan, looking up to the point of potentially breaking my neck. "We're a pack. We face challenges—and mothers—together."

****

I fully expected when we let Catherine Braker into the house that she was simply going to yell at Aidan and leave. Apparently, coming face to face with her son had her hiding her temperament. The fact she knew she had to hide her true colors should have alerted her to the fact she wasn't acting appropriately. Not that I expected an apology. But maybe some self-awareness.

Aidan's mother was beautiful, but it was to be expected when you looked at the specimen that was Aidan Braker. He obviously got his looks from his mother. They had the same blonde hair and face shape. Her dress was tight, highlighting her figure, and stopped at her knees in a way that screamed 'posh'. She had a matching coat the same length of her dress that I chose to believe was covered in faux fur. Nails done, hair immaculately curled, and makeup freshly applied, I wouldn't bat an eye if she admitted to getting ready and dressed specifically for the occasion of coming over to yell at us.

The male that stood behind her as a silent sentinel, Roger something, looked like an Irish stereotype with the red hair and freckles. His face was long and rectangular, matching the rest of his body. He might have smelled good, but his arrogance matched that of his mate.

Besides Roger, we all sat in the living room. Aidan was on the couch next to me, and Jenson leaned on the arm of the couch on my other side. Enzo had walked in when we led Catherine and Roger inside and immediately announced he was making dinner—for his pack.

"Some tea, Aidan?" Catherine asked.

I scrunched my nose at the request. This was a coffee house. And who didn't add 'please' to requests? *People who only make demands.*

"No mother, you are not a guest," Aidan said. "Say what you've come to say and then leave."

"Watch how you speak to your mother," Roger said.

"I did not raise you to be so disrespectful," Catherine said.

Aidan sighed but surprisingly didn't argue. I had no clue what kind of childhood Aidan had with his mother, but I could guess, based on Catherine sitting on the edge of the couch, her knees together and ankles crossed like she was the freaking queen.

Enzo came over and placed a small bowl of mixed fruit in my lap, then walked away without acknowledging our non-guests.

Catherine seemed to be reaching her limit as she glared at me while I picked up a raspberry with my fingers before popping it into my mouth. The entire room was quiet expect for the echoing sounds of Enzo cooking in the kitchen. Every swallow felt too loud.

"Betas," Catherine scoffed, finally breaking the silence. "Is this your plan? Simply act like an omega in the hopes of entrapping my son and his pack?"

I could feel Aidan tense beside me, but I didn't say anything. Words hurt, especially coming from someone I'd hoped would be like a surrogate mother to me, but if she thought this was the first time I'd heard this shit, she was woefully unaware of how betas were treated. Alphas had a tendency to think betas 'didn't know our place' and then also create the standards of education and society for us. I was more certain of how alphas viewed betas than I was on how I viewed myself.

Which meant I knew exactly how to deal with an alpha. I shrugged one shoulder in response to her question and then dug around in my bowl for a blueberry. I tossed it up and caught it in my mouth. I smiled up at Jenson, pride coming off me in a ridiculous amount because I'd never actually thrown food and caught it before.

"Aidan, you cannot honestly tell me you are considering bonding with such a creature. What about— what was her name?" Catherine asked, her wrist making invisible gestures. "Lana? No, Laura. She was a fine beta. Very poised and even came from a good family. Her mother tells me she's just heartbroken over your breakup, so she's sure to take you back."

"I dated Laura because her friends were dating members of my pack." To smooth over his words, or maybe because he felt my jealousy, Aidan's hand came up to the back of my neck. The skin was very tender from his claiming bite—which definitely needed a bandage soon—but it was his touch near the literal part of me that belonged to him that sent a shiver down my spine and raised the hairs on my arms. I had to bite the inside of my cheek to keep from moaning.

Roger gentled a hand on his omega's shoulder. "Son. When you first started dating betas, I'll admit, we were all shocked. But we've come around to the younger generation's way of things. Your other fathers and I think it's a good thing. Shows how dominant each of your alpha instincts are. We've already explained that to your mother."

I wanted to roll my eyes at the condescending tone Roger had toward his omega mate. It was stereotypical alpha-male-bullshit. They knew best. They calmed the wild omega. It was a weird separation of belief. Alphas like Roger thought dominance was in controlling an omega, when really, dominance was supposed to protect weaker designations from other alphas so they could be free. What was strength when you were already going up against a weaker opponent?

"This is ridiculous," Catherine said. Her scent was starting to flood the room, making me more agitated with every breath. "The three of you cannot share a beta. You will become too territorial, and the longer you are unsatisfied, the worse it will be. You are dooming this beta to broken bonds when you need to rut."

"Mother, I promise, you do not have to worry about my sex life."

I couldn't help but laugh at the awkward conversation even as my cheeks burned remembering how Aidan had taken my ass earlier. Let her interpret the blush any way she wanted, but I had no doubt I could satisfy my males sexually.

"Don't be crude," Catherine snapped. "You are being selfish, Aidan. Think of the beta's future."

Aidan growled. "All I do is think of Koda. And likewise, she can think for herself."

"Enough Aidan. We need to put that heinous article's rumors to an end. Let Jenson claim the beta, and we can find you an appropriate female if you're determined to settle down right now."

The entire room froze. Even Enzo who I hadn't thought was paying attention stopped cooking. Her words spun around and around in my head until all I heard was that single word: article.

"What article?" Aidan asked, earning a vicious grin from his mother.

"Apparently some students saw Jenson moving his bonded beta out of the dorms last week. Those same students then verified that you—Aidan—told some professor on campus you've bonded the same beta. It's even speculated poor Lorenzo will claim the beta, if he hasn't done so already."

Jen's hands tightened on my body in a gesture that was supposed to be comforting but just confirmed there was something wrong. The scent of a desert storm, mixed with the tang of anger, bled through the chemical scent on Aidan. I didn't know whether my alpha was angry over the article or his mother reveling in the pain she knew her words were causing.

"I think it's time for you to leave, mother," Aidan said, never breaking eye contact with me. He reached for me, pulling me onto his lap before finally looking over at Catherine. She seemed to struggle for words, and Aidan didn't give her a chance. Lifting my hair, he planted a full kiss on his mark on the back of my neck and that time, I couldn't catch the moan quick enough.

Catherine gasped. "You've made a terrible mistake, Aidan."

And then Catherine Braker and her mate left.

I snuggled into Addie, needing his warmth and comforting scent. Jenson took the seat I'd left, and Enzo made his way over with two plates.

"Here you go, Orsetta." Enzo handed me one plate before sitting on the coffee table in front of us. Then he pulled out his phone, already opened to the article Catherine mentioned, named, *Beta Student Breaks Social Norms and Claims an Alpha Pack for Herself.*

The article did more than quote students who saw me with Jen and Aidan, but also the female students from Jen's class talking about how they'd never been against designations mixing before but now their beloved teacher refused to help them because of my apparent 'raging jealousy'. The worst part wasn't even the inclusion of my name and the name of my alphas, but the end, letting the reader know the author would be following the beta's journey at the academy.

"Eat up, Koda bear," Enzo said. "You'll need your strength for this conversation."

Aidan and Jen grabbed their own portions while Enzo and I ate in silence. The lasagna was good. A different shade of yellow than what usually comes out of the box, but I was guessing it was homemade. I tried to enjoy it since Enzo had spent a lot of time and energy making it just for me, but the more I ate, the higher my anxiety rose until I finally took my last bite, and I couldn't stop the words from immediately coming out. "What does this mean?"

My alphas shared a look. They didn't know. We wouldn't know until we got into the fray tomorrow.

JOSEPHINE LIGHT

Chapter Thirty

For the first time, ever, I was actually awake before the sun rose. Not just up and getting dressed—but wide-awake. Although, that was putting it generously, seeing as I didn't sleep a wink last night.

After dinner, Jen received an email from the chancellor with the link to the article and a comment stating any protests would be met with my expulsion.

And that was it. All my hard work. My years of schooling put into the hands of strangers.

My alphas talked with me into the night, trying to apologize for whatever perceived guilt they had, but I'd put an end to that real quick. My admission to Braker Academy had been on the rocks several times, but my alphas hadn't done anything wrong.

The only good news was the article had clearly called me a beta. Braker Academy had been a dream come true, but if I had to leave the school, my true designation was still a secret.

All of my alphas were joining me on the ride to the academy this morning. This had always been the plan, but the car was silent with tension. Aidan was in the back seat with me today, occasionally bumping my shoulder to remind me to drink my coffee. I thought he needed the normalcy from me, so I obliged each time.

As we pulled into the professor designated parking lot, Chancellor Kelly was already waiting for us.

I sucked in a breath, feeling the tears forming before Jen had even parked the car. I felt more than saw Aidan unbuckling my seatbelt and pulling me onto his lap. The scent of angry alphas quickly perfumed the car, but I couldn't focus on calming them down with my heart breaking.

It was all lies. Lies that I could survive being kicked out of the academy. I sobbed against Aidan. I wanted to go home but was unable to get the words out through the hiccups.

"I got it," Enzo growled before he left the car, slamming the door behind him.

The tears came harder now that one of my alphas was walking away. My hands shook even as Aidan gently rocked me back and forth. Both he and Jen were purring, but there was nothing to do but let it out. Let out the sorrow and my dreams.

The car door opened, but instead of the passenger seat, it was Aidan's door. I couldn't actually see through the tears, but I would have known the brown blob in front of me anywhere.

"C'mon, Orsetta, I need you to calm down enough to listen to me. Can you do that for me? For us? Can you be a strong girl right now?"

"Let's just leave," Aidan said. His voice was calm even if his words were anything but.

"No, Kelly was adamant about talking to her," Enzo said. "Can I carry you, Orsetta?"

I didn't want to leave the car. Or have Kelly see me like that. Or go wherever he wanted. But I couldn't get the tears to stop, my nose to stop dripping snot, or lift my tongue to speak. So, I just reached my hands out and let Enzo pick me up. Wrapping my legs around him as best I could, I tuck my head into his chest, trying to quiet my sobs.

Two car doors slammed shut, and then Aidan and Jen joined us.

"What is this about?" Jenson demanded.

I thought he was asking Enzo, but it was a female voice I recognized that responds. "Tell the poor beta to dry her tears."

It wasn't the words themselves that put a pause to my sobs but the gentle tone. When I finally managed to control myself—wishing I had tissues—I looked up. My cheeks were definitely splotchy, my eyes red, and I didn't even want to discuss my nose, but I managed to make eye contact with Anne—Chancellor Kelly's secretary.

"Are you all ready?" Anne asked. The beta could barely contain herself, bouncing on her toes, but she did give me a sympathetic smile before bringing her pink thermos to her lips.

"For what?" I croaked. I didn't think I could handle a formal announcement I'd been removed. I'd prefer an email.

Or no announcement.

"For the nuisance I expect you to fix," Kelly said. "Now stop blubbering. You aren't being dismissed from Braker."

"I'm not?"

"She's not?" My alphas asked together.

Kelly exhaled like dealing with the four of us was bothersome. "Reporters have been patrolling campus since I came to the office this morning. They were harassing Ms. Wallen, demanding to know your schedule so they could meet you."

"Because of the article?" Enzo asked.

"Yes." That was all Kelly said. No more information.

"What the hell is going on, Kelly?" Aidan asked.

All three of my alphas were putting out aggressive pheromones, and while their scents calmed me, it did nothing for my sadness.

"The article gained traction overnight," Kelly said, turning to walk away and simply expecting us to follow. Anne walked dangerously close to the alpha chancellor, but he didn't seem to mind. "Koda has become pseudo-famous. Now everyone wants to watch her, learn about her, you name it."

"But protestors—" Jen started, before he was cut off by Kelly.

"They aren't a concern of mine, right now."

All my alphas growled at the disrespect, and Anne shrunk behind Kelly at the sound. The chancellor's woodsy scent became frustrated even as he pushed his secretary more behind him, as if protecting her from my alphas. "Enough with this. The beta stays because she is currently in the limelight. She can do more good for the beta designation just by continuing to go to school here than she can do bad if protestors were to show up. It was a 50/50 on which group would show up first. You lucked out. And for fuck's sake—put her down."

Enzo obliged, although he took my hand and let Aidan take the other, Jenson walking between Kelly and us like a guard. Instead of heading in the direction of Elder Building and his office, Kelly took us to the front of the school where a bunch of reporters were standing together, chatting to one another.

The moment someone noticed us, however, the shouting started along with flashes of cameras. I stared, shocked at the bright lights, before I managed to look at my alphas. They didn't look happy at all and even moved closer to me, completely blocking me from view. This only incited the group to be louder.

"Enough," Chancellor Kelly announced. The cameras continued flashing, and I was sure I saw a few video recorders between the gaps in my alphas' arms. "I have with me, the beta student, Koda Tucker, and her pack containing Aidan Braker, descendant from Braker Academy's founder, our own Quantum Mechanics Professor Jenson Fields, and Lorenzo De Luca."

Enzo grunted, either because he didn't get a title

or because of the use of his full name. The normal gesture had a corner of my lips turning upward which grabbed my alphas' attention so quickly, all three turned around to stare at me. At least my tear-stained cheeks hid the blush.

"Any questions you have, you may ask now, but quickly. We don't want to keep Ms. Tucker from her classes." Kelly seemed to survey the group before pointing out a reporter I couldn't see but could hear.

"Will Ms. Tucker be allowed to continue her courses at Braker Academy now that she's bonded?"

"Yes." Again, that was all Kelly said. Each question solely getting a yes or a no.

Had I bonded all three alphas?

Kelly looked to Jenson, who nodded.

Yes.

Was I truly a beta?

Yes.

Did I pick this pack?

Yes.

Would I be graduating from this academy?

Yes.

I didn't answer a single question, but that was the way the world worked. I might have won this battle as a beta at a predominately alpha school, but betas were still fighting for their rights to be equals to alphas. Omegas had an even longer war needing to be started. But that was someone else's fight.

My phone buzzed and I pulled it out, looking at a message from Hannah: *You're on the news, bitch. Smile!*

I was just a half-beta-half-omega member of a pack with three more semesters until graduation. I might have had the public's attention and be flying much higher on the radar than I'd wanted, but that was okay. I had my alphas. My education. And a new friend.

For what it was worth, I was happy.

JOSEPHINE LIGHT

EVERNIGHT PUBLISHING ®

www.evernightpublishing.com